Snow on a Raven's Back

Hiag Akmakjian

riverrun

IP – 5 March) Police reports indicate that the shopping mall's Happy Valley Foot Spa was operating as a massage parlor offering sex acts by women. It was said that the women, aged between 18 and 23, were paying off their "immigration debt". Few spoke English. The women are of Southeast Asian origin and are set to be deported to their countries of origin.

1

"Nothing is futile. What's wrong with people? Where's the fucking outrage?"

Roz, calling from Hollywood in that feminine-throaty voice that could get me to do anything.

"So if you'd kindly move your ass out here we'll get this thing going."

She meant our film idea. We wanted to make a film about women kidnapped off the streets – "disappeared" women.

The thought of going to the Coast had appeal but as it stood the plan sounded not easily workable and I really needed more convincing.

"Look," she said, "it'll move swiftly once we get Max on board," meaning Max Petrov, the film director and Hollywood icon: two Oscars, a few Emmys, a Palme d'Or, his early classics on TV. Not only was he Roz's favorite director, he acted as her advisor, and their names were so frequently linked that fans long ago had them in bed together. I wondered if that last detail was true.

"You think it'll work?"

"With a film project like this, once we get Max on board, it'll be like rolling off a log."

"A piece of cake."

"A piece of cake."

Which gave me even more doubts. But she was a good friend, it was a worthy idea and she had a reputation for making things happen. So I decided what the hell and began making arrangements to join her. I was fairly sure we'd make a go of it, and anyway it would be nice to go out to Hollywood and see how the other half lives.

•

Actually it was more than a good idea, it was an important idea. I think what set it all in motion was Roz's reading an editorial in a Mumbai newspaper sent to her by a friend. He knew of her interest and had sympathy for the cause. The editorial was about something that had happened in the mountains of Nepal, near Kathmandu, and the article wound up saying that this was neither the first nor the last time we would hear of such events.

The event in question involved a mother of two boys and their nine-year-old younger sister. Their father had died and the mother and the children were surviving in any way they could. Then one day a nicely-dressed lady from Mumbai knocked on the door, saying she had good apprenticeships in the city for children like the little girl. This woman had once lived in Kathmandu and knew how much poverty there was there and said she wanted to help the family.

Roz had clipped out the article and saved it and asked me to read it. It was really a very sad story about a woman who looked trustworthy and sounded genuine when she described the trade that the girl would be taught. She emphasized it would give the girl valuable skills in life and earn her enough money to send home a little bit each month.

To demonstrate the sincerity of the proposal, the woman gave the mother a small advance payment that covered the cost of a TV antenna for her roof, something the mother had long wanted so she could watch television programs from India. It made the mother very happy that this nice lady would see that her daughter was taught a trade, especially when the woman promised that the girl would write home once a week to say how well she was doing and whether she needed to have anything sent to her.

The editorial went on to say that a few months went by and when the mother had not heard from her girl, disturbing rumors began reaching her. She loved her daughter and trembled when she heard the worst of the rumors, which was that girls like her were lured away from their families and forced into prostitution in filthy brothels.

I could see how just reading this would get Roz all incensed. It was a very angry article and presented facts in an ironic editorializing way. The writer said that Mumbai was a city with an enormous population and had to maintain thousands of brothels to meet the needs of its male citizens. That of course would be of indirect benefit to women as well – by providing men with a safety valve.

It explained some of the mechanics of the brothel business. It told about how pimps and women procurers were always on the lookout for new girls. Very young girls were preferred because a customer could take a girl's virginity for $1000, which was certainly a lot of money to pay for a one-hour session with a nine- or ten-year-old girl. But in a big city like Mumbai you could always find some men who could afford that.

The girls weren't always sold just to American or English sex tourists. Inexperienced girls were much sought after because of the belief among some men that if they had sex with a virgin it would cure them of their AIDS. The men eventually died of the AIDS and so did the young girls they infected, but word of that never got out.

It's true, the article said, that people did hear of such things and knew they happened, but the facts were available only as government statistics and who ever read such documents? Also, no one knew who the actual girls were, what their real names were or where exactly they had worked before their bodies were found dumped by the wayside. That they had existed at all came to the attention of the authorities when their corpses showed up in the city morgue and in medical examiners' reports.

Shockingly, records were poorly kept and "woefully incomplete", the editorial said, and in the smaller morgues not kept at all. Most people didn't know such things even happened and certainly not among them – right there where they lived. It was the kind of thing they always read about happening elsewhere.

The editorial concluded that something had to be done about these terrible events that were a shame to any civilized people. Indian society was a decent society, and these criminal offenses should not be allowed to keep happening as though the community were helpless. The offenders needed to be punished and the time to act was now.

•

It was easy to see how that would get Roz started and I can't say I blamed her. Apart from everything else, that account from Nepal probably connected in her mind – I know it connected in my mind – with the story we were about to pitch to this Max Petrov. Ours was the story of an event of two years ago involving a 17-year-old Finnish fashion model. She had disappeared after becoming famous when a nude shot of her appeared in Vogue. This model, Karen Bryggman, was a younger friend of my lover Inge, which was how I learned about her. I didn't know her personally. On Karen Bryggman's disappearance, Inge, my lover, underwent so much self-recrimination that nothing could console her.

As people later pieced things together, this fashion model Karen had gone off on a jaunt to Morocco with a man she had met at a party. She said his name was Frank and in her not-very-good English she called him her "vunderfool Romeo". And that was the last anyone ever saw or heard from Karen again.

What happened next was this Romeo person showed up back in New York one day – alone. He said they had gone to Marrakech and he had left her at a café for just a moment to go make a phone call, leaving her sitting on the terrace. When he returned she was gone. He looked everywhere for her.

People who knew Karen didn't believe the story. Things like that didn't happen in life. Karen wouldn't just wander off without telling anyone. And in Morocco? Never.

The next thing anybody knew, reports began circulating that this "Romeo" friend had sold her to a local sheik for $25,000. According to rumors, Karen was by now probably imprisoned in a brothel somewhere. Or in a harem.

Friends found it difficult to believe such reports. But on the other hand, they didn't have much to go on and didn't know what else to think. There was some disagreement about the $25,000 figure. Some contended that young good-looking white teenagers were almost a commonplace nowadays. There were so many of them that the price could be as low as $10,000 for a girl. It was also possible that she could bring in a little more if she was still a virgin or could be doctored up to feel like one to the first man to have her, or think he was the first one.

•

So that in a nutshell was our film idea: the story of this 17-year-old fashion model Karen and the way she just vanished one day. We hoped it would raise people's awareness of terrible events of this kind and underline how common abductions have become. Our hope was that the awareness would lead to a search for Karen Bryggman and get her back and, more than that, act as a step toward liberating all such women and eventually – our long-range hope – work toward ridding the world of sex slavery. That might have sounded idealistic to some people but not to us.

"So what's our ending going to be?" I asked Roz.

There was no doubt that the idea was a good one but the story needed something more for it to work as a movie. It had to lead to a resolution of some sort. It was a true-life event we were dealing with but a film had fictional needs that life sometimes didn't supply and fictional needs had to be met if people were to want to go see it and believe it and – the important step – act on it. That was our goal, not to entertain but to get something done about the crime, at the heartlessness of lives destroyed.

"We'll work it out. The studio could always put word men

5

on it. They're good at endings."

I had never heard the expression before.

"Word men? Writers. Writers are good at coming up with ideas."

I didn't know what I was letting myself in for but was willing to go along with her – anybody would if you knew Roz. I remember thinking that the ending would come. There was no such thing as a story without an ending.

2

I knew that if anybody could get things going in Hollywood it would be Roz. She had the popularity and status Marilyn Monroe once had. But there was a big difference in personality between them. Roz was never late to the set. She never gave anyone any trouble. And she was never temperamental. Everybody said she was a dream to work with and studio heads considered her money in the bank. As a result she was sent as many as five or six of the choicest scripts a month to read.

Still it continued to bother me that an important element like an ending to a story was something that could just be "worked out later". Was that how you told a story?

It was only because Roz was a good friend that I let her pep-talk me into thinking our plan was viable, although I admit that at the time it did sound good. But apparently my response was a trifle short on enthusiasm and in revenge she leveled her heavy artillery at what she considered the great weak spot of my life: my job. She wanted to pry me loose from the paper before I gave it my best years. That was her line.

"This project could spring you from that pissy crap stuff they have you doing at the paper. Nothing personal, you understand."

"Pissy crap stuff" got no argument from me. That was my nine-to-five boring "journalism" at the New York World-Herald.

If you're not a New Yorker, there's something I should explain about the World-Herald. It's a rag. Emblazoned over a red-and-white Stars and Stripes and a black screaming eagle at the top left corner of the front page is its founder's sacred motto:" Informing America – Enlightening the World" – speaking of crap.

It was a broadsheet, one of the last of its kind, and my job was to write a column of entertaining quotes picked up, borrowed or just plain lifted from various sources. Honesty never fazed the paper, and more than once it was caught red handed printing stuff without permission and then writing a check in an out-of-court settlement probably under the heading of the Cost of Doing Business. I found it surprising at how much theft journalists got away with, and the number of out-and-out lies and flagrant misrepresentations they routinely regaled the public with as "news". Admittedly certain TV channels were more dishonest, so as bad as the World-Herald was, it wasn't the worst source of misinformation in town.

•

It was useless to tell Roz she had too flatteringly high an opinion of me. Really prejudiced, she was. But that was part of her objection: it wasn't just that I was throwing my life away on work she thought beneath me. Nor do I think it had anything to do with my being paid peanuts, which I was. She just didn't care for the column – "fluff and bat-shit trash" was how she dismissed it – although she admitted it could at times be funny and that it had a good title "Out of This World" (a title I thought it best not to tell her had been lifted by the paper from I forget which journal).

But her main objection was: "But it's so obviously incommensurate with your talents" – obvious to Roz and nobody else.

At least she acknowledged that I was a journalist and that that was a fine and respectable thing to be in life, not a hack – that is, not a prostitute. But the column itself was pure hack work, she insisted.

Frankly, to me it was just a job. The writing, if you could call it that, was old-fashioned three-dot journalism of quotable trivia to entertain the 1.1 million readers of the World-Herald and didn't pretend to be anything else. It was a way to pay the rent and so undemanding I could write it in my sleep. In informing America and enlightening the world, the paper specialized in partial truths and blatant larceny. It sometimes just swiped things from not-easily-traceable publications considered safe to borrow from. Some of the printed material coming across my desk were exotic periodicals I had never heard of, like the Punjabi Sunday Spectator (a particularly rich source) and the somewhat more esoteric Somali-Kenya Review, a stapled job of modest circulation that you would have to be an East African to have even known of its existence. And my favorite: the bluntly-named Edinburgh quarterly No! I liked its definiteness.

My job was to give an entertaining twist to the little verbal thumbnails found in them and make them if not jokey and bizarre then at least entertainingly rewritten to keep readers' eyes glued to the World-Herald and resisting any return to reality. The thumbnails were strung out along the right outside edge of the paper in one long column of alternating typefaces zigzagging down the page:

. . . A Manchester birdwatcher spotted a rare robin – one of only eight seen in Britain in the last five years – that had flown the 400 miles from Norway and watched too late as her cat Monmouth had it for lunch . . .

. . . A man sued police in an Arkansas town for refusing him a position on the force because his IQ of 125 was too high. 104 was considered the maximum intelligence to keep candidates from getting too bored to stay on as cops . . .

And for bizarre there would be nuggets like some from The Nepalese Evening Courier in what my managing editor described as a change of pace and I thought of as scraping the bottom:

. . . *Three staff members of a psychiatric hospital in Kazakhstan killed a prostitute and cooked her as a dish of dumplings, explaining they were hungry and all the restaurants were closed, so what choice did they have?* . . .

Junky froth was the way Roz also put it – in her kinder moments.

3

Few people could sling it like Roz once she got going. Especially about my virtues, so called. Despite how she felt about the work I was doing, I'm sure she got mucho mileage from touting it among her Hollywood friends as what her "New York journalist connection" was doing and I even heard her say once: "You'll like my collaborator – the World-Herald columnist? He's made quite a name for himself in Manhattan circles" – nonexistent circles, it hardly needs adding.

Her urging me to fly out and live in her guest bungalow gave me the edge I needed to get up the nerve to approach my managing editor for permission to go to L.A. I could work the column for about two weeks from there, three at most. I promised I'd keep a lookout for local anecdotes to send back so that readers of "Out of This World" would not experience withdrawal.

I didn't realize how ballsy the request must have sounded to the managing editor until I saw his Adam's apple rise to the top of his throat and do a u-ey before sinking back down again as he stared at this germ standing in front of him with the unbelievable chutzpah to ask for paid fucking leave.

"You've been working here how long?" he asked, his ears possibly deceiving him.

But as it turned out, everything worked out in the end, the laugh, so to speak, being on him. I have to admit he had the grace to tell me so himself, although, as things turned out, the truth was he had no choice in the matter. He slid past my desk later that day once the city edition had been put to bed to inform me that the fourteenth floor was not altogether opposed to a brief California work leave (great emphasis on the four-letter word) if while there I continued culling stuff from papers as column fodder and emailing them back to New York and – an extremely big AND – that I come back with an extended interview of Roz.

"And no little eight-and-a-half-column-inch piece of shit on whether she goes to bed with only her radio on," he emphasized.

"That was Marilyn Monroe – ancient history."

I had to laugh that the bigwigs on fourteen were shocked that I even knew Roz and that she was actually a friend. Obviously it was her name that had done the trick and part of their shock was that I knew her by her off-screen name Roz. Because to moviegoers she was Lorna Beach. That was her screen name, a tacky name Roz herself thought worthy of a women's deodorant "for those special days" and on a level of taste that was pure Hollywood. Old Hollywood.

The bigwigs were so impressed by my Roz / Lorna Beach connection that I had fun piling it on with Umpleby. That was the managing editor's name, Jonathan Umpleby. I said that while I was out in Lala-land I might even bring back an interview of her director, Max Petrov, "the Magnificent Max", aka the "genius movie director". He was the one we'd be talking to about our story idea. Roz was convinced that if we could get him to do our film on the trafficking of women, he could bring what we hoped would be an emotionally powerful indictment of the crime to the public's attention.

"The most effective thing we could do would be to dramatize the growing number of victims. The public may not be aware how bad things have become. We'll show that the crime is now more global than anyone thinks and we'll try to move people to act."

That was becoming our mantra: get people to act.

So, knowing I would be spending time on the Coast with Roz and Max, I felt pretty safe offering the added inducement of a profile on Max too. I could always fake it: his biography and the facts of his work were all in Wikipedia. In the media world it takes a certain amount of bullshitting people to achieve success and at the World-Herald you could multiply that by a factor of ten.

The thing was, if the film were done properly, it could be promoted with a lot of excitement as a cinematic event. Not just the usual opening-night searchlights crisscrossing the West Coast sky and stars parading tits and asses up and down red carpets or interviews and Academy Award presentations. There would be all that of course, but in addition there would be newspaper headlines and interviews of the famous and the mighty, including Congressional inquiries and investigative reporting. All stops would be pulled out.

When Roz talked about getting people stirred into doing something, she didn't mean just film buffs. She meant the FBI, the CIA, the United States attorney general, state law enforcement agencies, the U. N., the European Parliament, Interpol, the cop on the corner, your Aunt Tillie and anyone else who might conceivably be persuaded to do something. It was global consciousness raising in the war to end slavery and it could be won if everybody got behind it.

The more Roz and I kicked the idea around, the more the mechanics of it began sounding über-ambitious and I again asked whether she thought we could really make it work.

Roz was never of two minds about anything.

"It can't possibly fail. Providing of course the banks come through."

Banks, financial backing: they always popped up in our discussions.

"What if they don't come through?"

"They had fucking better – are you kidding? With Max's name plus his thirty-year track record in the industry, I doubt that they won't. Not as long as there's money in it for them."

I have to admit that when Roz was on overdrive she had a way of overcoming my resistance. Anyway, I thought, at the very least I'd enjoy a quickie California break living only a few meters away from the movie star Lorna Beach, national lust object and intelligent-man's sex fantasy – and my close good friend. (Not friend with benefits – to head that one off at the pass.) You'd have to see Roz not on the screen but in the flesh to know what I mean by the fascination she wielded. Men meeting her for the first time took one look and thought bed. Which was very uncomfortable for her. She was made constantly aware of this reaction and felt unhappy at being men's blatant sex fantasy, and some women's too. (She got about two marriage proposals a month from women.)

She enjoyed sex but disliked what people made of it. I once heard her elaborate on the "surprising power" of sex to an enterprising cub reporter who apparently had had the courage to pick up the phone one day and call her up. Something about that appealed to her, as she later explained to me. He was a journalism major in a junior college from some place way up in Idaho, interviewing her for the school paper. She let herself be interviewed on her patio facing the sea. He sat with a red-white-and-blue five-dollar giant spiral notebook called The Big One in his lap – the kind you see in ninety-nine-cent shops. She said he was charming. His questioning mostly turned on a fresh new angle that no one had ever thought of before: sex.

"He couldn't have been more than nineteen," she smiled remembering him, "and had that wonderful twelve-year-old innocence that men seem never to lose."

Pacing casually and feeling sorry for the kid and genuinely wanting to help, she accommodated him by breezing on and on about the things that draw men and women together, her eye slyly following his ballpoint pen as it scribbled along with her words.

"Sex has fantastic power and . . ." pausing to let him get that down: "sex . . . fantastic power . . ."

It was a condensation of interviews from the two years I'd known her and her comments about "today's woman" came out smoothly.

". . . yet it's amazing," she said, resuming, "that men just don't understand that instant intimacy isn't intimacy. You need to let feelings, you know, grow. You have to let emotions pass through layers of intensity before there's love. Are you getting all this?" A glance downward toward his notes.

"Yes, Ms. Beach."

"Because it's only when you have love that you have good sex. Really that's when you have the best sex and not just the gland thing. You, for example, I can see you're intelligent and I'm sure you understand, but just try explaining that to most males. They just plain don't get it. You know how they say men think with their little head?"

Shy appreciative laugh, fast scribbling.

"Yes, Ms. Beach."

"Well," Roz said, "if you ask me, that's an awfully flattering assessment of that head."

4

I had the same trust in Roz that she had in me, and not having the sex thing between us allowed me to concentrate on our project. I did have thoughts about what she might be like in bed and whether she, you know, shaved and the color difference between top and bottom, but those were thoughts I had about most women and nothing personal to do with her. (Inge informed me that you didn't go by the color on top of the head. You went by the color of the eyebrows, which was the same color as what was down below. Just to get that topic out of the way.)

The success of the project promised to be swift and easy. Few actors in the world had Roz's fame and I was convinced some of her self-confidence came from her pleasure at being publicly adored.

"We're bound to come up with backing," she said.

Hearing her say that as often as she did worried me.

"How much backing do you think we'll need?"

"Maybe a hundred million. Two hundred maybe. Not much. But we'll see as we go. And maybe we'll get a book out of it too when the film is out. Maybe you could be keeping a log as we go along. We could publish it later as part of our publicity campaign – you know, 'the movie log'. We need a title for the film."

"You have any ideas?"

"How about you?"

"Me neither."

"Don't worry," she said, "we'll get one."

"You honestly don't know have a title for this thing?"

"I think of it as Girl Missing? Just as a working title. What do you think"

"I don't know. It sounds okay."

"It's just a working title. Until something better comes along."

"Okay. Girl Missing."

"Once we have the money in the bank, the rest, actors, script, location, production, and so on, will be a snap. Even the title. The only thing standing in the way right now is getting Max to commit."

But that was the way Hollywood worked, she assured me, and it was perfectly normal. You had to sign somebody on with the kind of marketability and proven talent that Max had. If not, the banks would pretty much steer clear of the project no matter how worthy your idea sounded.

"They're not in the business of worthy. They're in the business of making money."

She cautioned me, though.

"When we make our pitch to Max, we should be prepared to hear he's not interested. Because with him 'no' always precedes 'yes'. It's an automatic Russian thing."

"Russians always say no?"

"You know, like at the UN. Nyet. That and the other Russian thing – every so often inviting me to share his bed. Although that's not Russian so much as universal."

"I thought his being Russian was a publicity story."

"There are more stories about him than the ancient Greeks had myths. The most persistent rumor I've heard is that he was born in Hoboken, New Jersey, not far from where Frank Sinatra was born."

I didn't know which of the many rumors about him to believe or anything about his character but she prepped me that we'd need several meetings to get the Great Max to the tipping point.

"But he'll come round in the end."

I still had doubts about the success of the whole thing. Why

17

I don't know. It was just a feeling.

She said we had to plug away at it. Which was the reason for getting me out to the Coast in the first place and getting set up in her guest bungalow. Like many big names in Hollywood, Max was so busy he was hard to pin down and we'd be putting ourselves in a position of grabbing him on the run in spur-of-the-moment get-togethers.

"That's how you get things done out here."

In Hollywood, she explained, there were only two ways of doing things.

"One gets you nowhere fast, that's the usual way, and then there's the Max Petrov way. The beauty of the Max Petrov way is that it has no rules. You just have to grab him on the run, and the good news is that he'd like nothing better than being grabbed, so there I have an unfair advantage. His libido not showing any signs of diminishing, there probably won't be a problem."

Her last-minute instruction was on how to pitch a film, which was the first time I had any notion there was an art to it.

"You keep it brief – five minutes – no details."

"Five minutes?"

"It has to work in five minutes. It won't get any better if you stretch it out to two hours. The idea is not to spell out the whole story. At this point, you're just throwing out a hook."

"And then?"

"No then. That's it. You present the idea and boom, done. End of story. And you're selling, so you have to put a little verve into it. But it's important to keep eye contact as you're pitching because it's in the other person's eyes that you will see the story happening . . . see whether it's working. If the people you're making the pitch to are moved, then you know you've got a story. You knock them for a loop. And the way you know you're knocking them for a loop is that they fall silent as they listen and stare. Then at the end maybe somebody says 'Wow.' And that's it. You've got them."

We would lay siege over several days and keep pushing the

18

agenda. That was the plan.

"Two weeks, maybe three," Roz assured me again.

The big names in the industry, they were called machers, were always tied up in conferences, and everyone knew that the only thing that worked in Hollywood was perseverance.

"That and luck, of course. You have to persevere right up to the moment of defeat. And be ready for defeat because – well, because defeat happens. And it happens more frequently than people like to think.

Roz said the streets of Hollywood were strewn with corpses.

But we felt that with a story like ours we could overcome the odds. That much I agreed on – I mean about the story. I shared Roz's conviction that it was possible to effect change in the world, given a concerted effort, and I liked it that neither of us thought that that sounded too idealistic or wet behind the ears. We both felt that only a powerful moral base got things done and without that nothing worthwhile was ever achieved. I know that sounded noble and all that but it was true.

With Roz's fame, looks and her place in the Hollywood food chain, plus the seductive power she exuded without even trying, I felt pretty sure we'd get our film made and also get some changes made in the world, the big changes we wanted to see. Fingers crossed, though, just in case.

•

It was a tall order but we were dealing with an even worse crime than the worst mafia excesses. We couldn't think of a more important story to tell, and nobody was telling it. That was a big part of our pitch, that nobody gave a damn about what was happening all over the world to these, so called, disappeared women.

Certainly there would be no difficulty convincing Max that the trafficking of women was a subject worth treating. That was too obvious to be the main point of the pitch. Our aim in telling about women being abducted and never heard from again was to get into the deeper story of human degradation. We wanted to tell of the daily horror of the lives of these women. No one ever spoke about that. We needed to get Max to do what we had spent hours trying not to do, which was to feel what those women felt – until they were either freed of their abduction or liberated by death.

Even apart from the circumstance that Max had a loving daughter and a wife who adored him and whom he loved and that therefore he would naturally feel empathy for women, it was easy to feel the deep compassion in him toward all human beings. Roz knew this about him. She was sure he would offer a sympathetic ear to any story of violence done to women. And not just women but boys and men too – and maybe worst of all to girls, some as young as six. Even four. Horrible tales – and horribly common.

By violence, we weren't talking about just some occasional Saturday night black eye between couples who were no longer married so much as not yet divorced. True, wife beating was terrible, but our story was about much worse than that,. We wanted to make people see and especially feel that what was happening to women was the worst violence a human being could inflict on another, even worse than killing. Women out shopping were lured by a gang and never heard from again. That was worse than killing because death at least was an ending. Nothing more could follow. But there was prolonged never-ending psychological pain when a girl was last seen walking home from school and bundled into a van and – in the part that was never seen but feared and read about in the news accounts of other abductions – sold to a gang who beat her and burned her behind the ears or made cuts on the soles of her feet, places that didn't show. Then after her spirit was crushed by daily rape and beatings and starvation, she was told that by cooperating and working as a prostitute she could earn her freedom back. Her family remained forever suspended in desperate hope.

Some of these details were new even to me. Did they really burn a girl alive so that the others would obey out of fear?

It was Roz's conviction that only a true account realistically told by a big-name director would get people emotionally aroused enough to act. People needed to believe that such things really occurred. They were not tales of horrors in remote parts of the world – like that Nepal story of the little girl. Karen had been living and working right here, in New York, in Midtown Manhattan.

"Where's the outrage?" she yelled. "What the hell moves people to act?"

In her angrier moments her face became luminous. She argued that the only way people could be moved to act was to make a film with real characters to identify with. They had to care about the people involved and feel pity for them – pity and terror, the ancient formula of Greek tragedies. That was what was lacking.

When I asked about the reports on TV, the docudramas, she said they were done for ratings. They were aired once and forgotten. They were public affairs broadcasts to comply with a licensing agreement for balanced adult programming. And the accounts were almost always about events in third-world places, like someplace in Asia: Thailand, Kolkata, Mumbai. Never Chicago or Boston or L.A. America was the land of life, liberty and the pursuit of happiness.

"Right fucking here, for God sake, right under our noses. If you want to get anything done in this world, you have to reach into people's guts. There's no other way."

In a way I agreed with her and knew what she meant and knew it would mean putting Inge on hold for a while – inconveniently. I had been preparing to pop the question to Inge but now that would have to wait.

"Well," I said, "it looks like we have a lot of work ahead of us."

Turning those famous movie-screen eyes toward me she replied, or snapped really: "Can you think of anything better to do?"

•

I knew what Roz was driving at. Popular opinion would be an

irresistible force meeting an immoveable object, but in the long run the object had to be moved and would be moved. We would get the great power of public opinion to effect the change. That was our aim.

Yet she complained that whenever she brought up the subject of abductions and the enslavement of women, or described how some women mysteriously vanished, everybody she talked to said they were aware such things happened but they wondered if maybe Roz wasn't exaggerating? -- just a little? Millions of women just vanish? If that many kept vanishing, didn't she think people would notice?

And another thing. It was hard to believe the figure that was always trotted out: twenty-seven million. It didn't sound real that there were that many slaves in the world. It was just too enormous a number. It was practically the population of New England. Somebody would notice if New England suddenly emptied out. Things like that just did not happen. Or they happened in dumb horror movies about aliens taking over the earth – creepy junk like that.

These reactions really got up Roz's nose. She considered the disbelief to be a measure of how wrong people's ideas were. I could see her point. It's an irony that to most people the simple truth sounds far-fetched. Around the world millions of girls and women are kidnapped and sold into slavery and never seen again. Sometimes it's their own families that sell them, as in those awful stories we kept hearing about. Families needing money sell their daughters so they can buy a satellite dish. She's their property. And what do people do when you tell them? They don't believe you. Or if they believe you they don't do a damn thing. Nobody ever does a damn thing.

What Roz kept coming up against was that the reality sounded like something out of pulp fiction. A woman allows herself to be lured away by strangers with a fake story and after she's drugged she finds herself in some cheap brothel in maybe some Central American banana port. It sounded like the kind of stuff you saw on TV forensics programs. Or she is somewhere being raped and as a prized white woman locked up in a Moroccan harem. The most lurid stories, even if they happened to be the literal truth, had the feeling of urban myths. Some people said to Roz: has anyone ever actually witnessed all those abductions? Have women ever come back to tell their tales? How could anyone know if this was true? – or as true as was being made out? All that anyone ever believed for sure were the stories published in Sunday supplements sensationalizing sex slavery in faraway lands, sex-touristy stuff almost, titillating, X-rated stuff..

Anyway, putting all that together was the essence of what we were out to convince Max of, that women and girls, and men and boys too, really did go missing, that was not some fiction, it was happening all around us, including right here, and nothing was being done about it. In America, 2000 children were reported missing each year. So after that, what? That was the question. Why was nothing being done?

Roz and I had kicked this around a lot between us before we decided that that was the story the film would tell. And as we prepared to make our pitch to Max, Roz was confident he wouldn't in the end say no. If Roz had any doubts – and she must have had some – she wasn't going to let me see them. But everyone who knew Max knew he was a decent human being and would come round in the end.

5

The press had Max and Roz coupled so often as the "Dynamite Duo" that I looked forward to their company in the little time I would have with them. It felt like a privilege.

"Is it really true that Max is a grand-nephew of Eisenstein's cousin?"

Roz almost choked at that. She couldn't stop laughing and seeing her I had to laugh too.

"That's a particularly elaborate lie, the brainchild of a studio publicist out to make a name for himself."

"Born in Odessa?"

"Odessa, Texas, maybe. Unless there's an Odessa, New Jersey. I think he's from New Jersey."

I had heard many stories about Max and never knew whether to believe them or not, that, for example, according to one persistent rumor, he had attempted to have a star assassinated because she and her leading man ran off to the Arizona desert to start a new life together. The contract on her was for five million dollars. I had trouble believing that one. From the little I knew, he didn't seem like that kind of person.

The great number of rumors made me even more curious to know the real Max. Roz's thumbnail of him was simple. Orphaned at two. A genius at filmmaking. Had an adoring wife and a Phi Beta daughter. Couldn't do enough for friends. And was a Guinness Book of Records philanderer. ("He'll fuck anything that'll hold still for a few seconds.") That last was kept below the gossip-column radar. Hollywood fortunes are interlinked and everybody knows when to shut up about whom if they knew what was good for them.

"He's very modest too. You know what he said once? He said, 'They tell me I'm a genius. But the only genius in my films is what I've stolen from Renoir and Hitchcock. And Citizen Kane.' You'll get along with him. He's immensely likable and easy."

As likable and easy, I hoped, as Roz herself. I had never met anyone less complicated than Roz, not counting my lover Inge. It was through Inge that I met Roz. Their friendship went back to their Bennington days, where they achieved overnight celebrity when they founded "The Courgette and I Society", a clandestine off-campus group that in that dim dark era of human history (a decade ago) would have had them expelled had the dean not simultaneously discovered that the teenage daughter of one of the college's benefactors had for two years in a row been acclaimed winner of the Golden Courgette Award, more affectionately known as The Zuke (zucchini). The incident threatened to make a stink after a pompously angry editorial appeared in a small local paper. But the story was squelched and all rumors abruptly stopped.

I think I had better say, before leaving the subject, that Inge – Roz's dearest friend and my lover – didn't have much of a licentious side in common with Roz and in that sense they could not be more different. More than anything else, Inge preferred a sapiosexual, after I explained to her what the word meant. A man was a sapiosexual if he was attracted to a woman for her brains, and Inge certainly had a good head on her shoulders. Roz was different, although she was as intelligent as Inge. Roz just liked men, indiscriminately. And she loved liking them and enjoyed them serially and didn't give a damn what others might think. She was especially partial to those who were good at what she cheerfully described as the Australian pleasures of lip reading down under, but I'd better stop before I say anything more. I wouldn't want to embarrass her, although I don't know if anything ever could. But you'd have to know her a while to know that (say about fifteen minutes).

•

Anyway, to get on with what happened next. Picking me up at LAX Roz sped north in some flashy late-model beauty from Europe, the jazziest I had ever seen – Maserati, Lamborghini, I'm not sure which but probably costing more than a two-bedroom house in downtown L.A. It was a crimson convertible with swanky tan-leather seats and a glitzy dashboard of navigational gizmos that lit up like a Christmas tree.

"I hardly ever drive it. The studio insists I get driven around in their chauffeured limousine for arcane insurance clauses."

Her foot seemed to enjoy the accelerator as a resting place, I noticed, and after we had whizzed skillfully around twelve million vehicles without hitting one, I could understand the studio's apprehension.

"If you have an appointment at Paramount at ten o'clock and let's say you live in Bel Air, you'd have to leave the house at seven forty-five."

After the close summer heat of New York the Pacific air felt refreshing on my skin. As we cruised freeways the speedometer seemed stuck just below eighty-five ("Lucky break – you usually have to crawl along here") and Roz explained my bungalow accommodations, saying I needn't be concerned about meals and shopping. Her maid Sophie would take care of all my needs – well, not all my needs – on days when she, Roz, would be working at the studio. Which reminded her, her other car was mine to use.

"Because L.A without a car is unthinkable. It's a fuchsia Mercedes. I hope you don't feel threatened by fuchsia."

She had already set up our kick-off meeting with Max at his place up some canyon or other. Movie people seemed to live in canyons or on beaches. Or glens.

"You're going to like him. He's an ageless Cary Grant type and nearly as handsome. Or like Clooney, come to think of it. A little older maybe, but at fifty-two he looks fortyish."

I hoped I'd get to hear him talk about film making – planning to include it in the profile on him and also for my own purposes. I'd always been interested in how movies are made and in my younger and more innocent years had for a while dreamed of becoming a film director.

"On Sundays he's as relaxed as he ever gets and invites me to his pool to read Anna Karenina – out loud – in Russian, if you can believe that. To give me the full flavor of it, he says."

"I didn't know you spoke Russian."

"Are you kidding – Russian?" Her features grimaced as though she had just glimpsed something hideous: "Good fucking grief! I have trouble with English, and that's my native tongue. He says the language doesn't matter. It's the feeling that gets through. Feelings, he keeps saying. I plead my weak bladder to get out of listening to more than two minutes of it, Tolstoy or not. And he comes out with his awful jokes in that fake Russian accent he likes to put on, 'Dollink, you shoot do eet een the pool.' 'Max,' I say, 'I'm talking about taking a leak. Piss, comprenez peepee?' 'It vill sveeten the pool,' Max tells me. Fortunately he's only kidding or you'd have to find somewhere else to swim."

I'm still learning Roz's ways as both a long-time friend of Inge's and as Hollywood megastar. "Megastar" is a phrase she dislikes as much as she hates "Ms. Box Office" ("although the box part sounds comfy and friendly"). She elaborates on her need to take what she describes as a wicked piss.

"They're the worst kind. And to listen to Anna Karenina on top of it? With all that pressure building? No, thank you. You're talking to Miss Thimble Bladder here."

I wished Inge could have been here with us instead of back in New York, but she was in the middle of a photo shoot for the spring fashion number of Vogue, which was a career opportunity not to be missed. It was a meaty editorial assignment that would practically guarantee getting her in permanently good standing with Vogue, and after that she'd be able to practically write her own ticket in the commercial photography world. Which in my opinion was about time. She was a damn good photographer, and although the assignment didn't pay much, the recognition it would bring would more than make up for it.

I was glad for another reason Inge had landed that assignment. It might take her mind off her gawky seventeen-year-old friend Karen Bryggman that our film idea was about – the fashion model who had vanished one day visiting Morocco with her Romeo, her new lover. Karen would stand in for every woman in the world who had gone missing – abducted, disappeared, sex-slaved – and the one victim Inge could never get out of her mind. She felt guilty at not having prevented her abduction even though everyone tried to convince her there was nothing she could have done to prevent it. Kidnappers don't send out announcements about upcoming abductions.

This was Inge's and my first separation, and in her easy Finnish ways (she had grown up in Helsinki) she sincerely was not bothered that I would be living in Roz's guest bungalow, or in other words, living with her horny movie-star friend bedded down on the other side of a swimming pool a mere skinny dip away. She trusted Roz – with me. Trusted me too, with anybody. In fact she pressed me to go to Hollywood and stay at Roz's place if that would help get the Karen story told.

Roz was never really a threat. She knew I was crazy about Inge and in fact hoped Inge and I would marry and couldn't figure out what the hell we were waiting for. To light a fire under Inge Roz once even told her: "If you don't grab him I will." Not meaning it, of course, but just, as I say, to tell her to get a move on.

I appreciated Roz's help even though it did no good. Inge was stubborn: "How can I be happy while Karen is still missing?" She couldn't get past the whole Karen abduction and I couldn't really blame her, in a sense. She was hit hard and I sympathized.

Listening to Roz going on now about Max and our plans, I kept studying that famous movie-star face that mesmerized audiences. If star quality was having a reputation independent of your films, she had plenty of it. On the screen she always had an amused-by-life look in a sophisticated Katherine Hepburn-ish way but with none of those high-cheekbone calcium deposits. She was way more beautiful than that, and in person quite different in personality and not the least bit demure. In fact, the last thing she was was demure. When we first met, her wonderful zaniness kept taking me by surprise. She made me think of the screwball comediennes of the 1930s – Carole Lombard, Jean Harlow, if anybody still remembers them – and she was just as earthy as those early stars were reputed to have been. When we first met she was a shit-faced alcoholic but now no longer. She still drank and the zaniness was still there but there was more control now.

"It's my rich fantasy life," she said, casually laying it on with a Size AA trowel. "I've always wanted to say to someone on the phone: 'Oh don't come over just now. I'm in the middle of a blowjob.' Then after a gasp of horror at the other end say, 'Naa, just kidding.' "

I bring these things up just to give some idea of her style. When she feels safe among friends she can get outrageous (calling it multitasking to leisurely blow somebody while chatting on the phone) and her studio's publicists have been known to complain of her frequent unprintability.

"Which is half my charm."

Listening to her, I thought if Inge felt some slight apprehension about my living at Roz's place, no matter how unfounded her anxiety might be, it would be understandable. Roz's younger fans admired her for not giving a damn what people thought about what she said or did. And they sensed, accurately, that her views were sincere and not just a flip attitude made possible by Hollywood fuck-you money. She apparently had enough bread piled up in the Cayman Islands and Swiss mountain vaults to guarantee personal independence for the next four or five hundred years.

"I'm stinking rich, what can I tell you?" is how she put it.

I asked if she'd ever had or was currently having a fling with Max. We were friends enough for me to come right out with a question like that and she took it in the right spirit.

"Max? Good God, no! I love him but I'd rather keep him hooked and happy. He likes being hooked even if unhappy. I'm on his short list of women he hasn't shacked up with. Yet, he thinks. He once asked me directly if we could have a happy little boff between friends and I told him there was nothing I'd like more, except that by one of those odd little coincidences God had appeared in a dream only the night before and made me promise never to fuck film directors."

For Roz it was an easy segue from this to life on the set:

"On location I sometimes get so jazzed up that to let off pressure I'll have a fling with one of the technicians or crew, like a grip. I mean, with your pussy throbbing, how can anybody think straight? They're usually good for a roll in the hay and they're just nice well-behaved hunks and don't hassle you afterwards. It's a way of, you know, getting rid of the physical thing, the tension, and they don't seem to mind being used, in fact they rather like it. I mean, what male wouldn't like no-strings-attached sex, right? One of them was really sweet, a dishy hunk of a guy. As he was pulling his pants back on he said he felt like he had just been awarded an Oscar. I felt so flattered I told him to take his pants off again, he had just received another nomination. It was a long break, we had at least another two hours of waiting around while they were preparing the next setup, so we had time to kill and it seemed to make him happy. Made me happy too. I mean, what else is there to do in Wyoming? Which reminds me, don't ever go to Wyoming."

6

Meanwhile I was enjoying Roz's guest bungalow. It was a handsome all-redwood job with her swimming pool just outside and along its length. Its interior design, after Manhattan apartments, was an architect's extravaganza of sitting room, bedroom, TV sets sprinkled all around, including one plasma screen the size of a school chalkboard. It faced the queen-size bed. Off the bedroom, a cedar-paneled sauna seated four, and next to it a glassed-in shower had twenty (I counted them) micro-nozzle heads that pulsated slanting jets of water at various body parts, including one powerful horizontal jet at crotch level that gave you a whole new feeling about life. After all this it was surprising to find the fridge unstocked except for quart bottles of Apollinaris, Evian, Vittel, Perrier (two each), possibly in the event of the next California drought or earthquake.

I washed up, shaved and, with nobody around, stepped bare-assed into the dry California air, inhaling the spicy medicinal scent of eucalyptus trees and did a few laps in the pool. It was very refreshing and nice.

Emerging from the pool I could feel a pair of eyes on me at the far end. Roz's housekeeper Sophie was standing at the open doorway of the kitchen of the main house. She was grinning. She shouted over:

"Breakfast whenever you're ready."

Toweling off, I put on my one pair of khaki shorts and my apricot polo shirt and a pair of flipflops I found in the bungalow's closet and walked round to Roz's kitchen. The inside of the kitchen glowed with the early-morning sun.

Roz was gone. A limo and union driver had delivered her to the studio for postproduction on something she had filmed six months earlier (for I think Scorsese but am not sure – somebody).

Roz must have given Sophie a list of things I liked because as I watched she prepared a breakfast of mushrooms sautéed with green onions and garlic. I ate it with a chewy-skinned sourdough baguette and commented on the tanginess of the butter's taste. Sophie said it was flown in from the Netherlands.

"The best and the most expensive butter," she said.

She told it with the carefree laugh of someone who enjoyed the best food in the best surroundings without having to pay for any of it.

"I get the butter at Henri's, on Sunset. Henri's is the kind of place where you pay a hundred dollars for three drops of balsamic vinegar. I won't tell you what I paid for the butter. Just enjoy it."

"That would have to be some vinegar."

"I get most of Roz's things from Henri's or from Farmer's Market. She likes to do her own shopping but sometimes can't go to places like the Farmer's Market even wearing a wig, a babushka and dark glasses. It's a pain in the butt having people recognize you everywhere you go. You know, fame. People don't realize."

Outside the kitchen windows I watched an elderly Japanese gardener with chin whiskers. He was snaking a hose skimming the surface of the pool. The water had seemed clean when I swam in it.

"Oh he does that every morning."

With a bamboo rake, the gardener scraped into a pile the scraggly ribbon bark that the eucalyptus trees had shed.

Then, as I was still watching, a rain squall shot upward from a scattering of invisible sprinklers under the grass.

Sophie laughed at my surprise. "That's nothing. At the base of each trunk a gizmo in the ground waters the trees intravenously. Welcome to Southern California."

I asked Sophie how it felt to work for a movie star.

"Oh it's not bad."

Her father had come over from the Pyrenees to work as a shepherd in Nevada. He didn't like Nevada and after a while had gone further west and with his savings bought a small spread in the Napa Valley. At sixteen, when her father divorced her alcoholic mother, Sophie, who preferred the Southland, left home to become a bit player in films before she became Roz's housekeeper.

"Bit player is another way of saying unemployed."

She had the long-jawed attractiveness of Basque women and seeing her in a black taffeta skirt and long-sleeved white silk shirt with ruffled collar I had trouble picturing her as a farmhand in some old John Wayne horse opera.

I was surprised at how much she knew about the old days. She talked knowledgeably about the "legendary Goldwyns and the Thalbergs" and even the feared, long-forgotten gossip columnists Hedda Hopper and Louella Parsons, who were now merely part of West Coast lore, the ghosts and caricatures of Hollywood's anecdotal past.

"Movie magazines still keep them alive," she explained. She read several magazines a month.

●

Though I was on leave from the paper, Umpleby sent me reminders to continue working long distance as he emailed me each morning a few newspaper clippings to work up into a column.

The recent cull was pretty dull. God knows where Umpleby got this one: a witch doctor in Liberia cast a "bulletproof" spell over a friend and fired a fatal shot through the man's heart. He admitted in court that his mistake was to forget to write the magic number three on the man's chest.

Another squib: a man with a winning lottery ticket died but it was not until after he was buried that the family discovered that his big win was $358,000. They asked that the body be dug up because they believed the winning ticket was in the pocket of the new suit they had buried him in. "I hope people won't think I'm doing it for the money," his widow said. "I'm gonna donate most of it to St. Peter."

•

Roz tried to trim my enthusiasm and the excitement at just being in California, and tried to restrain my eagerness to learn movie making by describing to me now what the trades had been doing to Max. It felt like she was breaking bad news gently and I was a little surprised she had held back on me. Critics had lately been raking Max over the coals for his recent film Millie in Love. It had been so expensive to produce that one wag proposed it as a candidate for A Short History of Hollywood Disasters. If we wanted the power of the combined reputation of Max and Roz to draw attention to a film about the abduction of women around the world, this recent battering came now as a complicating factor.

Looking back recently over the log, or the notes I had begun keeping over the events of this period, I note that I intended to go see Millie in Love, and if I still haven't got round to it, I wouldn't take that as a comment. A friend described it as "not totally puke-worthy" but it was generally known that this friend had become an uncommonly harsh critic after his bitter divorce had convinced him life was a prolonged shit feast, as he put it, so I wouldn't put much trust in his judgment. It had to be a better film than that, I believed, because it was Max's.

But with these revelations it suddenly became clear we couldn't have picked a worse time to interest Max in making a film – not even with Roz starring in it and not even if she did it for free, as a gift to Max, which she actually offered to do. She'd be satisfied to get points at the back end, if the film were a success. Up-front money was not important to her. Making the film -- that was what mattered.

For a while there were a lot of jokes about Millie in Love, and the kidding around on late-night TV was that the most it could hope for was the Dolly Parton Cleavage Award. Nothing against the friendly crowd in Dolly Parton's balcony – what Roz called her stuppendages. Dolly Parton was not in the film nor in any way associated with it and the only point of the jokes that dragged her in was the number of cleavages filling the silver screen (one of Max's trademarks), with Roz's own unenhanced breasts in all their breathtaking reality teasingly glimpsed once in a thrilling half-second of resplendent showstoppers, as attention-getting on the screen as the giant white letters

H O L L Y W O O D

were in the natural hilltop setting.

Don't get me wrong. I like Dolly Parton as a person (as I imagine her to be) and I also think she's one shrewd cookie, and lovable in her shrewdness, and that it's part of her successful persona to have you think she's just a sweet little ole hillbilly lady. Get into a business deal with her and she could probably run circles around you, tie you up in a nice pink ribbon and make you feel happy to have been screwed, blewed and tattooed – metaphorically speaking. Thinking these thoughts it crossed my mind that maybe she'd be interested in making the movie but I set it aside to concentrate on Max.

•

So the following morning, on our way to Max's place, we drove down a palm-tree-lined boulevard, then up some canyon or other. Every half mile or so I got a glimpse of a swanky estate behind trees and an elaborate electronic gate topped with iron spikes, and as she drove, Roz repeated her cautionary advice.

"No letting up no matter how much he says no. His style is to keep saying no and then in the end say yes."

Roz explained that critics had a high opinion of Max and continued to admire him despite this Millie thing, even though the way they talked about him you'd think he'd sold out.

"He's said to be one of our great cinematic geniuses, on a level with Hitchcock and Jean Renoir and a few other people they compare him to – not just compare him with, you understand, but actually compare him to – and they find it difficult to understand how he could have put his name to what his kindest critics are calling a vanilla washout."

"That bad."

"No. Not that bad. There's just no pleasing everybody. The critics'll come around to it eventually and it'll be 'rediscovered'."

In the past few weeks the film had started showing signs of a small financial return, but that was only because of Roz or Lorna Beach and her wide-screen cleavage. It was just a half-second shot of America's most famous boobs. But then, with Roz in a film, it never took much. She had only to appear in a scene for men to feel a certain pelvic happiness, or maybe unhappiness, and Umpleby, the great managing editor of the great New York World-Herald, said of her breasts that they alone made the world a better place to live.

But it wasn't just her boobs. It was her face. It made competition useless. Even the most rivalrous of her women admirers felt outclassed and succumbed to a kind of wonder that a set of genes in that precise combination even existed. It made me think of a story I had once heard of a Frenchwoman whose fellow townspeople found her so beautiful they passed an ordinance compelling her to sit on her balcony twice a week just so they could look at her.

Anyway, there we were, Roz driving up to a gate and saying "Hi" and returning a smile to the uniformed gatekeeper ("Af'noon, Ms. Beach") and driving on up a gravel driveway to a Gone with the Wind portico. A middle-aged lace-cap-and-aproned maid opened the door and led us to Max's study. It was a long neat warm-colored room of walnut-paneling, with three or four easy chairs and a well-used comfortable-looking velvet couch.

Max rose extending his hand and I saw him tall and tanned and wide-chested under his open-collared yellow polo shirt. There was great force in his handshake.

"I've heard all about you," he said. "Come in, come in, come in."

We each took an easy chair facing the other two in a triangle and Max spoke to Roz, "How's life, sweetheart?"

"Comme ci, comme what may."

"I love this woman. We always end up talking about life, than which nothing is more interesting, don't you think? We're born, we die, and the only question is why."

"A koan," Roz said.

"Yes. 'What's it all about?' as the old song goes."

"I forgot to tell you," Roz said to me, "Max is not only a film director, he's also a philosopher. A bad one but you have to give him credit for trying."

"And Roz is a flatterer. I'm quite content to be a film maker."

"The greatest art form ever devised."

"Exactly."

"Tell us again about the film you were going to make called 'From Bible Belt to Garter Belt'."

"I love jokes," Max said to me, "even bad ones. Like the one about the butcher and the cannibal."

"The butcher and the cannibal?"

"The butcher tells the cannibal that he sells lawyer's brains for $24 a pound, doctor's brains for $50 a pound and agent's brains for $100 a pound, and the cannibal asks how come agents' brains cost so much, and the butcher says, 'Do you have any idea how many agents it takes to make a pound of brains?' "

"Max has it in for agents," Roz said.

"Actually bad writers are worse. Way worse than agents," Max said. "With bad writing, the best acting in the world doesn't stand a chance."

"I think writers are terribly abused," Roz said.

"Oh I agree," Max said. "The average producer or director thinks that if he can hire six writers to write the same script the film will be six times as good. The result is it's six times crappier."

"Too many cooks."

"In the end it's the audience who is the author. Which is why there are previews. The moguls cater to the audience. They test the audience's reaction to certain lines and change the lines if the reaction is not what they had hoped for. The film is a commodity and they want the audience to buy it so they can get their money back with a profit in order to make another commodity and more profits – it's like making widgets. Is there anything wrong in doing that if the public wants to buy the crap? Of course not. Who's opposed to widgets?"

Encouraged by seeing them in a light, joking mode I took a chance and jumped in with my favorite Hollywood anecdote, about the screenwriter warning his friend that a certain film was so putrid he advised him to avoid the movie house where it was playing and even avoid the street the theater was on in case there was a sudden shower and he ducked inside and accidentally saw some of the film.

To this Max murmured approvingly, "Joseph L. Mankiewicz."

The way he said it made Mankiewicz sound like one of the saints of Hollywood, and I suppose in a sense he was. Is.

•

We were soon making progress, in a way. The ice broken, Max and I seemed to hit it off and I began to believe that our film could be made even though we hadn't mentioned it yet. Max seemed comfortable about my outsider's status, which from all I'd heard was regarded an achievement in Hollywood. As Roz said, "Nobody's more of an outsider than a Hollywood outsider."

Max seemed amused and interested to hear Roz call me Horatio and asked if that was really my first name. A touchy subject and my least favorite topic of conversation. He was polite, though, and didn't laugh.

"No, it's not, actually. My real first name's John, but I never use it. Horatio's my middle name, which is bad enough." I never tell anybody I have a second middle name, Hornblower, not wishing to shock people. I let them get used to Horatio first. Why I was saddled with these names remains both a mystery to me and a sore point. Usually a little bit of humor is enough to terminate further discussion on the topic of first names and good friend Roz saved the day by steering the conversation abruptly to our film idea. Watching Max's face I could see the first sign of resistance.

Speaking to each other as though the three of us had been friends for years, Max intimated flat out it would not be possible to make a film of the kind we were pitching. What he actually said – and said so many times it came out sounding like a mantra – was:

"Listen: no ending, no story." The dismissal was that brief. He said it twice. "No ending, no story."

He seemed to study the change in my face and then said.

"If that's your pitch, you might as well go back to New York."

"No ending, no story," Roz repeated, staring at him.

"You can't tell a story with just a beginning and a middle."

The criticism was irritating though certainly valid as far as the words went. No ending, no story. Of course. But then I had been forewarned: first Max would say no. But I also began to suspect that maybe I'd be going back to New York earlier than I thought. I was already missing Inge terribly, and I had that as consolation.

Roz wanted to know why some writers couldn't just tack on an ending, damn it. Providing of course the point of the film was not violated. Roz's voice here took on a pleading sound, which surprised me.

"I mean what are screenwriters for?"

She was not going to make it easy for him to slip away. She wondered aloud if there was another reason for Max's apparent unwillingness to make our film.

I was out of my depth here and having nothing to contribute

that would make the least bit of sense to them decided to just sit back and enjoy listening to a couple of motion-picture biggies argue. I was here as a break from my nine-to-five air-conditioned dungeon in an architectural abortion on Manhattan's Lower West Side, and I thought to myself I might as well enjoy a few nice balmy days in California and let the two friends work things out. It was a pleasure seeing a beautiful woman venting anger on a beautiful day, providing of course said anger was not directed at me.

Because Roz, not giving up, was well into Super Foul Mode, tossing high-velocity f-bombs – not quite fuck this, fuck that but getting there – I mean, totally incensed. She was one of the few people in Hollywood who could explode at the great Max Petrov and still find employment with him. In fact, I think Max loved it coming from her.

"How much more of a fucking story do you want?" It sounded as though she was suppressing the words "You idiot!"

Max, ever unperturbed: "In a story, the idea is to show people doing something. With twists and turns in the plot and not just constantly talking about doing something. And their action has to lead to some resolution. There's a problem, the problem is solved and that brings you to a nice ending. Film 101."

Roz looked at him, her mouth open a little.

"What is the climax?" Max needled her. "Where is your climactic scene? If you don't know what your climax will be, then you don't know where you're headed and you wander around lost. You have no ending."

Roz started yelling at Max. But Max came right back at her:

"No, you listen to me. Family stories are what you want. Family stories are worth more than all the statistics and official documents in the world about disappearing women. So the first thing you need is a story about people you can identify with. They have to have lives that something in you enjoys following."

This was old familiar ground so I only half listened as I took in the beauty of the semitropical surroundings outside the wide picture windows at the garden end of the long room. I kept thinking: I'm in Hollywood. I should be thrilled.

It was a fine September day, one of those cloudless California days that a poet friend who had moved to Big Sur described as "achingly beautiful". Once he got past the pain of beauty he called the blueness of the sky "an obstinacy of azure", and just when I was hoping he'd give up poetry and try writing advertising copy for ladies' hairspray or foundation creams, he won a John D. and Catherine T. MacArthur Award for his "important" poetry. I could never figure out what "important" means in that context or what it takes to make somebody an "important poet", but it certainly was a handsome award and netted him a quarter of a million bucks a year for five years. The conferring of such awards is a wonderful help in living allowance, but many believed that in his case it turned out to be a mistake. Everything he wrote after that came out turgid and tedious (alliterative too), and lost him the approximately three and a half admirers he had had before then, counting his wife as the half.

Anyway, it was a lovely day. High overhead the sky was blue above a low luminous morning mist at ground level, and I didn't think a climate could get better than that. Especially after New York, where the steamy days of sopping heat inspired thoughts of ending it all or moving to Finland, which was where Inge's family lived in the middle of a hundred million lakes. And they were always talking about a little town in Lapland called Ii – not included on most maps of northern Europe, if you were thinking of looking it up – a place I suspected her family liked because of its name. I'm not sure whether Inge said it was twinned or it should be twinned with a cutesy town in France called Ôo, and the family had many jokes about the marriage of Ii and Ôo, or Ii-Ôo. (Tea for two, me for Ii-Ôo.)

Inge once likened the sound of Ii to the cry of an animal horribly caught in a life-or-death struggle and desperately hoping someone would hear and come save its life.

•

"Before we go any further let's take this outside," Max said. "It's stuffy in here."

So there we were, the three of us, Roz, Max and I, lounging around his pool, legs comfortably stretched out under a large wrought-iron-and-glass garden table shaded by a lemon-yellow Nieman-Marcus umbrella with little white-tassels dangling in dippy fringes around its edges. Real Hollywood piece-of-shit umbrellas. I counted twenty-two of them around the pool, each umbrella probably costing two months' of my pay at the paper. I felt happily decadent and wished only that Inge could be here to enjoy it too.

A hard-working maid from Russia, or Moldavia, or possibly Central Casting, silently entered and exited bearing canapés and knickknacks and frosty pitchers of summery drinks. She carefully arranged everything on a white-tableclothed table at the edge of the pool.

It was all a very cheerful and nice-looking scene in a movie. At the far end of the pool spaghetti-straight trunks of palm trees were spaced in a mathematically even line against the sky. The row of fronds at their tops made lazy curls. Tall neatly-trimmed shrubs at the foot of the trees concealed a distant L.A. sprawl of eight hundred square miles of freeways ribboning over the tops of houses and empty lots, open-air drug deals, bodies in dumpsters, a rape-in-progress – other stories in need of an ending.

7

I helped myself to some lemonade.

"Marya makes great lemonade," Max said.

"Delicious," I said.

I had made up my mind that Max's resistance to our idea was not going to stop me from enjoying my Hollywood break. Just visiting Max at his home and sitting around the swimming pool of a twenty-seven-room house. was providing an education in film history. He described it as a "formerly owned" residence.

"What's 'formerly owned' mean?"

"It's code," Max said. "It means a place with a pedigree going back to some famous 1920s movie star. The pool's kidney shape itself tells of a bygone era of custard-pie films and old-fashioned ritzy stars like Pickford and Swanson and Garbo."

"Some or all of whom might have dipped their highly-paid asses in the water right here where we're sitting," Roz said "It's a wonder somebody hasn't bottled some of it to sell on eBay."

"How do you know it hasn't been?" Max kidded along with her.

"So our story needs more work" – terrier Roz never giving up.

"It needs a lot more work," Max murmured, but then gave her a friendly word-to-the-wise: "Look, I don't want to discourage you – I like your idea. It's a very worthy idea. But if you want to bankroll this thing you'll have to be more realistic."

We were trying to impress on him that the kernel of the idea was a true story of what had happened to a friend: Karen Bryggman. We went over it again. A young fashion model, a sensation at seventeen, had mysteriously vanished and that was the whole story. It had been in all the papers about two years ago and even now there was an occasional reference to the famous young fashion model's unexplained disappearance from the scene. The story was no longer fresh in people's minds but seeing the film they would remember her.

For Roz, obstacles were just things to be removed. Her response to Max to the problem of getting money to back the film was "Balls!" What powered her was that no subject in the world was more important to her than the abuse of women. She and I had had many long discussions about it, and Inge too, the three of us feeling we were in this together. And Roz was getting worked up about the subject again. Women were abducted, sold as sexual slaves, or murdered, and it was happening daily. Right now, right fucking now, while we were sitting around this fucking swimming pool doing fucking nothing.

Roz was growing passionate making the pitch. Lives, whole families, were being destroyed. Like a lawyer arguing a case, she demanded to know whether there could possibly be a more important story than this. The worst of it was – did Max want to know what the worst of it was? – the worst of it was that it was happening with the knowledge of everybody in the whole fucking world while the criminals were getting away with fucking murder. It was a film that had to be made. What was wrong with people?

"Prostitutes are arrested as criminals. They are seen as the problem, not the traffickers who forced them into prostitution. For every 500 prostitutes arrested – for every 1000, for every 10,000 prostitutes arrested – you know how many traffickers are arrested? None."

I enjoyed seeing her in this mood rather than the screen persona of Lorna Beach honored on television news with a star in that bullshit Hollywood Walk of Fame. Also it was impossible not to enjoy looking at that beautiful head when she got mad, a cliché idea about women, admittedly, but you could fall in love with just the way a woman's mouth moves when she's, as they say in Hollywood, emoting. And this was no role she was playing as she went on and on about women being kidnapped off the streets. What especially bothered her was that parents sold daughters into sexual slavery. Was that true? Parents knowingly sold their little girl to a brothel? Well, maybe in poor Asiatic countries.

When Max sounded callous about nothing being new in the trafficking of women I could understand Roz's feelings.

"I do get this whole thing," Max said, "but movies can't correct human injustice. Movies can show you the things that are wrong in society and they can move you – which isn't bad for a medium that started out as a boardwalk novelty showing still photographs of people suddenly surging into motion as if they were living human beings and not two-dimensional images." For an uneasy second I thought he was going to launch into a history of cinema. But he stopped abruptly.

It was self-evident of course that in film making, a story had to have something new in it. Which was part of his point. Not just the ending, but what happens?

"It's no longer 1910," Max said.

"1910?" Roz asked.

"What made Hollywood possible was the boredom of the masses. Their only entertainment in 1910 was to stand at the train station and watch the 7:02 arrive and then leave again at 7:04."

"I think I'll have a gin and tonic," Roz said..

"To entertain, you have to hold the audience's attention. You have to give their inner chaos, so to speak, a path to some sort of emotional resolution – a resolution they're expecting."

"Jesus. Make that a double."

"That's what a story does. Women are trafficked, but then what? Where's the twist in the plot, in other words? And what does it lead to? This is where good writers come in. Am I boring you with this?"

"Oh don't stop now," she told him, "I was just beginning to drift off."

"You know," Max said, "there's only one thing wrong with Hollywood."

Roz: "You're kidding."

"They're all good people here and mean well but they suffer from brain rot."

Roz: "You're kidding."

Max was a movie maker and however convolutedly he put things he was only being realistic. He was not interested in ideas for dollar-a-dozen documentary shorts presented on the evening news. He assured us of that.

The meeting was definitely not going well. Max was giving us a definite No, just as Roz had predicted. And it didn't matter how sure she felt that the subject, looked at purely for its commercial potential, yelled box office. It was to her one that a studio, any studio, would grab and run with. But now, after talking to Max, Roz and I were no longer certain we were getting anywhere with our good intentions, and her getting pissed off didn't help.

She complained to Max how infuriating it was that no one seemed to give a fuck, and she was getting fed up with the whole fucking human race, and so on, piling on all the fucks she could work in – I mean, so pissed off I had trouble not laughing. What impressed me was her use of the word "fuck" as three or four parts of speech in one memorable sentence – as intensifier, verb, adjective and noun – and of course the compound noun expressing the tabooed relation with mother. I forget how she worked that one in.

"Only simpleminded assholes don't care when you tell them what's happening when you'd think that the bare facts alone would enrage people into action."

Max, with his usual modulated tones: "Anger, the great motivator." His attitude wasn't helping. "Listen, I'll tell you a deep dark secret. People are not going to do a damn thing unless you send chills up and down their spines. And sometimes even then."

Roz turned disbelieving eyes on him, and then on me.

But Max showed no sign of being drawn in, commenting, "Life is cutthroat, brutish, nasty and short, as Shakespeare said." Then: "And it doesn't help that these migraines are killing me."

And that was the other part of our unfortunate timing – his migraines. It was a recent development that Roz had been aware of but not given much thought to its effect on his receptiveness to our idea.

When a migraine struck, his suffering was enormous and all work stopped. I suppose he couldn't help it but with his director's talent he turned the very real local pain into Greek tragedy. The ancient Furies were hot after his, Max Petrov's, ass. Or rather his head.

He was a sensitive and kindhearted man, though, that much was obvious, and besides, as someone who couldn't take even a slight headache, I felt sorry for the poor bastard plagued by migraines. It had to be murder. And on top of all that, he had begun to suffer these days from sleep deprivation. Really his life at the moment was a mess that I wouldn't trade places with, Hollywood or no Hollywood.

He sounded resigned. "You have no idea how slowly time can pass until you lie awake all night staring at the dark."

Roz – perhaps just a tad too sweetly: "Don't curse the darkness. Take a sleeping pill."

•

Max was Hollywood aristocracy and liked life italicized and with a capital L: Life. He spoke of the beauty of Life the way the elderly do who are close to departing from it. His plan for the future was only to make movies until he collapsed one day, ideally while cranking a camera, and preferably cranking it at Roz. Roz was not just his favorite actress. She was also his most steadfast lust object. But he kept his emotions under control and she felt comfortable with him – and felt reassured she would never be out of work. Her "handsome Crimean prince" was protective of her and that was a good feeling to have in cutthroat – and nasty and brutish – Hollywood, even if "in the horizontal department" they would never "consummate a happy-ending boff."

She had another reason for boff nonconsummation. It didn't take much feminine intuition to know that in the long run it would be politically smart to keep bed and work separate, especially in her profession, where so much happened horizontally that at times the little back pocket of West Coast known as Hollywood resembled a whorehouse on steroids.

As the winner of two Academy Awards and two or three Golden Globes and I forget what else – Cannes, Berlin, the whole schmier – she appreciated the electrifying effect that she as Lorna Beach had on men and allowed for exceptions among certain less-experienced leading men who, surprisingly, turned into nervous ingénues during a climactic love clinch when cast as her costar. She would invite the poor bastard into her trailer for a quick boff, or, as she put it to them, "a private conference to go over notes," as the swiftest way to put him out of his misery.

"Not exactly Stanislavski but it works."

"I don't know how anyone can bear even the tiniest headache," I heard Roz saying now to Max. We were back on headaches again. "A migraine would drive me up the wall."

"Right now a tiny headache would feel like two weeks in the Bahamas.".

I wondered if he owned property in the Bahamas too, along with his residences in Gstaad, Cap Ferrat and Malibu – and this incredible spread here, which was either up some Beverly Canyon or Beverly Glen or Brentwood or Bel Air. Possibly it was Holmby Hills. Or maybe it was Hidden Hills or Beverly Hills. I only knew for sure it wasn't Hollywood Hills, at least not the part of it where you see all those giant white letters along the top of the cliff.

This whole part of California was a glamorous geography of glens, hills and woods with names made romantically familiar by a million filmland bios. The drive from LAX had passed through or over several of them, or, as somebody once said, through six suburbs in search of a city. It felt more like thirty-six suburbs. A number of L.A. homes grew lemons in their backyards – a fact I noted for possible use in the column someday. Lemons and, I think, lime trees but curiously no oranges.

It was seriously worrying that the project Roz and I were attempting to get off the ground might not become a reality. Max had all the clout anyone in the movie industry could wish for, so when he sounded casual and indifferent, it made it all the more painful to hear him doubt we'd ever see our film made.

"It's terrific as an idea. And certainly it's an idea whose time has come. But . . ." His voice trailed away from the "but" – the thought apparently not worth completing.

By training and experience Max was hard-nosed, and what Roz and I were proposing just made no sense to him, and that was what he was telling us, openly and forthrightly, in a dozen different ways. No ending, no story.

•

To be honest, I hadn't really wanted to come out to Hollywood in the first place – I mean, not all that badly. I was a little curious about it but that was about all. The idea was Inge's and Roz's and it didn't help much now thinking Max might be right about its not being workable as a movie the way we told it. There was nothing more fatal to a story than not having an ending. What happened to the girl? Whether abducted or sold, women disappeared, and then what? Well, they vanished. OK, they vanished, and then what? That was the question we kept coming up against: then what happened? Until you had an answer to that you had no story.

I honestly didn't know what good I was doing here helping Roz, or supposedly helping her, because in pitchability I was worse than hopeless and felt the only smart thing to do would be to call it quits and head back to good old Manhattan. California weather was wonderful and swimming pools were pleasant but I preferred Midtown, even if it would be difficult to grow lemons in backyards, assuming Manhattan still had backyards and assuming I might someday feel like growing lemons.

For Roz it was quite different. There was her, as I say, terrier aspect. There didn't seem to be any letup in her excitement about the project. This was not some commonplace story we were proposing – another drug-running flick. Drug movies were yesterday. Even putting things purely on a mercenary basis, the smart money now was in stories on the sale of women as sex slaves.

Slanting it commercially to get Max interested, Roz went into a serious pitch about sexual slavery as a trade in billions a year and safer than drugs. There was nothing illegal in having girl babies and growing them into adolescent girls. It wasn't cocaine or anything clandestine. They were girls and they came of ordinary families and each year there was another new crop of females ready for marketing. Young more-or-less attractive women appeared in life one day, were abducted and then sold, and ditto juveniles eight years old and some even as young as six. The younger ones were sold by their families, from the little research we had done. That occurred mostly in Asia. They became income-producers for their families by being taken in hand by some nice people in a big city somewhere to "do a little work" that would earn money to send home – like the little girl from Nepal.. These families never learned what happened to the young girls when they got a little older and outlived their usefulness at "work". Those were the bare outlines, and surely Max could see it was a story that didn't need embellishing.

He could see it, all right, but he was intransigent.

Roz started getting incensed again. Just outlining the story, her voice rose as she explained that you could only hate parents who destroyed the lives of their own children, and especially in those other cases that she was thinking of now, where fathers killed their daughters for something they called their fucking honor, and on and on. Even carried away she had a very smooth pitch. Not having her talent, I could not possibly reproduce it, but it seemed persuasive to my way of thinking, although it apparently made little impression on Max.

But that didn't deter Roz. Nothing deterred Roz.

"Did you know that five thousand teenage girls are killed each year by their fathers? And their brothers? Five thousand women are stabbed to death in their own homes, by their own family – can you imagine the horror of that? – for their fucking family's fucking honor?"

I had this gruesome picture of a knife entering a girl's chest, and I could tell from Max's face he felt Roz's passion. She was getting through to him. Yet strangely, his response seemed unemotional. Maybe in the elegant surroundings of palm trees and swimming pools the subject seemed unreal. He nodded, quietly agreeing, yes, yes, terrible, he was sympathetic to the idea, very sympathetic, yes, he understood. Still there was no budging him. He even tried changing the subject to something that did concern him, and concerned him very much. He too had a movie in the back of his mind, something he had long wanted to make.

"I know what you mean, in a way. Death and disappearance have a great fascination for mankind. It's a truism that in old age you risk death every day," he said. "And –" scoring a point with her – "death is the greatest disappearing act of them all."

Max's style of communication was similar to his film technique: shock to keep it all moving. Roz stopped dead here, looking at me, as I suddenly felt we were all in a Chekhov play, with Roz talking about the abduction of women and Max going on about death in old age and me thinking about citrus growing in Manhattan.

Suddenly Roz seemed to realize Max was talking about his own death. Or that's what she thought, anyway.

"You gotta be kidding! At fifty-two you're old?" Roz turned to me, her sleek fingers gracefully flicking sunglasses from forehead to the top of her head "Women start their bidets running as soon as they hear Max is in town."

I again looked at the face that columnists running out of ways to rave about lazily summarized as "legendary", stating it to be their belief the ancient Greeks were right in elevating beauty to the rank of goddess.

"What are you thinking about?" Roz asked taking in my glance. Still cross.

"Lemons," I lied.

"Mine are bigger than that," she said.

Max turned to me: "So you're a writer. Have you ever read The Death of Ivan Ilych? Fascinating story about a man dying."

I had stopped thinking of myself as a writer but as a journalist. A point of pride – well, a point of sadness: aside from wanting to be a film director, I had always wanted to be a writer, but having nothing to show for it I didn't like admitting it.

I told him I had heard of the Tolstoy story but had not read it. About Tolstoy I knew only, or had heard only, that he was a horny old buzzard who humped anything that wasn't actually furniture. And then when he was done he would run into his study and confess it all to his diary as the sinner that he was. No – there was another fact I had read somewhere. He had been orphaned at two and at seventy-eight still yearned to hug the leg of a mothering person and cry.

Max, undeflected, brushed aside my reading gap.

"In old age you risk death every day. It's Russian roulette, and believe it or not, there's exhilaration in it. It's exhilarating because you win every time. When it comes time for you to lose, as of course you inevitably will, you won't know about it, so what is there to be afraid of? All that you will ever know is that you wake up each morning and see that you're here. Which is maybe why the elderly smile so much."

Roz: "Could we maybe talk about something else? Perhaps even the subject at hand. Or even, hey, I know – how about the weather?"

"Just imagine, when you drop dead, you will be the only one among family and friends who will not know you just died."

I don't know if Max had even heard her.

"And so what is there so depressing about that?" he asked.

"Excuse me while I go pee," Roz said. "And not in the pool."

8

That's the way it started – not exactly auspiciously. Roz asked if we could have another meeting and when Max swiftly agreed, it said a lot about his feelings for her.

"Love to see you again, dollink. Trish will set it up." Trish was Max's secretary at East-West Studios.

The next morning, having breakfast in Roz's kitchen, I told Sophie I missed seeing a daily newspaper and she informed me Roz didn't subscribe to any and if I didn't like reading them online I could go down to the Strip and buy one. So to kill time between meetings I took the Mercedes down to the Beverly Hills library, figuring I could always do a little research browsing the stacks once I got done with the papers.

It turned out to be a nice modest-sized library. It was in the Spanish-baroque city hall area just across from a church. As I walked in and looked around, a librarian came over and asked if she could help. She was a blue-rinser, with shoulder-length straight hair and bangs that fell at an angle to either side of her forehead. She led me to where newspapers were hanging on rods. Making talk to thank her, I commented that it was an interesting-looking church across the way and she agreed it was charming and a fine example of Art Deco.

"It's the Church of the Good Shepherd. The locals call it Our Lady of the Cadillacs."

I got a copy of the L. A Times and opened it out on a table to read. It had a front-page story about a woman last seen a couple of years ago as she hitchhiked along the Coast Highway, and the police were saying they had exhausted all leads and were declaring the case cold. They had no clues nor did they have suspects or persons of interest, only conjecture and suspicions. Maybe the woman was kidnapped and was now somewhere in Asia – as far-fetched as that sounded. Or maybe butchered and her body parts left in the Mojave Desert. Or, quite possibly, she was in the next county living a happy life and choosing to remain as far from her family as she could get.

The police seemed reluctant to admit they hadn't a clue but wouldn't comment on the little they did know and were asking for the public's help. They said: "We don't know whether she met her demise. That would take us into matters of speculation, which we don't feel it is our place to do. It's still pending. We'll only go so far as to inform the public that there's much work to be done."

I love police talk and collect it. I especially liked it that the women's demise was still pending. That went into my new notebook.

●

Involved in reading the papers I lost track of the time and when I got back to the bungalow Sophie relayed the message that Max had asked to see us and Roz was already on her way to his place. So I got back in the car and sped over to Max's, remembering the way to the gated estate not that far away. A gold plate on the tall surrounding iron fence said Great Cotswold. A guard looked up my name on a list and let me through.

I was quite a few minutes late, but, as Roz had hinted, Max was a forgiving person. He seemed permanently courteous and a great talker and, as I found out, interviewed beautifully. A maid brought me out to the pool, leading the way through a lavish room that could have contained a three-room Manhattan apartment and began deep inside the house and with no visible external wall kept going until it morphed into a spacious flag-stoned patio and the swimming pool. The setting was something out of a four-color two-page spread in an architectural magazine.

As soon as I arrived Max turned to me.

"Ah, there you are. I was just thinking about you and wondered what your dreams are," he said.

"My dreams?"

"You're smiling but people's dreams may be the most important subject in life, as crazy as that sounds. What do you want from life? What do you dream of – of having or doing?"

Thrown by the question I said the first thing that came to mind. Which was that when I was young I wanted to be a writer – like the writers I admired: Joyce and Hemingway and Fitzgerald. Just knock off novels and short stories as I globe-trotted around Paris, the Riviera, maybe down to Amalfi, mailing back manuscripts to an impatient publisher. It embarrassed me to tell my naïve adolescent fantasy but strangely I felt comfortable with him.

"Ah, a romantic. You wanted to be a writer so you became a news reporter."

Roz jumped to my defense. "He's not a news reporter. He's a journalist and a damn good one and has a lot of experience at it. Glad you got here. We were just talking about the Karen story." (Roz: Staying On Message.)

Max was supportive. "There isn't a subject in the world that can't be made into a movie."

He sounded seriously engaged. Roz, going on with the subject they had apparently begun just before I arrived:

"Women are bought and sold in India like animals. Were you aware of that?"

Deep into working on Max, she was not letting up, telling me:

"We were just talking about how these women are locked in big cages in the marketplace – grown women, for heaven sake – like your wife, Max, like me. Can you imagine women in a cage and men going down to the market and looking them over and picking out one that appeals to them and taking her home? They take home a woman. Like grocery shopping. Can you imagine the misery of that woman? She's now their property. They own her – how much is that little doggie in the window? How much more drama could you ask for? It's the same in Africa except that in Africa it's more clandestine. There they just kidnap you off the street and sell you to mafia-like people. And these things are done every day."

Her voice ended in passionate pessimism. Amazingly Max looked skeptical. Then, speaking reasonably: "That's something for the U.N. to be concerned about, wouldn't you say?"

"Yes, and that's part of the story too. The U.N. is fucking helpless." Roz indignantly turned to me. "Tell Max the figures – you know, from the other day."

On cue I recited: "A report says that there are twenty-seven million slaves in the world today. And that's supposed to be the low figure, and it's also historically the greatest number ever."

For once Max looked shocked. "That many?"

"Four million new women are added to that number each year. Isn't that horrific?" Roz asked.

"It's pretty horrific, yes," Max said. "But I don't make documentaries."

"You mean you're not interested?" Roz yelled.

"Of course I'm interested," Max replied. "It's a subject of enormous interest. But not in making a film."

"Why not?"

Enunciating carefully: "Because to make a movie you first need a story and a story needs an ending." He looked at her as though he was tired of repeating himself. "I thought you were more professional than that. You must know that." Then as a concession: "Maybe I can get Jake Carpenter and Rob Rubinstein to come up with something and see if they can make a story out of it. I mean a story with an ending. But it's only because I like you. I'm really trying to help you."

It went on like that for a while but not for very long. Max had another meeting coming up, and as we got up to leave I asked Roz about this Carpenter and Rubinstein. She said they were two of the best writers in Hollywood (Max nodding concurringly) and usually worked as a team. She seemed encouraged by the news. Carpenter and Rubinstein might come up with something. They could save the day.

As we left, Max had a thought. He suggested I attend a business meeting at the studio to learn how things worked in getting a production going – or (a small laugh) how things didn't work. Maybe then I'd get a better idea of the reality of film making.

•

Max's preoccupation with death was not new, apparently, because for several years Max had been wanting to film that Tolstoy story, The Death of Ivan Ilych. Hollywood was full of surprises. There, now, was a film he'd be happy to make. It at least had an ending. The hero dies.

The trouble was he had been finding it difficult to locate a writer for the kind of script that that particular story needed, someone who understood what Tolstoy was after. Also to put his, Max's, stamp on it. The rest – casting, direction, production design – all that would easily fall into place once he had what he called a solid story on paper. Listening to him I wondered what was wrong with Tolstoy's own solid story on paper but said nothing. There were probably important things to learn about translating a story to the screen.

All the same I secretly admired Max for his choice of death as a subject. Death, of all things. I gathered that much of the story happens in Ivan Ilych's mind and you can't photograph that without flashbacks, dream sequences.

In Hollywood, to think seriously about doing a film about dying, you would either have to be looking to commit professional suicide or be a Very Big Name – and Max's name was certainly one of the biggest. He could count on Roz to come aboard to play the wife and she was bankable, but what about the male lead? Now if he could sign up Brad Morgan the film would practically be in the can. There seemed to be a general feeling that with a package that included not only two stars but top-notch script writers and a solid story on paper, even Tolstoy could fill a theater.

But the trouble – here too – was Max's Millie in Love. It had been in distribution for many months now and the CEO of East-West Studios, who had pulled the strings in bankrolling the film, recently described it variously as "a flopola, a disaster, or a fucking dud, take your pick." From what I gathered, this CEO, Rutledge, was not easy to deal with, and it was said that after Millie came out, if you mentioned Max's name in his hearing

Rutledge gave you a dirty look.

It hadn't helped that the opening of a really terrible Magnox film, released at the same time and expected to have an appeal limited to the late-teen market, grossed an impressive $38,000,000 over the same four days. Bad luck, that was. Millie in Love had cost $68,000,000 just to have the negative, and it was obvious now, nine months later, that the picture would be lucky if it broke even at the end of three years. Or better give it five. In the film world that represented disaster – a flopola, a total fucking dud, take your pick.

With those slow returns, the studio had cooled toward Max since Millie in Love opened – or in Hollywoodese, hadn't opened. It was considered to have bombed in its first weekend, and there was no worse fate for a new release. The studio gave it limited distribution before Christmas to qualify it for Oscar nominations for that year (which with his name he was certain to get), with a rerelease date around Easter. But over a weekend of the balmiest December days that New Yorkers could remember, the film grossed a mere $15,000,000, and there were jokes that that was almost enough to cover the producer's cigar bills. Nobody could believe that a Max Petrov film could do that badly, and a buzz began about the end of his career.

None of this, of course, helped our cause, and Roz whispered to me as we were leaving, "Shit, we've gotta think of something," adding, "He's right about an ending, of course."

Which caught me off guard. "I thought the ending would come to us as we went along. I'm a little confused here."

"We're not gonna get anywhere without an ending."

"So you're agreeing with Max. He's right, then, about an ending."

"Of course he's right."

"Was this something you knew all along?"

"Well, you know how it is."

"Jesus, Roz."

"For crissakes, let's leave Jesus out of this."

9

I have to admit the World-Herald was being patient with me. It helped that Umpleby had been a great admirer of Petrov's ever since he had read one of Max's favorite quotes somewhere. It was a funny whining complaint made by Darryl Zanuck: "I know audiences feed on crap, but I cannot believe we are so lacking that we cannot dish it up to them with some trace of originality."

Umpleby fed on stuff like that and with quotes exchanged between us, he and I got along. At least on the surface and at your place of work that was all that mattered. Although Umpleby had attended Yale he wasn't educated but regular attendance at classes had attained the desired diploma. What kept us together was a common love of quips and a new favorite of his, something he called para-something, I never did get the word straight, but they were little one-liners with a surprise in their ending, and he never got tired of quoting his favorite: "I like going to the park and watching the children run around because they don't know I'm using blanks." A knee-slapper for the old bachelor. Runner-up: "The sex was so good, even the neighbors had a cigarette."

My job depended on Umpleby's favorable assessment of me. He kept telling me that my writing showed potential and suggested I read the collected works of George Carlin. Umpleby was a nonpracticing Catholic, and he elevated Carlin practically to the level of saint. Carlin fit in with the way he saw my modest role at the paper, which was to pass me squibs, little anecdotes culled from newspapers and old secondhand books. My job, as I've already explained, was to write them up in a light-reading feature using the tone of gossip columnists. It was corny stuff but so easy I didn't mind doing it, reminding myself that a great writer like Hemingway started as a reporter in Kansas City on the police beat. The daily tripe he wrote was so undistinguished that after he had become famous he disowned the journalism of his earliest years. A big mistake in my opinion. Some of it was rather good.

Anyway, our movie had, as we thought of it, a worthy purpose and our hope was to get people motivated to stop sex slavery the way the TV program "Most Wanted" helped catch criminals. And for us, Max was the ideal director for the job. First, because he and Roz were pals. Second, he knew the up-to-date technologies in modern filmmaking, and the well-known excellence of his work would command appeal. Third and most important of all, his authority in the film world was practically unparalleled. People paid attention to him. And with his influence we would not have trouble getting backing, and after the film was made, we would be assured of the widest possible distribution. Despite the specter of Millie in Love, we hoped.

What inspired us to hope for our project's success in spite of initial rebuffs was Max's affection for Roz. He listened to her even when affecting indifference. The close warm feeling between them did not go unnoticed in the press or by cinema lovers. Film addicts had Max and Roz so coupled in their minds that once, while they were on location in the Brazilian rain forest, a whole continent distant from the nearest gossip columnist, they were the subject of a daily string of rumors of sharing a double sleeping bag that the crew romantically arranged for them at the edge of the moonlit Amazon while topless tribeswomen fanned cool air over them during bouts of nightly boffing.

Once during an idle moment I tried to piece together Max's love affairs. I listened to every tale being told and I have to admit I believed them all. Friends joked that he had to have a different woman every night, or given his energy level, the first thing in the morning.. The women had to be brunette, with matching top and tail (a well-bushed tail kept neatly trimmed but never shaved). A superdiscreet cathouse named Jasmine sent them over as "production assistants" at three thousand per assist, although no one was taken in by the deception. Dress code: decorous, never whorish. The women were required to wear the perfume Shalimar, which was what Max's wife wore, and they were schooled in discreetly vanishing after a sunrise breakfast à deux as Max turned his attention to work and his see-no-evil maid Marya came to clear away breakfast jams, cream pitcher and silverware without asking questions she had no need to ask. She herself had laid the daily table for two while also serving Mrs. Petrov breakfast in bed off in another wing. Marya was a very valued employee.

•

Very early on I got in the habit of phoning Inge with updates on The Project. I usually did it at dinner hour in Hollywood and late evening in New York,

Out of sympathy, I asked if she was feeling horny – first things first. I had never known Inge not to be at least mildly horny or about to become horny or just finished being horny. She had quite a set of hormones, which was great, because hers and mine got along just fine.

At the moment, she claimed, she was indifferent, a new category. I took it on faith.

"Sometimes I go for long periods without even thinking about it."

She told me that while I've been away she has not removed her Finnish reindeer-skin chastity belt, a device I didn't know she owned. Or even that such a thing existed.

"They have chastity belts in Finland?"

She laughed. "Yes but not like in Sweden, where they use cement."

I reported the day's progress, or its lack. Max has been reading Tolstoy and that brought us back. The whole idea of death had apparently become an obsession with him and he seemed to want to talk about Tolstoy, an author I had so far succeeded in not reading.

"How come he wants to talk about Tolstoy?"

"I think his mother just recently died. Possibly thoughts of her are bringing it on. Maybe thoughts of Mother Russia, hard to tell."

After some reporting and talking, we hung up more or less simultaneously, neither wanting to be the first to leave the other.

I could feel at her end not just some sadness at our separation but more like sorrow, a sadness dragged down by an older and deeper feeling that seemed permanently there. It was the Karen sorrow: Karen not found, Karen dead – Karen alive but dying each day as someone's slave. In Africa. In Asia. South America. The awful subject.

•

Max had a reverence for Hitchcock, placing him second only to Jean Renoir, whom Max idolized. So Roz came up with a new plan of appealing to him: frame our abduction idea as a Hitchcockian suspense story.

"How do we do that?"

"We'll figure something out."

We met for another meeting poolside. People in Hollywood all have pools but though they mostly don't swim in them, from I could see. Max stood fussing with his beach umbrella to change the angle of tilt, jiggling the flippy little white tassels as he listened to Roz going on and on about a film they had once made together. Getting the umbrella tilted at the correct angle, Max sat back down again in the new shade he had made and said:

"Yes, you were really good in that movie."

"But don't ever give me lines like that again," she says.

"Lines like what?"

" 'Such innocence is ephemeral.' Remember that beauty?"

This, said affectionately to him while she turned toward me: "I told him people don't talk like that."

"What do you want her to say? 'My virginity was a bubble – one prick and it was gone'? That's crap dialogue."

"Oh Max, that joke has whiskers. But even that sounds more natural than 'Such innocence is ephemeral.' "

I was enjoying their joking criticism. Max appreciated her acting. Said it came across as ordinary speech, not acting, in lines that sounded like ad-lib responses to what the other actor was saying.

"Out of her mouth even the stalest dialogue sounds believable."

And Roz admired Max's direction. "When he comes up close to quietly explain a point, I know from his eyes what he wants me to do. You think your ideas are yours but they're really his. But he lets you think they're yours."

"If only all actresses were as easy as you."

"He directs the movie, not the actor." She turned to me: "I'll tell you a secret about screen appearance. You let the cameraman and the director develop a crush on you. That way you can be sure they'll make you look good."

Max gives her the privilege of working with the cameraman of her choice – a rare privilege. Roz's favorite was Mickey Rosen. He knew how to light her face when she was having her period.

"You remember Janet?" Max asked Roz, and like the old friends that they were, they laughed in private happiness at the name. "Directing her was like trying to direct a typhoon. So now I have it in every contract – never work with Janet Greerson."

"Does she really have a microchip in her left buttock?"

Me, believing her: "Really?" I took everything they said seriously.

"It connects with a GPS system that locates her on a bender."

"It would take a chip," Max said.

It was a journalist's dream, this humorous banter. An article about them would be easy to knock out. I noted down that when Max, speaking about plots and the idea of inevitability, said, "Over human history, some things never change," Roz replied:

"For example, when you eat beans, you fart." Max smiled and said he was thinking more of religion, that "we move toward the light." Roz: "So do flies." These were cheap shots, of course, and I would probably never use them but I wrote them down anyway.

"So what about our idea?" Roz, bringing Max back to our subject.

"The abduction story? As soon as you get an ending, dollink."

"Max" – Roz patiently hammering home a point gone over before – "do you know how many women disappear each year?" And we were back on subject.

For the first time I saw Max irritated: "Don't go into all that again. Please. I've thought about your story, believe me I have, and I have to say, yes, it's an interesting idea. But the trouble is you have no ending. Do you capisc' no ending?"

"But Max" – now Roz looking irritated too – "that's the fucking point of the story."

"That's just too amusing. You want to make a movie that has no ending and that is its whole point."

"No – that women disappear and nothing is done about it. That's the ending. It's the one big crime that goes unpunished. Don't you see the awfulness of it? When I think of it, I wonder what's wrong with the human race."

She waited for him to reply. He merely looked at her. She went on.

"In the hands of a good writer the possibilities for pathos are enormous – great pathos. The women are gone. They fucking disappear. Shit! What part don't you get?"

Max, not budging. "Sorry, dollink. Let me say it again, as succinctly as I know how. No ending? No film."

"What do you mean, no ending? What did I just get done saying?"

"You're asking me to believe a story that, after a beginning and a middle, stops cold. What the hell kind of Aristotle do you call that? 'Sorry, folks, the girl we've been watching has just vanished and we can't locate her right now – but, hey, have a nice day'? You expect people to pay good money to go see that? Even the best acting in the world couldn't bring that to life. I'm surprised at you, dollink, a professional. I thought you were more experienced."

Whenever he called her his 'dollink' he was being affectionate, adopting a Russian accent as something more consistent with the name Petrov. I think. Anyway I was impressed at how often Aristotle's name came up in Hollywood.

"Okay, look," Max said. "The plain fact is I owe the studio. My contract with East-West calls for one more film and what the studio wants is a sequel to Millie in Love."

I looked at him to see what I wasn't getting. I didn't understand. He was in trouble with the studio for his most recent film because it was not making enough money, yet the studio wanted to front him money for another film. It didn't add up.

He saw my look. "Like God," he says, "Hollywood moves in mysterious ways."

"God probably got it from Hollywood," Roz says.

But the explanation was simple. Max was famous for staying within budget. Woody Kilgallen and Max were among the two or three directors who respected budgets, and investing in them was financially safe and, depending on cast and production elements, even attractive. Hollywood Reporter did a feature on their respect of budgets, it was so rare. And that was why the studio was cautiously willing to take another chance on Max – but only for another and, it was hoped, more successful Millie film.

•

Roz was the owner-operator of the world's smallest bladder, as she herself was the first to point out, and she made a quick trip to somewhere inside and returned. She called it taking a nerve-pee, something she was afflicted with especially during filming.

Roz: "With my new agent, bless him, my deals are now in the low eight figures, and Maxie here wants me for The Randiness of Millie. Isn't that wonderful? The studio's willing to pay any amount within reason. Plus the usual."

I asked what the usual was.

"A percentage of the film. Of the unadjusted gross." She explained that meant starting with the first dollar, and she would, of course, accept. "One small job like that would buy me a small island somewhere in case I ever need a small island somewhere."

"The Randiness –?"

" – of Millie."

And I enjoyed her performance as she launched into one of her screwball riffs, meant purely to entertain.

"It's about a diamond merchant on 47th Street named Mendelssohn – Felix, if I'm not mistaken – who when you take him away from his gems has the IQ of a brain-damaged brick layer. But he's a very lovable character and falls in love with lovable me, a former, I think, nymphomaniac, or currently a nymphomaniac, and he can't accept the fact that I'm deeply in love with my new husband Rodney, chief rocket scientist at Berkeley. It's a documentary about the space program."

"Roz, Roz": Max smiling, his eyes in love with her.

I had the impression that to him all females were in heat – and maybe they were when he was around. I looked at her eyes looking at him. They showed she was tempted but strong-willed.

•

I phoned Inge. She was unhappy at how things were going – or really not going – on our Karen abduction film and I tried to cheer her up by mentioning Max's invitation to attend a business meeting as a fly on the wall. It could help in writing about him and about Hollywood and the projected film – really a golden opportunity. He would let me know when.

I could understand Inge's irritation at having so little to report but I didn't know what I could do in the circumstances.

I thought it might soften things by coming out with one of my favorite quotes to her. An ancient Greek named Menander: "We live not as we like but as we can."

Unfortunately I remembered too late I had quoted that one before.

"Oh fuck Menander!"

Maybe I had quoted it once too often.

•

In Hollywood everything starts with meetings. Then there are what's called pre-meetings.

Before the business meeting rolled around, Max and I met privately one morning for a pre-meeting, and, installed in his comfortable study, he told me he was taking our idea seriously enough to suggest I meet the two writers he had mentioned. They were currently working on a project that was in development: Carpenter and Rubinstein. He thought they were the best and he liked them very much. It might provide some insight into how things were done, how stories were put together, directors' problems, and so on. I suspected maybe my proposing to him that I do a profile on him for the World-Herald was having an effect.

The phone interrupted. Hearing both sides on speakerphone – which I think he deliberately left on – I pieced together that the Studio had, astonishingly, a hundred projects either in development or in production, involving sums that kept being referred to as ballistic. I listened to some talk about current principal photography being done in Equatorial Africa, Alaska, and Southeast Asia that was leaving the Studio gasping and new projects on hold.

Max motioned across the room to me, miming an apology for keeping me waiting. Tactfully I turned to a far wall and studied an elegantly framed drawing of a Matisse charcoal nude. Next to it there was a delicate Pissarro landscape, a Utrillo Montmartre scene and on a table below them a bronze Epstein figure. I guessed that in that room a total estimate at Sotheby's would come to a few million.

Listening I felt sorry for Max who was getting annoyed at whatever bad news he was being given. He reminded the caller that he, Max, had made $1.5 billion for the studio in 23 years of films, video, cable, DVD, TV, "ancillaries and toys and assorted crap." He could understand a need for austerity, but he said he had a longing now to bash in the skulls of the austerity nuts, who were the top-ten schmucks and biggest pussy freaks of all time that he had wined and dined at his table and supplied with Jasmine's choicest girls to fuck and whose kids he'd patted on their fucking heads. Why didn't the studio cancel some of the fucking slop it put out and get its corporate head out of its corporate ass.

"Goddamn it, Max –" a squawk at the other end – "listen, Max, I – "

Max: "No, you listen!" Then, almost to himself, quietly, "Naa, on the other hand, forget it."

Hanging up abruptly, with no goodbye, he explained that apes and slime balls were taking over. These certified schmucks were not interested in making films. They were interested in overnight fortunes. Parking attendants and hairdressers were producers now, people who'd never even heard of Eisenstein, or Vigo. Or Renoir.

"Most films you forget before you even pass the popcorn machine on the way out. Are you changed by a film after seeing it? That's the question to ask."

He said a few more things about the fucking moron he had just been talking to – apparently a fellow director – who had to be reminded that he had to agree to pay cost overruns once filming started, and if he hadn't learned that yet then he didn't know shit about making movies. I listened to all this and wondered how Roz had the impression he never lost his temper.

To me: "You see how things are." He shook his head, not at all embarrassed by his outburst, and said, "These things don't do much for headaches." He smiled at his own feeble joke and added to me: "Do yourself a favor. Don't ever get migraines."

He winked as he said that and I could see he was pleased that I had just had a glimpse into some of what he had to contend with. It wasn't all act. Something was troubling him.

•

Conversations with Max wandered all over the lot. He might start with actors, move to agents, producers, and then call girl rings and whatever else popped into his head and end with a lecture on the respect to be paid to writers and how so many films that were made were so lousy and often merely because of the writing.

"It's not even that they're written by committee. Even one writer working alone, which means enjoying freedom from interference, can make a lousy film. It's done all the time. Producers, front office people and even most directors don't understand writing. That's the core of the problem."

"What do you mean?"

"They think that by remaining faithful to some original text they will make a beautiful film – Gatsby, say, or Hemingway. But the result smells, just like practically all the films that have ever been made. Why? Because they miss the point. Gatsby ultimately is a feeling. It's more than the text. When you say "Gatsby" it conjures up something – that's what needs to be caught – the feeling of the book as a whole, the feeling that stays with you after you've read it. And it's exactly the same with a film. When all is said and done, a film creates a feeling – it leaves you with a feeling. That's all that the acting is about, and the writing and the direction, the music, the costumes, the production design, the sound – everything. It's all conjured to effect that one outcome, the feeling you're left with. And what is the feeling? The sense that for a moment you looked into life a bit more deeply. You saw something you never saw before. Get

69

that in film."

I had no idea he felt so deeply about writing and had so much to say about it.

"You know how writers are thought of out here?"

I expected the standard comparison with prostitutes. He must have guessed my thought.

"I've never liked that comparison. For one thing, prostitutes do an honest day's work." He laughed. "No, out here writers are thought of as malcontents, a necessary evil. And greatly overpaid."

"Isn't that how all directors view them?"

"Not all. I have a deep respect for writers, a great respect. Like they do in Russia. Did you know it is the tradition in Russia that you are not allowed to sit down in the presence of Pushkin's manuscripts? Just his manuscripts, you understand. You are required to stand up if you're in the same room with them. But I have to say that writers out here are a timid lot. They're timid because of their new house in Malibu and the mortgage that's killing them. But they're not the problem. The problem today is agents – C.A.A., I.C.M., all of them. Their strong-arm tactics are destroying the way films are made. Agents are even sewing up writers as part of package deals. Can you imagine Jean Renoir making A Day in the Country by being assigned writers and actors in some package deal?"

"Did screenwriters do a shooting script for A Day in the Country?"

Max looked to make sure I wasn't pulling his leg.

"Writers come to Hollywood to make their fortune. Practically since childhood they've wanted to come out here and live as part of the movie colony. With their first pay check they're thrilled to make a down payment on a house in Malibu, maybe up in one of the canyons, somewhere not too cheap. Then they begin to make it but at the same time feel an awful Hollywood cultural vacuum setting in and miss New York. They consider themselves a real success only when they move back and buy a townhouse in Manhattan, which is where they really wanted to live all along. But first they wanted the

Hollywood experience, you know, the cashay. Malibu was a way station on their way to conquer New York. Of course some of them fall in love with the California climate and stay. De gustibus and all that."

But nowadays there was another kind of writer. I mentioned Mamet.

"Yes, writers who aren't of the old mold – true. They don't get strung out on drugs, nor do they drink while working. They know how to write and they deliver the goods. On time."

Remembering it from some magazine bio I said: "You know what Mamet says is the hardest part about writing for the movies?"

Max smiled expectantly.

"Stashing the finished script away for three months before submitting it so the studio'll think it's getting its money's worth. The work actually took a weekend."

Max laughed. "Yes, but do you know how most films are really made? You think somebody sits at a desk and types words all day? Scripts are sewn together like patchwork quilt, but the problem is you can't know how a line will read until you hear an actor say it. And even then, it could be a good line but not for that actor. And everybody knows about how Casablanca closes. And Some Like It Hot."

"Written on the set."

"And the lines were thrown in till somebody could think of something better. Some of the best lines in movies are ad libs made during retakes."

He told me about a film he was involved with a few years earlier.

"The original director quit. The studio was furious at him for making an 'art film.' So they brought in a new director, a flavor-of-the-month genius."

The genius apparently agreed to do another set of tests and reshoot a couple of critical scenes. He replaced two of the actors and when Wolfson, the studio head, saw the dailies, they even gave him some hot-shot new writer to help him out with a couple of other scenes that were giving trouble. Two weeks later the director got dumped and they brought in Lawrence Wertheimer – fresh off Calico Weather – to direct and reedit what was now a hundred and sixty-two hour's worth of exposed film, threatening to make Greed look like a short subject."

"So what happened?"

"I had to take it on, to free myself later to work on the Tolstoy.

"So I directed this jumble of crap as fast as I thought I could get away with it.

Another pause, another thought:

"Maybe you should put this in your article too. Movie makers make good films occasionally – sometimes by accident. People don't go see a story by some great screenwriter. You think the average moviegoer knows the name Mankiewicz? They go to see Cary Grant. They go to see Meryl Streep. They go to see Richard Pryor being his usual inept con artist self. They want to watch him hoke things up – the same as the last time they saw him hoking things up in his usual bungling way. They want to see Spencer Tracy's goofy fuck-you smile at Katherine Hepburn, eyes all wrinkly-twinkly, as she comes back with a blithely clever retort that wipes the floor with him. They've seen it before and they want to see it again. When you come right down to it, most Hollywood stars are stock characters doing stock things, with, meanwhile, some unimportant story happening around them, and in a certain sense you don't really give a damn what the subject is. All that matters is that the plot is taking you forward without your being aware of it, and as for the rest, even before the movie starts, you know that Boulder Dam is going to be built, and Krakatoa is going to wipe out the island, and the cheap crook will get caught in the end by Sam Spade. Most films are shticks. They're Dean Martin and Jerry Lewis cracking the dumbest jokes in the world: 'Did you take a bath this morning?' 'Why? Is there one missing?' You laugh."

Looking at my face he said:

"Don't judge. Aristophanes wasn't any better. The audience is amused not because the joke is funny but because they enjoy seeing Martin and Lewis horsing around together. Especially on

TV, because they're two old friends right there with you in your bedroom, entertaining you by cracking the same old dumb jokes and having a good time. It's like having pleasant company over except that you're in the comfort of your bed."

"A script is almost incidental, it sounds like."

"No. You need a script. A story, not just an idea. But the script is just the beginning. Then while you're filming, things happen – insights, unpredictable ideas, lines that pop into your head – and those bits make the film as much as the structure does, or as much as the well-crafted dialogue does. A director is concerned with two things. To make the film as believable as possible and to do this by breathing life into the scenes. Do you understand? And those are not things you can map out in advance."

Noting all this down, I recorded a few more bits about film making, stocking it all up for the profile:

"You have to be excited by what you do. And if you're excited, the audience will feel your excitement. It's what makes a thing come alive."

And: "It doesn't matter if a work has faults. Did you ever read Gatsby? My – God! The book is so riddled with so many faults and pretentiousness that you have to laugh in spots watching this kid from Minnesota attempting to write a grown-up novel. But it has life in it. Which is all that matters. He knew how to write."

Some of this came close to Inge's view of things. She once told me that she had read somewhere that people stave off death by telling each other stories and do the whole Scheherazade thing. At least I made that connection in my own mind between what Inge and Max were saying and made a note to mention it to Max. I thought he might appreciate it. Scheherazade was about staving off death too.

Umpleby would probably want to know how big her tits were.

10

In keeping with Umpleby's suggestion to keep the trivia column going by email, he began sending more little squibs for readers of the "world's greatest newspaper." Two letters were recently sent in to the paper asking why the column didn't run in the daily edition rather than just the weekend edition. So my job was safe, the theory being that two letters sent in by readers translated into two thousand letters not sent.

But Roz was still going on about my doing a column that to her was just trashy stuff, amusing though it may be. She again said it was beneath me. That kind of journalism was worse than prostitution and, in her view, a waste of the talents she flattered me as having. And to make matters worse, I was working for a "fucking pittance". Although she exaggerated my talents, I did agree about the pittance.

But despite her violent reaction she saw no solution except for me to write longer pieces and by making a name for myself write my ticket to freedom.

"And get the fuck out – not to mince words," she said.

Real articles of the Max-interview kind that she and I would be putting together were more my style, in her view. And just on general principles, I should in any case ask for more money. What was I, a wimp or something?

I appreciated her concern but felt she overvalued me out of friendship. I told her I was lucky to have a job. I have always found it to be true that family and friends were always the worst critics: they love everything you do. If you write three pages of dialogue you're Shakespeare. I never realized what a scold Roz could be.

"If newspaperman is what you want to be, then be a newspaperman, not some minor hack. Think of Inge. Don't you two ever want to get married?"

Roz knew I was mad about Inge and that I felt lucky our paths, Inge's and mine, had crossed. In my post-university years of one-night stands and summer romances I never once met anyone like Inge, and I still had trouble believing my luck. She was sometimes a little strange but always wonderful, and maybe the strangeness was part of it – hard to tell. I recently proposed marriage and her usual playfulness with the English language caught me off guard. She mused that in the old days it was women who wanted to get married and now men did. I asked if that was a yes or a no.

"Why spoil a good thing?" she asked.

I told her I felt I had just been given the task of finding an irrefutable answer to a rhetorical question.

That stopped her, but only for a moment. "What's the rhetorical question?"

" 'Why spoil a good thing?' "

Inge's view of marriage was that it was too legal. It was a binding agreement that could conceivably strangle you.

"If anything goes wrong and you want out, it drags in judges and lawyers and a whole legal industry system plus a lot of old laundry you'd rather not look at, and that only upsets you when all you want is to be free. You just want to get on with your life, and there are all these people suddenly telling you what you may or may not do with it."

She'd never been married so how did she know that? Being in dismissive mode she came out with her latest English: "Tut tut."

I don't know where she got that one from but she was always learning new expressions in English and now everything for a while was tut tut. Anytime she learned a new phrase, new to her, she worked it into the ground. The next time I talked to her about getting married she said, "Tut tut."

As an answer that didn't make sense. So as a tease I said: "Tut tut?"

"Definitely tut tut," she responded without explaining further. She didn't see the point in marriage and giving up your freedom and all that, and reminded me again. "Nowadays it's men who want to get married. Women no longer do, or not so much anymore."

"Sounds like a case of tit for tat."

I knew it was coming even before she said it.

"Tut tut."

•

Roz's prompting me to become a good journalist and not a hack, saying I should find things to write about and send in to the paper, had me thinking about Inge's former lover, the fashion photographer Hal. So I sat down and wrote a story about him and a self-assignment of his about a little-known cathouse near Coenties Slip. People like to read about cathouses, especially puritans, they eat that stuff up. The women let him do full-length portraits of them all dressed up in their Sunday best. I explained how he originally set out to do these full-length portraits for himself, for his own private collection, but he gave each of the women a print and they were so happy to have pictures of themselves, especially the madam, who seemed bossily elegant but charming, and offered Hal one of the women in trade. As graciously as he could, he declined the offer on the ground that he was in love, which they all thought was noble of him and he thought was practical and cautious of him in avoiding the clap. Or AIDS. The women really were photographically charming to look at, posing as they did with middle-class gentility in a peacock chair brought in for the occasion, all decked out in lacy white froufrou underwear as they gazed at the camera in a kind of demure innocence. With their permission, he put several of the portraits into a show at the Waldenstein, and of course they were inevitably compared with E. J. Bellocq's work. Which made sense except that Hal's photographs were better felt than Bellocq's. Well, that's just my opinion. It'll take museums decades to see that and maybe admit it. The Bellocqs have greatness, no question about that, but if you should ever see a Hal North photograph you'll immediately see the difference – his personal work, I mean, not his bread-and-butter magazine-assignment crap, which though crap is still good work. It – the commercial work – has to be good, but it's only Vogue-magazine good, and magazines like Vogue are as slightly removed from reality as the women who buy them are. My two cents.

After I wrote it I put it away in a file box for some day. I didn't want the paper to think I was cheating them by writing articles on their time.

●

As promised, Max set up the meeting at East-West Studios and invited me to go with him and "kick ass." It was bravura but I loved it because it was Hollywood bravura.

A chauffeur arrived from his studio to pick us up, each separately, and deliver us through Los Angeles. We didn't use one of Max's cars. His Mercedes was designated his wife's car, and she used it mainly for lunching and shopping, which was practically her hobby. For himself he preferred his lavishly-outfitted Land Rover – when he was not working on a film. He had, I had heard, other cars, but when he was filming or, as now, doing studio work like attending a meeting, East-West's insurance insisted that a teamster chauffeur pick him up and return him in the studio's Bentley with blacked-out windows.

Luxuriating in the car's air-conditioned opulence I took in the part of L.A. that we were passing through where everything looked lovelier in a morning mist that had not quite burned off yet. We could have been in Cairo: pastel bungalows with boxed air conditioners in windows, TV lights flickering in empty rooms, pennants flapping over used-car lots, hot dog stands shaped like hot dogs, a city junkyard of butane tanks, billboards, kebab shacks . . . On a long street of tall, inward-slanting palm trees a white-stucco motel's neon "VACANCY" sign nervously flickered orange, more off than on. The Nile wasn't far away – on the Universal back lot, along with a Sphinx or two.

Max in a talkative mood spoke of his proposal to the studio to do The Death of Ivan Ilych. They wanted him to use Marilyn Blanchard, to give her image a needed boost.

He said to me: "Don't let anybody tell you any different

about studios. They all have the same philosophy: if there's no
sex scene, there's no box office. I tried to explain to Burt – Burt
Wolfson – that Ivan Ilych, the poor bastard, is dying. That's all
that happens in the book. Practically from beginning to end Ivan
dies. So where would Marilyn Blanchard come in – climb into
his death bed? So this genius comes back with, 'Don't you think
the poor schmuck had no youth? You do a flashback. He must
have gotten laid before he got married. And who did he lay?
Marilyn Blanchard. That gives you an opportunity to show
Marilyn Blanchard getting in and out of her underwear and
there's your sex scene.'"

Elaborate scorn on Max's face to me as he went on.

"So I reminded him Marilyn Blanchard doesn't wear
underwear. Anybody who reads gossip columns is aware of
that. 'Nah nah,' this genius says, 'we don't want no X rating.
She has to have underwear on.' I said, 'So then she takes her
underwear off? – on camera?' 'Exactly. Now you're getting it.
There's your sex scene.' 'Do you slip in a pussy shot?' I said to
tease him. 'What are you crazy?' he said. 'No pussy shots!' "

He spoke too of actors. "Extremely successful actors play
the same role over and over again once they've discovered
they've become bankable. Being bankable they tend not to stray
from what got them there. But up until they make it as big-name
stars, they're just as scared shitless as anybody else out here.
Especially the women."

Mentioning women made him stop and think. "I'm not a
womanizer. It's just that I'm one eighth Hungarian. It's my
Hungarian blood."

"I thought you were Russian." I had the feeling I might be
on the track of one of the myths about him.

"My genitals are Hungarian," he said, laughing.

Me, getting into the spirit: "They say all genitals are
Hungarian."

He laughed again. "Except for Hungarian genitals. They're
more Transylvanian."

"What do Transylvanian genitals look like?"

He was saying "You don't want to know" when the Bentley arrived at the studio gates that now majestically opened wide before us as the car rolled up.

"Morning, Mr. Petrov," the unformed gateman said, fingertipping his eyebrows, as we drove through to the heart of East-West Studios, the lion's den.

Another day, another hundred thousand dollars.

•

It was unusual for Max to use his office to work in. Most often, his staff, meaning principally his personal assistant Trish Hooligan, came to his home. It was she who told me he had this special arrangement in his contract, that he could work at home even if he had to use a union chauffeur to drive him around during normal working hours. Most mornings, when he was engaged in working at the studio, a chauffeur brought him in in the morning and drove him home again in the afternoon, and I calculated that the chauffeur made more money in those two hours of work than I made at my newspaper job in a week.

His studio office was almost as comfortably furnished as his study at home. With a few differences. You entered past a wet bar that looked like it was never used and then a desk about a mile long. After that came a hidden bath, but I didn't discover that until I had to take a leak and Trish showed me how the door worked. The whole place was almost spooky. A hidden device silently closed doors behind you as you moved from room to room in a display that out here didn't appear to be anything special, just the flaunt factor, or Hollywood conspicuous consumption.

Trish was there, smiling, alert, black hair tomboyishy cut. In New York she could have been a clothes model: beige blouse, white linen miniskirt, and the tallest heels I've ever seen in a workplace. She looked about twenty-seven or twenty-eight years old, not shy, California bright. He introduced us.

"If you need anything typed up or whatever, Trish here would be happy to oblige."

"Absolutely. Be delighted."

"She's expert at what she does. If you'll excuse me for just a moment" – and he said something about a one-minute stand-up meeting with a producer named Schnelling. "You know, they say producing is the hardest and least rewarding of jobs. All you get in return is box office – if you're lucky."

At this the phone rang. It was Burt Ringle, head of publicity, saying he needed to see Max. Urgent.

"I'm never sure what a producer does," I said to him after he had hung up.

"A producer? He keeps all the plates in the air. And you have to always appease him. Meaning you have to protect the producer's illusion he's working for a living."

Trish made a small loyal laugh.

"He gets to sit on his own folding chair, name on the back and everything. His job's on the line every minute. He has to be seen to meddle, interfere in things, fuss over a detail about the heroine's shoes, otherwise he would not be doing his job. How are you this morning, dollink?"

"Fine," Trish said.

"You're so desirable."

One of the more pleasant things about Hollywood was that it was a relaxed superego zone.

He said, turning to me: "I make it a principle never to fuck stars working for me or any of the employees. It complicates the work environment." He winked at Trish.

Not batting an eye she said: "But, of course, you're willing to make exceptions."

"Of course."

As Max left she whispered with a laugh: "Of every woman he meets."

Max gone, I asked Trish what she thought of him. Oh, she said, he was wonderful to work for. "He's a legend."

In the land of hyperbole, anyone who's been around for fifty years and is still active is a legend or if now dead was once a legend. She mentioned the "legendary days" of Louis B. Mayer and "the moguls of the golden age" and you could almost see their ghosts flitting around the sound stages making "legendary" films. Hollywood likes to live up to its fantasy.

•

Minding my own business waiting for Max, I examined a small shelf with three volumes book-ended: Remembrance of Things Past, The Complete Plays of William Shakespeare, and Walt Whitman's Leaves of Grass. On the wall above the books a crocheted motto said: "Think Jean Renoir."

I opened the Proust. Trish seeing me said, "It's a good read."

Snobbishly surprised she was familiar with the book, I asked: "Have you read it?"

"I haven't quite finished it yet."

"You read a lot?"

"Not really. Jackie Collins mostly. I like the way she understands life."

"Life out here."

"In general. You know, the way people live."

Max reappeared and as though there had been no break picked up our earlier conversation

"You know what producers do? They take a perfectly good idea and 'enhance' it into a nice little vehicle for – Minnie Mouse. Then, as though that weren't bad enough, in place of Minnie Mouse, they offer the role to Meryl Streep, or someone at the top of the food chain."

"Someone bankable."

"Believe it or not, this guy I just saw? He said to me: 'We have to get just enough story in it to suspend disbelief.' But I know him. He's not a real producer. He's a legman for the front office. What he normally does is snoop around to see if you're staying on schedule and also to make crucial decisions, like the one he made yesterday about the heroine's hemline needing to be a half inch longer in the church scene. He said, 'You don't want the audience to keep concentrating on her pussy while she's listening to mass.' "

I asked Max what he thought of the Proust on the bookshelf.

"It's got a good plot. But I haven't read all of it yet."

•

The pussy reference reminded me that Roz once told me that Max's movie called The Food of Love was privately called Eating Pussy.

"True," she said. "Kid you not."

Max to Trish: "Do you like your job?"

"I like working for you, Max, yes."

I didn't believe Max's pretense at celibacy with respect to staff. It was pretty obvious he was enjoying impressing me with it to influence the profile. He was giving me A Glimpse into a Director's Life.

To Trish: "Interested in a nooner?" – waiting for the response, me standing there, taking it in, a little embarrassed by the obviousness of the maneuver.

"Oh no, Max, I don't think that would be a good idea."

Then the insincere blessing: "You're a good girl, Trish."

While he was gone to the can (Max's word) she quietly corroborated that it was a routine they had.

"With anybody else it would be offensive. But he's such a nice man and we have such deep respect for each other."

"Would you ever go to bed with him?"

I instantly regretted asking her the indiscreet question but it didn't seem to bother her.

"If he were to ask, you know, in a sincere kind of way, who knows? But I don't think so. I think he needs me to say no to have the feeling that some people are not easily available. Funny, huh?"

"But secretly you would,"

"He's very good-looking."

•

Over the phone Inge has a name for Max's way of speaking:. She calls it a Maxism when he says things like, "No experience is ever as good as the telling of it. That's why we have films." And, more obvious: "The single most important thing in life is making it last." I thought that was ho-hum, but Inge thought if my life were ever in jeopardy I would reorder my values – or words to that effect. She was probably right.

I began making notes on everything, especially Max's responses to leading questions, like how he got into the movie business.

"I wanted to become a film director so that I could boff every woman I met, starlets, typists, society women, the hostess of next week's party – all of them."

"Society women?" I had always imagined them as well behaved. When I told him that he laughed so hard he began coughing.

"Society women are some of the easiest pushovers in the world. They have nothing else to do while hubby is playing the stock market. Do you think Marie Antoinette spent her days knitting? In those days fucking is what people had in place of TV. And still do, some of them. People talk about sexual addiction, but don't make me laugh. That just means you don't make a pass at your wife as frequently as you did during the first week of your honeymoon and you turn to a little outside variety. Addiction? What addiction? You just like to fuck. It's built into us by nature. If you want to get scientific about it, it has survival value. Keeps me alive, anyway."

I wrote it all down later from memory – a bit stiff but pretty much verbatim – and wondered how much of it would survive editing at the World-Herald. There were too many sexual references. Reading back, I got the idea to write the profile as cheerful unprincipled chatter, just as it came out, unchanged. Not in any way to hurt Max but just to give Umpleby a laugh out of reading it, then censor the good bits in anticipation of the unacknowledged and biggest puritanical censor of all, the reader.

Max confided things like: the married state, apart from providing plentiful sexual opportunities, was a safety convenience for someone in his position. He was "legally committed". Which meant that bimbos were forewarned: hands off – spoken for – wife. Temporary lovers were not tempted to angle for marriage or have illusions of anything more than momentary recreational sex from him: "Kiss, strip, fuck, bye."

Regina, his wife, conservative by nature, put up with a lot but had respect and lové for him of the Old World kind. Their marriage too was legendary as any marriage in Hollywood lasting more than thirty years would be.

"She loves me still, she admires me. And she needs me. I could never do anything unkind to her. She knew me when we were both nobodies and in our early years never complained when we didn't know if we'd have food the next day. But you know, I sometimes look at her and think, 'When all is said and done, we're really still strangers to each other.' Odd, isn't it? It's an awful way to be. But I wonder if that isn't true of many marriages."

•

Friends who knew them well said they were more affectionate with each other in this current stage of life than they had been as newlyweds. Regina learned to accept the casting couch – understanding that you couldn't be the wife of a film director and not be complicit in it, however unhappily. She accepted it, I was told, not in some hysterical movie-heroine way, bravely crying into her pillow at night, a description that would have given Regina a laugh. It was merely the cost of doing business and a way of keeping her marriage intact and solid – if you could call that a marriage, and the indications were she did. Max was as dependent on her emotionally as she was dependent on him financially and emotionally, and that, in her view, seemed as apt a definition of most marriages as you would ever find. Her love was genuine, though, and made it possible for her to forgive him. She sounded interesting and I would try to work her in some prominent way into the profile on Max.

I remember one time she whispered to me: "Men are like boys, and if we love them we have to learn to take care of them."

"You sound sincere."

"Oh but I am."

•

There was so much yet to learn if I was going to write a credible profile of this much-honored Hollywood figure – the kind of man he was, his temperament, his shortcomings, anything of popular interest and especially to cinephiles. Did he have enemies? Was he known to regret telling people off? Had it meant giving up past hopes to reach where he was? And what was his daughter like? How did she feel about him, and about her mother, and about the gossipy lives of their famous friends?

Umpleby, the author of some of these questions, was pushing to know how the profile was coming along, and I stalled him – surprisingly easily. I explained it was slow-going because Max Petrov moved cautiously, being respectful of the living Hollywood legend of himself – The Great Max. He protected his public persona and hoped his indulging me would end in a fat article further enhancing his reputation as America's Most Loved Film Director. Most loved for now.

Umpleby's concern was to scoop the Times even if the "scoop" happened only in his own mind. As a result he allowed me a bit more time if needed, as long as, while getting material for my interviews, I kept sending the paper the amusing anecdotal little piece-of-shit things that I didn't exactly have a wild longing to get involved with but on the plus side could knock off in my sleep.

"Just don't take forever."

He was being exceedingly kind and knew I knew how patient he was being. Umpleby could fire me any time he wanted. He could always find another drudge, fast too.

●

Unlike Umpleby, Inge was not being patient with our progress. She sounded upset most of the time, in fact angry. I had a vision of her pacing up and down the apartment, phone at her ear as she ranted at the universe – vodka gimlet in her other hand. I wish she could learn not to get angry at the world. What good did it do?

To Inge all that mattered was that the Karen story be made into a film – by Max. Max himself, as a person, was irrelevant and utterly unimportant. He was a means to an end: get a film out of him. And he was the chief subject and a bit of comic relief of our nightly phone calls.

I stressed that I didn't think Max could be rushed. To me, journalists, even some of the good ones, were intrusive and rude, and what was being expected of me now was to turn into one of them and I couldn't. I kept telling Inge I didn't need pressure from her. Roz was doing a good job of that. It was merely that I was the wrong person for this kind of work.

"Well, I hope you don't make that into an excuse not to get on with it." She sounded so cold I felt sorry for her, as well as for myself, and after I hung up went around with only the one thought of helping her, of giving her some good news. But there was no good news.

11

One morning after I'd been there a little over a week, Max, not having had a headache for several days, declared a need for a holiday break.

"A day off," he said, which turned out to mean joyriding in his helicopter. He contended that flying his beloved "Betty Boop" over Death Valley and the southern wastes of California never failed to clear his mind of cobwebs.

"You two are coming," he commanded.

I suspected that his inviting Roz and me together accorded with his secret view that we were having an affair. He knew about my feelings for Inge but maybe the idea of duplicity had appeal and would confirm his poor opinion of human morality. Or maybe he just needed the infidelity of others to rationalize his own.

Trish made it a foursome. Her secretarial presence might act as a solid alibi he wasn't just off screwing some hopeful starlet or gone to Vegas with a new Jasmine "assistant". With Trish along, it was work.

She was excited, as I was too, as we took off from Santa Monica Airport and whirled over Tehachapi to the Sierra Madre and from there up to Montecito. It was wonderful getting around so fast, high above traffic and nature. Wealthy estates appeared on the horizon.

"Look. Santa Barbara."

Among the mansions far off, Max pointed out landmarks, happy at the controls, and suddenly whirled us out off the coast and then traced back along the wave-breaking line of Pacific shore. He dipped once to just above the waves and grinned at our nervous excitement. The low swoop toward land startled the few surfers who were out so early.

"Isn't it against the law to fly this low?" Trish shouting against the helicopter's noise and Max nodded conspiratorially happy. They were being two kids enjoying soaring over green forests and rolling hills and sandy beaches.

Max, never off duty, commented on the California coast, like a director discussing notes:

"What you want in a film is beauty. Never forget that. Not beautiful shots of this" – inclining his head toward the magnificent landscape. "That would be too easy. It could be a story that takes place in depressing surroundings, like a ghetto, but the film as a whole would have to leave you with a sense of something beautiful. More like an afterglow."

Roz, shouting over the helicopter sound: "You mean like His Girl Friday and Casablanca."

"Yes. You remember bits of a film, and those bits become a part of your life. It's a good film that can become a part of your life."

Flying past a roll of hills he tapped Trish's shoulder and jabbed a finger toward a beach house in a setting of picturesque pines and eucalyptus. Trish smiled and silently nodded at the manicured real estate. It belonged to him. It was home territory.

Approaching Malibu he swooped low to a lone woman stretched sunning herself on a striplet of beach.

"Hey, she's on my property. Let's give her a thrill."

As we dipped offshore but near her she jumped up enthusiastically and yanked her top down at us and waved.

"Woo-OO!" Trish shouted.

Max laughed. "Some lousy boob job, huh?"

Roz, in a loud, happy mutter, "Too fucking much."

We waved at the woman frantically waving back at us as she grew smaller in the distance.

As we parted ways back home, Max declared that that had definitely cleared his cobwebs. Roz let it be known that her bladder had never been pushed to such limits, and Max asked Trish: "Was it good for you too, darling?"

"Oh Max, come off it!"

•

"Was that your first helicopter ride?"

"It may be my last one too," I said.

Sophie, Roz's maid and cook: "You're always holed up writing. You should get out more. Like that helicopter. It must have been fun."

It was pro forma talk. She liked it when I stayed holed up and had already told me she hoped I wouldn't leave California but move in permanently – some place nearby. I'd be good for Roz.

"She seems happier when you're around."

"Are you matchmaking?"

"Why not? Roz used to have this terrible lover Laszlo – so wrong for her. But she finally wised up, and you should hear her talk about him now – my god, the language. Well, if you know Roz you know the language."

Language that made the studio publicity department dread her appearances on talk shows, never being sure what she was going to say next.

"Afraid of lawsuits," Sophie said, agreeing. "Playboy wants to do a major thing about her. So right now you still have a chance to beat them to the punch."

I explained that Roz and I were already committed to doing an interview for my paper. I was fairly sure we'd beat Playboy.

"If I can help in any way . . ."

" 'Hollywood Maid Tells All!' "

She laughed. "Well, not all."

•

As the days went by, I learned quite a bit about Roz from Sophie and about Sophie from Roz. Roz had already informed me:

"Sophie has a tendency to steal. She thinks I don't know."

She told me with a kind of awe that Sophie's view of life seemed to involve underwear.

"Underwear?"

"Yeah, hunh?" Something about that secretly pleased Roz.

"Her own? Or underwear in general?"

"If she doesn't like something, she says it's yesterday's panties. Interesting way of looking at things. I think it's her way of saying it's no good. Or it stinks, possibly. But anyway she has a thing about panties."

"What do you mean?"

"She missed her calling. She should be in sales."

"Selling what?"

"Panties!" she said exasperated. "I'm serious. She steals mine. There's actually a market for panties out there."

"What, on eBay?"

"No. Here in town. Although – hell, I don't know, maybe eBay too. Maybe some of mine are in Australia by now. They've got panty fetishists down there too."

She swore she wasn't kidding.

To catch her in her theft Roz put a dot of indelible ink hidden in the band of one of her panties and then rinsed it in a mild bleach to see if the mark survived. It did. It was pale but if you knew where to look you could still see it. She wore the marked pair and put it in the laundry and then checked through her chest of drawers for it and never saw it show up again.

"And I wasn't wearing it."

"You're sure?"

"I can assure you I'd know if I was wearing panties. Besides I mostly wear either thongs or nothing."

"Why are they called panties?"

"I don't know. Why do the British call them knickers?"

"Short for knickerbockers?"

"Hardly. Or possibly maybe."

"Okay to include this stuff in the interview?" I asked. "A nice little fable about Hollywood?"

"It has a sociological interest, so yes. America is longing to find out about movie stars' underwear. You remember what's her name?" She mentioned an actress I'd never heard of and didn't quite catch the name – Marie something. "She says there's a demand for these things. Not just hers or mine. Famous stars'."

"What do they go for?"

"I don't know but the ones that have been worn and not laundered sell like hotcakes. As a male you would understand these things."

"It's the not-laundering part. They get seasoned, you might say. It authenticates them."

"Jesus."

"The ripeness is all."

"How can they tell who's pussy's been in it?" she asked. "I'll bet there are thousands of fakes out there. They must have underwear meets. You know, Sunday morning panty swaps."

She has never said anything to Sophie, taking the view that Sophie probably considered this particular petty larceny a minor perk for working for a celebrity. Roz felt it would be too stingy to object.

•

On that evening's phone call I told Inge about it, glad to have a different subject to talk about. She asked if this sort of thing held interest for me.

"Because if you like, I'll hang on to some – it'll save on laundry." When I suggested she Fed Ex them out, she asked if I had preferences. "Frilly? Lacy? I bought a nice new thong this afternoon, the palest of blues. Do anything for you?"

"As long as they're yours. Worn once."

"For Sharon Stone that would be a problem, wouldn't it? – going commando."

But she brought the subject back to Karen again, keeping things on a serious level, so after we hung up I remembered something and after a few minutes called her back. Determined to amuse her before calling it a night, I told her of the story the papers were carrying about the disillusioned members of a local doomsday cult. The subject was one I knew appealed to her anthropological interest, confirming her view of the human race as composed largely of nutcakes. One day this particular cult's leader, gathering his followers around him, made the big announcement that the final days they had all been yearning for had at last arrived. It was here! Were they ready?

I could hear Inge's smile over the phone and feeling her pleasure I went on. Cult members went through moments of pious jubilation about the end of life on earth and looked expectantly toward the next Thursday morning, which was when The Moment would arrive, at approximately nine-forty-five, Pacific Daylight Savings Time. That was when they would hear the purifying thunderclap announcing that the end had now officially begun.

"So what'd they do?" Inge asked.

No longer needing worldly goods, they began giving away their possessions, closed their bank accounts and blew their small savings, and as pantries and fridges ran out of provisions they didn't restock. Then, on the fateful Thursday morning, they all sat around on empty orange crates, looking at each other in eager expectation, waiting for – they weren't exactly sure what they were waiting for. . . . Would it really be a thunderclap? Anyway, nothing happened and they waited some more, and still nothing. Thursday afternoon came and went – and they were all pretty hungry now. Toward midnight Thursday the awful thought occurred that the report was a false alarm – a dreadful misinterpretation of some sort. Or somehow the dates had gotten mixed up. Then, as the realization crept in that they were destitute, that with no furniture in the house or money in the bank or food in the fridge they had to nevertheless go on living, they went out looking for their leader and hanged him.

I knew she would like that. She laughed. I told her I loved her and lied that I'd get Roz and Max to get the lead out of their respective asses – and of course had no such intention, knowing we were all doing the best we could. But it was just something to help keep Inge going.

"He's still looking for the ending. We'll find something." I hoped I was sounding reassuring.

"Ending, ending," she says. "Maybe Aristotle was wrong. Maybe in life there is only a beginning and a middle. Followed by death."

"A beginning and a middle and then you drop dead?"

"Something like that. Isn't that what happens?"

•

Sometimes just talking about our progress, minimal though it was, aroused a feeling of virtue, although I distrusted virtuous feelings and thought of them as danger signals. But I got to thinking about the model Karen who had disappeared and wondered where she might be and what might be happening to her, and then started to feel rotten all over again. She went to Morocco with her lover, her Romeo, she called him. At a café he left her for a moment, saying to wait right there, he'd be back. I tried to tell myself that whatever was happening to her, at least she was not dead. But then I thought maybe she was dead. Maybe in the circumstances being dead was the better option – better than living as a slave. A slave where? In Morocco, or wherever she was.

I had to stop thinking about her.

•

Max said to meet again and we did. He was feeling a little down – not down, bored – and he entertained me with his account of a recent visit to his M.D. He acted out their conversation, and I recorded the little playlet:

Max complains to his doctor, Sam Lifton, that he's been having migraines. To come clean and keep Lifton abreast of the latest, Max confesses he's also been seeing a shrink, somebody named Benenson. This shrink feels the cause of the migraines might be psychological and discusses its etiology.

So this Dr. Lifton says, "It's certainly possible. I wouldn't rule it out." The professionalism and interdisciplinary support pleases Max. Doctor Lifton sagely warns: "You'd be surprised at the physical harm caused by suppressed emotions."

Max wants to know if there's something he could take. "Like morphine? Heroine? A little coke maybe? I wouldn't mind becoming a dope fiend if that would stop these migraines."

Lifton gives a kindly smile. "I'll set up a scan."

Max tells me all this as a scene in a film he's directing, elapsed screen time thus far: ten seconds.

Scene Two (still to come): the brain scan. Max continues the narrative:

"In the old days we took painkillers. Now we don't take painkillers anymore. Nowadays we go for an MRI. We've got all these advances now in medicine."

What happens if the migraines don't go away after an MRI?

"Ah. Then we take the painkillers."

•

I wasn't altogether sure I liked the way that read. I tried to get Max into profile mode, and to give our talks a kick start, I resorted to the usual banalities, like which stars Max found likable as people and which were difficult to work with, blah

blah – public-pleasing drivel. But trite though that tradition was, it led to anecdotes involving well-known actors and directors and the daily deities of the entertainment world – Sunday-supplement fodder that for modern readers replaced ancient myths.

Giving him verbal nudges to steer our talk toward Hollywood in the sixties, or even better, the fifties, hoping that reminiscing about the past and old myths might tug his thoughts back to his youth in Odessa, or possibly St. Petersburg, my attempts brought a relaxed dismissive wave of his hand and some casual remark about having left Russia too early to remember much. No matter how often I tried, we never arrived back in Odessa or the days of his Black Sea youth, or wherever. About that period I learned only that his mother died when he was two ("Same as Tolstoy"), and during his childhood his father never showed the physical closeness or love Max felt he needed – which, he added, all men need, at whatever age. He commented further that some critics claimed to see in his films evidence of his early emotional deprivation . . . he of course was not in a position to say.

I felt pleased at how increasingly easy we were finding each other's company, cracking jokes as much as talking about the project. I had no sense that there was a gap of not quite a generation between us. The moment I suggested, at his insistence, some "ideas" for projects ("As an outsider you're bound to have fresh ideas"), he laughed with gentle ridicule as he declared that I just didn't understand how movies were made. "That you call a movie?"

As he said this he downed the new painkiller he'd been taking and complained about the damned nuisance of a headache – no, not nuisance, the bloody inconvenience of it.

I asked if he was willing to talk about it.

"There's nothing to say."

Having forgotten to charge my iPhone, I wrote all this down in a tiny notebook with a stub of a pencil.

His first migraine had struck after the weekend that *Millie in Love* opened and he thought it was a hangover from the opening-night party. Normally he never experienced so much as a mild headache, ever, so he thought it wiser to just ignore it. His shrink wondered if it was connected with the disappointing reception of the film, but Max thought it more likely it was the two large brandies he had taken after dinner in place of sleeping pills. A bad habit – he remembered a doctor in Paris telling him exactly that.

"You saw a doctor in Paris?"

"This Docteur Bertrand said he discounseled the practice of brandy as a soporific. It damaged the heart, to say nothing of the liver." He sounded almost French reporting their dialogue.

Max said in France everybody had a bad liver. Even those who didn't have a bad liver had a bad liver. Mal au foie.

Dr. Bertrand never really addressed the matter of the migraines or its possible remedies, and Max felt the consultations had been a waste of time. But he kept going back. Why? Well, the nurse was a knockout. He could easily have slipped her into his next film, providing he could slip it into her. If only she were not devoted to Doctor Liver Quack.

His talk seemed to ramble, and as he indifferently observed me taking notes he fell back to an old theme, that it was possible that his youthful habits were catching up with him. Not that he could blame it all on aging, fifty-two was not exactly aging – though things had been going downhill for months, and thoughts of one's mortality were always there. Probably it would be good to get away, just go off somewhere, maybe a longish break in Gstaad – no, not Gstaad, Cap Ferrat. The good old French Riviera.

"Meanwhile, though, we're not going to let a headache stop us from work."

I had to smile whenever Max said "work". The term was so relative, meaning in his case poolside meetings with lunches worthy of Babette's Feast, starting at noon and lasting through the afternoon. His Moldavian (Russian?) maid Marya took away plates and returned so regularly with replenishing trays of French and Russian delicacies that you could almost believe they were being hourly flown in from Europe. It was quite a life, and I could see how some Easterners, having had a taste of it, might lose all desire to return to New York. That is, if you got invited to the home of a famous director and had a taste for that kind of life.

Becoming aware he had been thinking aloud, Max's thoughts about the Riviera tailed off as he saw me waiting for him to continue.   Clearing his throat he gave a warm Petrov smile, one that implied everything was fine and thoughts of mortality were unwarranted and he apologized for any worry he might have caused.   What was wrong was that he had not done much work for a while, that was the real problem, and it was time he got down to it.

12

Pressure from Inge was growing, so with my increasing closeness with Max, I chanced reminding him that only one story concerned me and that was the one he always succeeded in avoiding. I didn't say "avoiding". I said that "eluded" us.

He didn't become angry, as I had been afraid he might, but said he understood. But his position about our proposal remained unchanged. A story without resolution was just not a story. It was becoming a mantra: no ending, no story. Must either find the missing girl or at least say what happened to her. You couldn't just say she disappeared and let it go at that.

He thought of Jake Carpenter and Rob Rubinstein again. They were both good at treating serious themes without getting too heavy. They might just be the ones to do the Karen story – and maybe come up with an ending.

"They're good word men," Max explained. "And they haven't had screen credits for a while."

I asked what he meant by treating a serious theme without getting too heavy and he explained that movie audiences wouldn't sit still for a lecture, which was the point he had been trying to get across all along. They paid money to be entertained.

"I don't need writers. I need storytellers."

And he came back to what I was beginning to think of as the Scheherazade moment.

"Tell me a story that will keep me from falling asleep. Get it? Whatever else you do, you have to tell a story."

If in the days of the civil rights movement a movie had been made in the form of a documentary that gave the public all the facts and figures about the terrible things that were happening to the blacks down South, it would have had little effect on the civil rights movement, and things might not have changed as they did. That was his argument and I couldn't disagree.

"You must connect emotionally. If you don't reach people emotionally you will never get them to do anything."

Which of course was what Roz and I had contended from the start. So maybe in a roundabout way we were getting somewhere.

•

The two screenwriters Jake Carpenter and Rob Rubinstein met us in Max's study. Long before a film is authorized there are preproduction talks, some of them lasting a year or more, when ideas and stories are tried out. The meeting today would go down in somebody's account book as a preproduction talk.

"These conferences," Max said, "sometimes degenerate into chitchat about little Johnny's measles, but something always comes out of them."

The men arrived together. They were both in casual California dress. In introducing me Max gave me an unexpected promotion: I was suddenly the World-Herald's hot new Sunday feature editor and I had come out to Hollywood to do a major article. I tried quickly to adopt or at least look the part as we exchanged nice-to-meet-you greetings and shook hands.

I had read that writers enjoyed working with Max because he discussed things with them down to the smallest detail of character and motivation and listened to what they had to say. He even described camera angles, and had suggestions for sound mix, wardrobe, and production design. He had some scenes so meticulously worked out in his head that it was said that the actual shooting of the film was incidental. Inevitably, of course, Max's method was likened to Hitchcock's, but Max was credited as the more rounded director. He devoted attention to character development, something nearly absent in Hitchcock's films. And: Max's films were not repeats of each other with only the names changed, as Hitchcock's films were – at least that's what critics said about his films made in Hollywood, not the early English ones.

"Hitch never gave a damn about character. He would have

worked with puppets if he could have found a way. For him it was all plot and camera angles." This was from Max.

"You didn't mind, though. His films were good box office," the writer named Rob said, and Jake Carpenter concurred.

"I could never work that way," Max said.

Max's "method" was to focus on the face and move the camera as little as necessary. This gave his images power the way Bergman got power, by filling the screen with the human face and its incomparable expressiveness.

"Max gets involved with each character as a human being. That's why his films are liked," Carpenter said.

"The secret of showing character on the screen is that people don't always exhibit their feelings. Mostly people try to hide their feelings."

It was going good and I gathered that the two writers were happy to be working with Max and felt it a special pleasure to be invited to his home. It was the Hollywood equivalent of an invitation to the White House.

They went off on a tangent about devising new plot twists for boy-meets-girl situations. When I expressed surprise they all assured me that at bottom most stories are boy meets girl, "even Dracula." Love interest and sex were the eternal ingredients of storytelling.

"Oedipus Rex too," Max contended. "It's boy meets girl – in a somewhat extended guise."

"Oh, come on, Max," Rob said.

"Hey!" Carpenter said. "How about a musical of Oedipus Rex? 'I Want a Girl Just Like the Girl that Married Dear Old Dad.' "

"Oedipus Rex meets his Shady Past."

Carpenter seemed perpetually cheerful. He let it be known he hoped they would be working with Max on the next Millie film – obviously word was out that such a film might be made. As old friends they kidded around as much as they talked seriously. For a while the conversation turned interestingly to stars that one or all had boffed and which of the women was the best in bed, praising one famous star, a BAFTA-award winner and recent import from Britain, for delivering the best blowjobs in Hollywood.

"A place known for industry blowjobs," Rob Rubinstein reminded everyone.

There were some standard jokes about the casting couch, Carpenter describing it as classic a piece of Americana as the rocking chair or Shaker furniture.

Max: "The most successful casting-couch line I know is the truth."

'What do you mean?"

"You say to a starlet, 'You understand, I can't promise you anything,' and it's almost like asking her to take her clothes off."

"Undress for success," Jake said.

"They somehow hear you to mean exactly the opposite."

"They're anxious to please," Jake said. "It's really sad."

"Or desperate to pay their bills."

"Or they think they're the exceptions."

Max's maid Marya came in. She had earlier laid out a mini table-top delicatessen on a long teakwood table, and her small watchful eyes were quick to supply what, if anything more, was needed.

Nobody needed anything. Carpenter began to make a pita sandwich of English kippers and asked Max if the bread was made with flour that had come from organic wheat.

"Distrust the writer who is a health nut," Max said to me. "Drunks deliver the best product."

The conversation turned serious as they discussed a script in development. Apparently this was one they'd had informal discussions about before. They went over a scene a dozen times to work out a motivation or a small bit of character development, and I listened as they fought for minutes over a single phrase ("Would she say 'labor over' or 'get the job done'?"). Then an entire passage would be dropped, made suddenly irrelevant by some new change. Some suggestions bumped the story in a new direction, but at this stage none of that mattered. They were here to hammer out the "straight dramatic line", which was also called the story's "arc". I was getting quite an education.

"A film loves reality." I think it was Rubinstein who said this. "It creates the reality of the world and in doing so it creates another reality. The reality of a film has in it the reality of the world plus the reality of the film."

"Sounds Platonic," Carpenter commented.

"Hey listen, Plato was no asshole."

On a nearby coffee table I saw the script of a film from a few years ago, Ups and Downs. A notice stamped on it read: "Revised Temporary Final". Max seeing me looking said such labels didn't mean anything, that in the end Ups and Downs was rewritten on the set.

"From beginning to end," Rob said with an ironic laugh.

"You know those old movies where the dialogue used to be so good?" Carpenter said to me. "You can't expect that kind of dialogue anymore from Hollywood writers – you know, witty, lighthearted et cetera dialogue."

"Why not?" I asked.

"Because if they could write that well, they wouldn't be in Hollywood. They'd be on Broadway. Or they'd publish their stuff in a book. A novel maybe."

"For a given film, there's no such thing as an original idea or an old or a new idea. Just good or bad ideas," Rob said. "Sometimes the ideas are blatantly lifted from newspaper headlines or taken from novels – even swiped from old movies. Fairy tales too. It's all fair game."

Apparently most of the dialogue in Ups and Downs was ad-libbed by the actors, with Max modifying the personalities of the characters as they went along. When the film was in the can there was so violent a dispute over the writing credit that the matter went to arbitration.

Which corroborated the hearsay that Max liked to improv.

He enjoyed being surprised by what developed between two actors and what they brought out of a scene. He said that in one film he was as surprised by the ending as the audience was.

So much, I thought, for knowing the ending before making a film.

If the scene allowed, Max even mixed professionals with nonprofessionals and permitted emotions free play, providing only that the actors stayed in character and respected "parameters".

Much use of fancy language in Hollywood-speak: "The story's problem is that it goes outside its parameters."

Just as there was a Lubitsch touch, there was also the Petrov touch – according to Hollywood's Petrovologists. Max was one of the few directors to have the right to a final cut, with no one to tell him he had too many wide shots or too many closeups, and he and his favorite film editor, Sam Shapiro, understood each other's intentions and worked well together. In the hands of a good editor, a whole film was sometimes built out of little moments of life found in footage a director might too hastily have removed, and Shapiro was one of the best.

"It's almost a coauthorship," Max explained.

•

I was fascinated by the talk and watched now as each writer dramatized an idea he was submitting to the others. He jumped up to act out a part with so much energy and passion that one of them joked that more good acting was performed at these sessions than would ever appear on the screen. He said there should be an Oscar for story pitching.

It was almost as an afterthought that Max brought up Karen's abduction – or her having gone missing, which, he explained, was all anyone knew for certain. Rubinstein immediately asked what was at stake.

Max turned to me. "He means the basic story is who's concerned about the missing girl?"

"Also: what does it mean to them?" Rubinstein said.

"What do they do about it? Why are they concerned?"

These apparently were standard questions.

Carpenter: "The old basic 'Who do you root for?' "

Rubinstein asked me: "Who've you contacted? Have you gone to the FBI about the girl? Or the Missing Persons Bureau? How far are you in the search?"

I told them what I knew. I passed along to them what Inge had said, that she had been discouraged by the government agencies that she had hoped could help. The FBI almost dismissed it as a missing person's report. There was no evidence of a kidnapping and therefore legally not something that would concern the FBI. Was there an abduction leading to murder – and was there proof of that? Because even if there were proof, murder was not in the FBI's domain. The Bureau would come in only if asked by a lesser law-enforcement agency. Murder was a matter for local police – city, county, state. Had Inge contacted the police? Yes, that was the first thing she had done. And? She was told what she had been told at the outset, it was just a missing persons story. Missing persons are needles in haystacks. Back to square one.

Carpenter asked about Interpol.

That too. Inge had already talked with an Interpol representative. And? The man she spoke with had offered her his sympathy, saying he understood the pain she was in. Which sounded like a brush-off but something in his manner told her the feeling was genuine, that he could do nothing.

Cases like hers reached them every day, she was told, but sad to say the agency had little success in, for example, tracking people along known African slave routes. There were so many places to look – all so overwhelming and complicated. There were crime networks everywhere, there was Southeast Asia, there was Central America and South America, and then there was the special case of the United States, where much more trafficking happened than people realized, and law enforcement was kept busy infiltrating criminal rings and exposing and arresting everybody it could.

"And no results?" both writers asked.

The man she spoke to wouldn't say there were no results, only that it was an uphill battle and they were understaffed. What could anyone do? He said if he knew he'd be doing it. They had to work with limited funds. They had only a billion or two dollars a year to fight world terrorism, which currently was their main concern and a full-time job. To look for a girl who was missing was low priority.

"Local matters keep the police pretty busy."

Carpenter said it was a sad fact of life that women were defenseless. Even right here in L.A. There was the case of a woman who stopped to fill up her car at a San Pedro station. The cashier, behind a glass booth inside, made no move to switch on the pump but stared across the forecourt at the driver. The driver waved her arms but the attendant merely stared back at her. It was surreal. Finally the driver went over to the cashier and the cashier urged her not to go back to her car while she dialed 911. She had seen a man slip into the woman's car and crouch behind the driver's seat. When the police nabbed him he confessed he had planned to kill her as a test that would qualify him for membership in a local gang.

"The woman was a complete stranger to this guy."

I thought Max would be annoyed seeing this discussion shift the meeting away from the subject at hand, but actually it seemed to prove his point. If there were a coherent story here with an ending, these men would see it. And they just weren't seeing any.

The meeting ended with Max suggesting that Carpenter and Rubinstein take home the germs of the scenes they had earlier discussed, to try to build them into a solid story – into the blockbuster the studio was hoping to book into the Radio City Music Hall for Christmas of the following year. If all went well, of course . . . If there were no hitches. If they got the green light. If this. If that.

It sounded so complicated. So much depended on getting the right cast, which meant getting involved with agents, and that meant hassles – "so unnecessary . . . such things never happened in the old days . . ." et cetera.

As they were leaving, Carpenter jokingly mentioned Gloria and hinted with a laugh that I should investigate it for the profile as a part of Hollywood life.

"A major part," Rubinstein said, laughing with him.

"Gloria the brothel?" I asked. Was that what they were talking about? I had heard about it.

"The clients call it The Oasis."

Max described it – tall white-columned mansion mimicking the antebellum South. A black maid in a smart black uniform greeted clients at the door. Hollywood seemed to have a lot of white-columned mansions.

Rubinstein dismissed the suggestion. "That's all passé now. People prefer home-delivery hookers. Nobody goes out to get laid any more. And especially not The Oasis."

"Why especially not there?"

"The madam is L.A.P.D.'s best informer."

"Which is why it still exists," Carpenter said. "It's an arm of the police. Nice girls though."

•

I learned a few things from the meeting. Roz asked me questions and fixed on the detail about Hollywood agents.

"The whole question of agents is Max's fatal flaw," she said. "He said he would bring them to their knees, which is hubris-and-a-half."

It was a huge mistake to boast about the upcoming "David and Goliath battle," as Max put it, and bragging that his side would win.

"His position of power used to be unquestioned."

"Used to be?"

"It's become shaky. You don't go around making threats,

and certainly not against big agencies. I forget who said this, I think it was Warren Beatty who said it, about friendships being functional, that in Hollywood you don't have friends, you have only deals. It's a gossip-addicted town. So word got out, and the Reporter ran an exposé of Max's plot. The fact that Max had never taken out so much as a small $50,000 ad in the Reporter didn't help."

She compared Hollywood to the old Wild West. The fights were no longer with masked bandits and cattle barons. It was now despotic agents and tyrannical studio heads pitted against directors. The old-fashioned shoot-outs of big-sky country took place in air-conditioned offices.

"Hollywood has one concern and one concern only: get the highest returns with the lowest risks – just like Wall Street."

And what Max was hoping to do was restore balance to film making by loosening the stranglehold of the schmuck agents and breaking their fucking balls and returning costs to reasonable levels. No more routine eight-figure fees to stars.

I asked Roz: "Did you know about all this before we decided to talk to Max about making a film?"

"Well, in a way, but I thought we had a chance. I still think we do."

What was facing Max was the task of making a film without depending on the services of the giant talent agencies that controlled big-name stars – William Morris, CAA, ICM. Max always had Roz, of course. Thank God he could always count on Roz. But to make money in Hollywood you needed two things: story and cast – and leading men would be the problem. He wanted the actors he chose, not those forced on him as part of a package that rendered the movie he hoped to make an impractical dream.

I had never heard Roz so gloomy. "Sometimes actresses go begging for work while men can be choosy, waiting for a juicy role to come along."

"Don't you like actors?"

"They're worse than writers. First they demand you give them scenes with good lines to speak. Then they demand you give them scenes with no lines to speak so they can show off how they can tell the story without any dialogue."

She suddenly switched gears and told me to tell Inge to come out here to live.

"Why?"

"Women need women. Men don't know how to talk about nothing."

"Why do you want to talk about nothing?"

"It's important for sanity."

Without agreeing with the reasoning, I thought Inge would be good for Roz. Having only Max and me as friends was not enough to fill Roz's need for sympatico people.

And certainly that description did not fit Laszlo. Everything I kept hearing about lover-boy Laszlo was that he had a torso like Tarzan's and the brain of a chimp. ("But" – Roz – "with a dork that's the size of a paper-towel tube.") There was something very Hollywood about Laszlo and I would try to fit him into my profile of Roz – like Laszlo's miniature palazzo that his friends said was a cross between Early French Romanesque and Malibu Laid-Back. The locals called it popcorn architecture. They said if that sounded too weird to imagine, it was even weirder when you saw it.

I guess I didn't have much faith in Rob or Jake. I felt more and more convinced that our project would wind up nowhere and maybe it would be wise to start preparing Inge for the ultimate disappointment. The odds were against finding Karen. It was really best not to think of the beautiful young life. She was lost. She would never be found.

What we had to come up with was an ending to a film about her, which was ironic. Our focus was now the ending to a film, not the missing girl. There was something profoundly wrong about that, and now I felt pissed off, as pissed off as Inge was.

I didn't tell Inge about my pessimism. I decided instead to research women's disappearances. Maybe I could devise a story having an unambiguous ending to move Max to push East-West to consider making the film.

•

That night, when I phoned Inge, she was in one of her blacker Finnish moods. But she had a new theme now.

"I'm weakening. Paska."

The new theme was her weakening, not the paska. Paska was just an expressive Finnish word meaning shit. It was an expletive Inge used frequently, speaking it with verve and a certain passion except when depressed. When she was depressed she muttered the word sullenly. Right now she was in sullen-mutter mode.

"What do you mean 'weakening'?"

"I don't know. I just need you to tell me you love me."

"Oh Inge, you know I do."

"Not like that. Men seem to feel that if you tell a woman once that you love her that that about covers it."

Really in a bad mood. I must admit though she had a point about my telling her how much I loved her. I made a mental note to say nice things to her more often. Women seemed particularly needy about repeated assurances, and although I had learned that long ago, I was always surprised each time I came up against it.

After saying goodbye I lectured myself: "Listen, me bucko, if you're ever going to get to 'Reader, I married her,' you'd better get off your ass and do something to make her happy." Which in a depressing free association made me think of an article the paper ran recently about the brave mating habits of the male spider. I get weirdo thoughts and when I'm in one of those moods, spiders can get me going. In wooing a female, to make sure she isn't so starving for her next meal that she makes an hors d'oeuvre out of the horny schmuck standing in her doorway, smiling with his social-friendly dick flamboyantly hanging practically down to his knees, he prudently throws a freshly-paralyzed fly into her web, the idea being that after she has pigged out on fly-under-glass and is feeling a deep postprandial satisfaction, they can settle down and enjoy a nice tête-à-tête. That in human terms is the equivalent of the dinner-before-boff ritual — except that spider road kill is cheaper, although it doesn't come with wine. And in the human ritual, one of the participants always runs the risk of experiencing the medical condition known as vasocongestion, known to the vulgar as blue balls.

One thing I've noticed about spider stories is that one way or another males get shafted. They're doomed before they begin and all because of the spider equivalent of testosterone, which the poor bastards never asked to be given but got endowed with at birth — got saddled with. After that it's a lifetime of being on the hunt, and not a long lifetime either. And only one principal governs them. If she has a skirt on, boff her, and if on arrival her skirt's already off and there's a little friendly twinkle in her eyes, well, then, what the hell are you waiting for? It seems like such a limited life, but then they don't think of it as a life. The little head has only one objective: slip it in. It's cold outside. You have to have some sympathy for the poor little schmuck.

13

After the phone call I warmed up some leftover KFC, and wondered why L.A. KFC tasted better than New York KFC. I ate it half-reclining on the bed watching TV and thought I would doze while watching, maybe sleep and call it a day.

A Petrov rerun was on, an oldie called "Cream", but I wasn't in the mood for it even though I remembered it was a good bank heist thriller. I switched channels to something called "Yesterday Today". This turned about to be an episode describing a trip to America once made by the late Princess Margaret of England. The mini documentary included a shitload of instructions the staff had to follow at all the hotels where she stayed. Her entourage passed out stuff like cards saying the princess didn't like heights, helicopters, or police sirens. And she had to have a double bed with a soft mattress, but – relenting here – the sheets could be of any color. She preferred soup, lobster, prawns, crab, egg and cheese dishes, and an occasional steak. But – major but – she did not like to eat oysters and American or Canadian salmon. It was her royal wish that no autographs be asked of her, ever, nor would any be given if asked. Then the refreshing detail, that if her national anthem had to be played whenever she popped up somewhere, then please, for God sake, play only six bars of it. (The program didn't say "for God sake".)

I decide to bail out of this boring shit rather than wait to see what happened after the commercial, when we would learn what her favorite hideaways around the world were. We were promised that was a secret she was prepared to reveal to her American friends.

To get ready to sleep I switched to the evening news and learned the good news that the six-year-old girl that had gone missing in the north woods was found. Hikers in northern California on an impulse had wandered off the trail and saw her next to a tree. It seemed so unreal – a little girl standing near the trunk of a tree way out in the middle of a forest somewhere. Just standing there and waiting. They had trouble believing what they were seeing. She was waiting for her mother. Her mother had left that morning, she said, instructing her not to move from the tree until she returned, because if she budged from the spot the mother might not find her again. The mother explained they were lost and said she was going to go for help and would be back as soon as she could. The girl had been there since morning and it was getting dark in the woods when the hikers found her. She pleaded with them not to leave her and asked one of the women to hold her by the hand, and when the woman took her hand the girl cried quietly.

In bed later, falling asleep, I was still thinking about the girl in the woods. I woke up twice during the night, each time after a dream. Afterwards I couldn't remember either of the dreams except for the one detail common to both: I was wandering through unfamiliar city streets and wondering where the hell I was. The dreams felt unusually real.

•

My new routine now was a morning dip, then make my own breakfast of two scrambled eggs and toast. The skillet and plate washed and put away, I hopped down to the Beverly Hills library for some more research on the disappearance of women. I had to come up with a story with an "ending". There was no way round it. An ending had to be found.

But I couldn't help thinking that if you went missing you went missing and if you were never found again you were never found again and what was there to be said after that? Wasn't that the ending? But I could see Max's point. A movie required something more. It wasn't just Max. Aristotle insisted too.

The library had practically a whole shelf of books on kidnappings and sexual slavery. It was really surprising for so small a library. Some of the books had practically whole chapters of facts and figures, boring amounts of it. Citing statistics was obviously not going to be a problem. What would be a problem was giving the facts shape and devising the story of a good straight movie, not a late-night docudrama called "Abducted: White Slavery in Thailand." The purpose of a documentary was to inform, but I've never known any that got people to do anything. We were right in thinking only an emotional shift in people got them to act. And I rehearsed to myself Max Petrov's advice and our mantra: need ending, need ending.

One book I skimmed through was as packed with documentation as the annual report of a corporation and almost read like one. It tallied up girls missing or raped. It reported that to satisfy the sexual appetites of Western countries, between 100,000 and 200,000 teenage girls are lured from Russia to Europe each year. In Europe kidnapping and prostitution were an annual $12 billion business. The same number of teenage girls were said to be exported to Israel. I didn't realize the Israelis boffed so much. I suppose that was one good use for shikses.

But this book at least was written interestingly. It said that forced slavery was the third largest crime in the world. In most countries it paid higher profits than drugs did and was much safer to traffic in. Criminals got more mileage out of girls than they could get out of drugs. Kidnapped girls could be sold and resold many times, and while they were in your control, if you put together the incomes of all the girls you owned, they came to a nice steady several thousand dollars a day. Multiply that by 365 days and you had a million or two a year. And your only expense was feeding the girls to keep them in condition.

Some teenage girls were used until they became experienced prostitutes and then were sold on to gangs in Britain, where apparently there was quite a demand for them. Girls and women kept being shuffled from brothel to brothel or country to country so that the men using them would always have variety, and the girls would be held in permanent debt to brothel owners as each move got them in deeper. This debt was of course fictitious, but the girls couldn't do anything about it, any more than they could escape: from the very first moment they were duped into accepting a job as "bar hostess" their passports were taken from them. Sometimes these same girls were kidnapped by rival gangs and sold to competitors on the Continent, and often to vice rings in Italy, because Italy was a country where the government operated something like 30,000 brothels and had a steady need for new girls, especially fresh young ones. One report said that half the income of these state-owned brothels went to the Vatican, the Church justifying brothels as safeguarding the honor and purity of Italian women, but I didn't know how true this was.

The business in trafficking followed a pattern. A report said that a London government agency making a study of abductees followed the trail of one sixteen-year-old western Siberian girl forced to become a "sex worker". Having read a bunch of reports, I was getting a little bugged by that phrase. There were so many mentions of "sex work" and "sex worker" that the words sounded like euphemisms, a sanitized view of the reality of a girl's life. More accurately her life was morning-to-night rape. As she was serially raped, some man or men collected money. Her "sex work" was performed on an unmade bed servicing forty to fifty men a day ("We hardly had time to sleep," one girl said), and that was another euphemism: "servicing" men. It sounded as if the men were having sex with her, but they really were not. They were fucking her body. They were sticking their meat into her meat. Sometimes a customer was already on top of her as the man who had just been "serviced" by her was still pulling his pants back on.

The story of one Siberian girl told how it all happened in an inconspicuous row house in Hackney. As an illegal immigrant she couldn't leave where she worked and was even barred from getting fresh air by attempting to stand near a window where a neighbor might see and report her. After putting in a year of this "sex work" in Hackney she had market value as a highly experienced girl and was sold for $3000 to a Balkan network operating out of Zagreb. The gang that bought her was known for its quick turn-arounds and immediately sold her as a prized commodity to a large ring in Kosovo at twice the amount they had just paid. Her story ended suddenly the following year, the eighteenth year of her life, when her unclothed lifeless body was found among trash bins in a back alley in Brussels. There was evidence that she had been beaten to death, but Belgian authorities could offer no clue about how or why it had happened. Some speculated that she had been killed trying to escape. But with insufficient evidence, the official police report declined comment. The worst of it was that no one could say who she was. A small name tag sewn on her underwear identified her as Karina, and I wondered if she had sewn it on herself or if her mother had sewn it for her while she was still living at home. Her being from western Siberia was surmised only from certain small clues, and when it was suggested that she might be identified by her teeth, it was pointed out that her dental records, if any existed, could be in any of a thousand villages in Siberia. And besides, there were so many like her that if they stopped to investigate the teeth of each girl turning up in some trash bin in Europe . . .

•

The librarian, Ms. Highsmith, asked if she could be of any help. She had a friendly outgoing manner, with middle age pulling gently at her face. I told her what I was looking for – a very abbreviated version of it. She steered me to two books. One was a directory of U.N. Reports about world sex slavery. The other was a compilation of government statistics on missing children. The subject was one that interested her, she said. If I needed any assistance . . .

"It's not just women, you know. Boys go missing too. And not all are runaways or murder victims. And the boys are used for sex too. You might check the internet" – she pointed to a computer on a table near her desk and suggested some sites.

I sat in the chair in front of the computer and got on line and the first thing I learned from the web was that the figures I had just been reading were outdated. The actual numbers were larger – much larger and expanding.

One site linked to another and I learned there was a subcategory: the "comfort women" of the Japanese Army during the Second World War. It was a side track but it got me interested, especially as it brought back a memory of news reports in the World-Herald a couple of years ago.

"Oh yes," the librarian said, remembering the reports. I guess other papers had carried them too.

It was really a short history of the several hundred thousand Korean women, and Chinese and Thai too, kidnapped for the sexual "comfort" of Japanese troops. Teenage girls vanished, abducted from homes or waylaid going to school and shipped to "comfort stations" in China, Taiwan, Malaysia, Vietnam, Thailand, the Philippines, Indonesia – to wherever the Japanese Army had troops stationed. Few of the girls were ever heard from again. They were quite useful in maintaining the fighting spirit of the troops and thought to contribute materially to winning some of the battles of the war.

Another reason to have a supply of "comfort women" had the moral aim of deterring the soldiers from raping civilians or sexually molesting prisoners in their care. And, in more remote areas, where morale was more difficult to maintain, it stopped soldiers from raping each other.

When the war began to go badly for the Japanese and they began retreating, the army decided to do the humane thing and bayoneted the comfort women. That spared the women from suffering a slow death by starvation if they were just left behind in the jungle. And too in the jungle their corpses would rot quickly, so there wouldn't be any problem about burials and things.

Overall, the grand operation Comfort Women was pretty much a success. Authorities calculated that after six years of war in Southeast Asia the number of sexual assaults on women was lower than many had expected, and that was a cause for some gratification. The number of assaults on females in cities and countryside was remarkably low. It was generally agreed that in all, only 20 million women were raped.

•

I picked up another report. This one was about the women brought from Mexico into the United States each year, about 15,000 of them, and they were forced into sex slavery. That surprised me but at least it wasn't called sex work but sex slavery. But that number was only a fraction of the two million smuggled into the country each year. Which surprised me also. Another report told of an annual hundred thousand Polish women entering the U.S. to become prostitutes.

A third report: Asian teenagers were sold to North American brothels for $16,000 a girl. It generally took the brothel owner two weeks to recoup his money and start showing a profit on his investment.

Another one was about girls taken from Nepal to India to work in brothels. At last count, it came to more than 200,000 girls aged 11 to 14.

•

I looked at all the books to read. The reports seemed endless. I had no idea so much documentation had been amassed. In Thailand alone 60,000 children are sold into prostitution each year. I checked the figure again: 60,000 children. Each year. In Thailand. Forced into prostitution for the enjoyment of men. One report corroborated that more than 100,000 women had so far been sent from Russia to Israel to safeguard the purity of Israeli women. The boffing apparently never stops down there.

More figures . . . women . . . girls . . . children . . . Sri Lanka, Myanmar . . . Cambodia . . . the UN . . . Interpol. . . .

I kept reading, finding it difficult to stop. According to the Department of Trafficking, the abduction and slavery of women was the fastest growing illegal industry in the world.

And it paid enormously well. Total annual revenue for "trafficking": $5 billion to $9 billion – figures unreliably old. The Council of Europe estimated that in the past decade "people trafficking had reached epidemic proportions, with a global annual market of $42.5 billion."

Recruitment techniques were coercion, deception, fraud, and corruption. All these abstract terms blurred the simple fact that one day a girl was out playing with her friends and didn't return home. Her family experienced a grief that those without children can't understand or feel.

A case in a government file: a 16-year-old Guatemalan girl kidnapped to California was forced to work in the fields. Each day, when work was done and the farm laborers were locked in one big room together, she was systematically raped by her coworkers. After several months, she wrote begging her mother to come and take her home. She explained she was in Central Valley, California, and to hurry because she was being treated badly and knew how much her mother loved her and to please come and get her. She gave the letter to the ranch owner to post and for several days it made things easier for her to take, knowing that her mother would soon be there to take her home.

•

I handed the books back to the librarian.

She held out two other volumes, and I told her maybe later.

"You can take only so much," she sympathized. She was very supportive and gave me a big understanding smile as I left.

She said, "We really have duties as citizens, you know, societal obligations, don't you think?" She said it was all so monstrous. Most monstrous of all was that there didn't seem to be any way of stopping what was happening. "Like, what does the U.N. do?"

She suggested a name to look up: Department of Trafficking in People, Washington, D.C.

"Why is it always called trafficking?" I asked.

They were lives destroyed, not trafficked. In the U.S., 300,000 women were "trafficked" each year – "trafficked", not broken in spirit or broken physically. They were made slaves of their fellow human beings, forced to perform sexually, beaten for minor infractions, left in a ditch, dumped into some tip somewhere, killed. They had been "trafficked."

"It probably wouldn't do to call it the Department of the Abduction, Sexual Slavery and Degradation of Humans, would it?" Ms. Highsmith said.

"Why not? That's what it is."

•

In an email Umpleby sent some newspaper clippings for the column. Fodder to encourage me. I was not only not in the mood to work on them but I was out of the habit, and then remembered Umpleby's comment that Western civilization did not depend on the column's regular appearance in the paper but my employment at the World-Herald did.

These, the latest items, were the worst kind of trivia to be worked into humorous anecdotes. It was especially difficult working on them after reading of comfort women used by the Japanese army and girl bodies in trash bins.

One amusing news item described a submerged bridge to be built under the Sea of Galilee so tourists could recreate Christ's walking on water. Another was the recorded phone message a Sussex scientist left for callers: "I can't come to the phone at the moment for, you see, I'm dead." Where the hell does he get these things from?

One caught my interest, though, because it sort of tied in with what I had been reading. A Tokyo mother sold her sixteen-year-old daughter to a geisha house. The mother was desperate for money to keep playing pachinko, a Japanese pinball game. She and her elder daughter, aged 27, got $10,000 for the teenager, enough money to cover thousands of games. Unfortunately the girl escaped the geisha house and returned home and the geisha house demanded its money back. The mother, furious at losing what to her was the equivalent of a once-in-a-lifetime lottery win, felt a sudden upwelling of moral outrage at her daughter's disobedience, took a stick and beat the shit out of her. The girl then went straight to the police and reported the whole affair. Which so royally pissed the mother off that it ended in another round of violence. After all the girl was her daughter, and who had any right to tell her that she couldn't sell off a piece of her own flesh and blood? The police listened, patiently at first and then impatiently, and, not buying any of it, angrily advised everybody to "just go home and act like grownups for a change – end of story." Ah, I thought, a story with an ending.

14

The next time Max and I met I could see his favorite subject was obsessing him again: making The Death of Ivan Ilych. For us that signified meant more delays – or not delays so much as protracted nothingness.

I had started to think our project was dead on arrival but then things got even worse. About the Tolstoy I asked Max stupidly-dutifully: "Isn't that an unusual subject for Hollywood – a film about somebody in bed,? Just dying? I mean, just visually, wouldn't that be dull?"

"It depends, of course. MGM once almost made Tolstoy's The Living Corpse, the same Tolstoy story but with that title. With John Gilbert as star. This is true, by the way. This was way before your time and in fact way before my time. Louis Mayer and Thalberg were the big names then, back in the early days, and they went so far as to authorize production. This is all true."

"What happened?"

"Nothing. The film was never made," Max said. "But it was all set to g-."

The word "go" was never completed. The vowel sound lengthened into a groan and simultaneously as I turned toward him I could see his wife Regina coming through the door. Seeing Max half bent over now and fumbling for the back of a chair to grab to keep from falling over, she rushed to support him.

"What is it – Max!"

As she tried to hold his body up, a series of events followed so swiftly we all seemed to be actors in some speeded-up film. Mrs. Petrov's chauffeur Llewellyn stepped into the room from the garden as if he had been waiting for this signal to appear and seeing Mrs. Petrov struggling, rushed to her as she meanwhile shouted to the flustered maid to for god sake call 911 – "Give them directions! Give them directions!" – as I meanwhile looked around for brandy, remembering that that was what people in movies did. I recalled seeing a bottle in Max's study, and by the time I returned with a big ship's decanter, Cedars-Sinai was phoning back to confirm an ambulance was on its way and requesting that the gatekeeper be notified to allow them through and not think it was some elaborate Hollywood prank. And it seemed only a minute later that two white-outfitted paramedics, contributing a new mix to the chaos, were lifting Max onto a gurney while a third medic restrained Regina from clambering into the ambulance behind Max, the medic telling her no, and there could be no diagnosis without tests, and reassuring her, yes, notification would come soon . . . careful, your hands . . . yes, we'll take care . . . watch door . . . ma'am, please . . . yes, no, yes, soon. . . . and they were gone.

Llewellyn's arm encircled Mrs. Petrov's shoulder protectively as she whimpered, "Damn it, Lew, we must get to the hospital," his comforting words beginning to calm her, while I, stranded in the middle of the mêlée and feeling superfluous, wondered whether to leave or find something helpful to do and recalled that people in movies usually knocked off a brandy at this point, and I thought why not, it seemed the right thing to do and it was damn good brandy.

●

Waiting to hear from the hospital I began putting together a short history of Max Petrov, knowing I could compose it in bits and pieces from various sources and then running the facts past Roz for accuracy.

Max and Regina, though deeply fond of each other, had stopped sharing a bed fifteen years ago. But nothing had changed their mutual respect even though Regina knew of the "assistants" her husband took on his trips. She described herself as an "old-fashioned homemaker and mother"/ She took comfort in knowing that although these trips were frequent he remained devoted to her. "Home is what he returns to."

I learned many things about her. For one thing, Mrs. Petrov left town frequently to go to New York. She would go for two-week stays to see the latest Broadway shows, always taking her chauffeur Llewellyn with her. He was close to her in age and the poor dear needed a break as much as she did. Besides, having her own chauffeur in a New York and renting a car by the day was less expensive than hiring a taxi for drives out to the country – not that she and Llewellyn did much driving out to the country, or even around town. Or driving at all.

No one believed her, including Max. He was tactfully blind about the whole thing and probably felt it was a small price to pay for his own more frequent deceptions. The strategic cost included jewelry from Van Cleef Arpels, plus what some wag of a friend once described as enough Shalimar to fill a five-gallon drum – "the perfume, never the cologne" – and an "eighth of a ton of beluga a year." And too, each Christmas Max approved without questioning a bill his accountant paid for things like a half-dozen white silk shirts with an embossed emerald "L" monogrammed over the breast pocket.

•

With our meetings temporarily suspended and while Max was in hospital I worked on the Roz bio also. Sophie, always eager to please, took the lead, asking:

"Are you getting dirt on her?" Seeing my reaction she said: "I don't mean dirt-dirt. Just little hidden things – human interest stuff that sells."

I told her that if anyone had "hidden stuff" on Roz, Sophie herself was ideally placed for it. Her laughing look said she was on to me: I couldn't fool her into unintentionally revealing anything.

"I would never tell anyone anything even if I knew something."

"Like what?"

"Oh, unimportant things. Like Tiffany's once. They let Roz

use a diamond brooch for a film and she thought it was a gift from them – you know the way they do at the Oscars, and then when the ceremonies are over, the jewelry companies all come back and collect the goodies. But Roz wouldn't return hers."

An argument over one of the brooches resulted in a settlement and a handsome compensation figure. Not compensation, Sophie corrected herself, some compromise figure.

"But that was in all the papers so I'm not revealing anything. But then she turned around and sold the brooch to a soap opera superstar for quite a wad. Not Joan Collins – the other one with all the money."

I was wondering who the other one with all the money might be when Sophie moved on to Roz's clothing. It surprised me that Roz preferred buying Banana Republic except when the studio wanted her to make a formal appearance. Then it was all Valentino or Versace or Ungaro. Or Vera Wang or a Donna Karan – Sophie named a whole raft of them, names as familiar to her as though they were neighbors.

"They give her things to wear because where she is now, fashion people need her more than she needs them. They get their names in People magazine and in the tabloids because of Roz. She's worth more to them than full-page ads."

Inspired by my interest, she switched to: "Did I tell you that Playboy wants to do a big spread on Roz?" She thought the idea for it came from Laszlo. "Heffner nearly flipped when he heard the idea and offered her a million. No, ten million. No-no, just one million – well, anyway, those were the rumors. But that Laszlo – he's awful, he's shameless and exploited her to get his own business started."

"Laszlo the lover-boy?"

"Former lover-boy. He was a wrestler in Australia and retired at thirty-two, broke. Now he's a food caterer to the studios – you know, when they go on location? – he calls his business Noshville. And he also has a small limo-renting business, so nowadays he has money spilling out of his pockets, I mean it's really nutty. He's nutty. He passed a kidney stone last year and showed it to people so they could admire its size.

He carried it around with him like a pet rock. It was so tiny you could barely see it. Roz refers to him as Crocodile Dundee and calls his –"

Sudden anxious stop, eyes reading mine.

"– you know, his . . . uh . . . schwanz – his . . . you know, the . . . Roz says that on a scale of ten, it's an easy fourteen, but she exaggerates so much you don't know when to believe her. Still, it does make you curious. . . ." Her eyes go down, shy dimpled smile spreading over pink Basque cheeks. An afterthought: "Of course it's not all just size." Another afterthought: "Well, size too."

•

Inge on the phone advised me to give priority to the Roz interview.

"And the more outrageous it is, the more the readers will love it. I don't see why you feel you should hold back."

I was hesitant. There would be no point in writing something unpublishable. "You know how Roz gets when she's on a roll."

"The paper could always edit out the four-letter stuff."

"Like what?"

"The fuck stuff. Although do you know anybody who doesn't say fuck anymore?"

"I met an old lady once."

"You shouldn't meet old ladies like that."

"What's wrong with old ladies like that?"

"What's wrong with old ladies like that is that they don't say fuck." That topic done with: "How's the weather there and don't tell me it's gorgeous."

"It's fucking gorgeous."

"Yes but can you get a Nathan's fucking hotdog out there?"

"No, and no fucking sauerkraut either. They only have fucking onions out here."

"I don't know how you're able to survive."

"The hotdogs that that guy sells on the corner of 86th and Third are better. He's got the best. And that papaya drink?"

"I agree, he's the best."

"The best in New York or the best in America?"

"He's the best in the Western Hemisphere," Inge said.

Easterners claim to be unimpressed by California weather but really they love it. They always put it down with the usual crap about how much fun it is to go walking in the rain and how great it is to see the changing of the seasons blah blah. We talked about that for a while. Inge, being Finnish, didn't like winter in New England, where it was colder than Finland. Finland has the Gulf Stream curving way up there. We reminisced about the cold look of the sea in that tiny place in Massachusetts where we stopped once, it wasn't even a town, just a place where we holed up one weekend, and the weather had turned bitter. It had been a mild winter but overnight the pond behind this little house froze over and we squeezed together in our large sleeping bag in the corner of the room near the potbelly stove ("Fucking cold," Inge said, wearing a scarf in bed) and were snug and happy all night.

I liked talking with Inge about that trip and other trips and I thought we were getting into Nostalgia Mode when she brought up the Karen project. So we were back on that again. I filled her in, padding it a bit to keep her hope going, and it helped but not much. Our pace was too slow for her, she was unhappy, and I could tell that the old anger was bringing her down again. Or resurfacing. Actually the anger was always there. She wasn't at all the Inge I knew when we first met but seemed to be turning into a bitter person.

15

To kill more time and get away from the depressing library research, I tried working on a preliminary sketch for the Roz interview for the paper. In taking notes for it Roz, in irrepressible mode, gave me her preferred opening: " 'Warm and radiating a glow of happiness after having just been boinked into blissful satisfaction by several members of Hell's Angels, Lorna Beach greets me at her door purring with gratified desire, face shining pink in a well-fucked look, ready to take on life.' "

We were going to have trouble.

"If that doesn't grab them nothing will. What do you think?"

"It'll grab them."

"Or" – another thought: "How about: 'She was discovered sitting around cultivating her finer feelings and found one she particularly liked.' You know, ham it up with a lot of horse shit, make it into a fun thing. You writing that down? I'm only kidding."

We've barely begun when she switches to her earlier lover, the painter Bill Joachim. He had apparently mattered a lot to her. He was a bigger name now that he was dead. His work was compared, favorably, with Jackson Pollock's, and even more so after his suicide a couple of years ago. Sotheby's recently complained it couldn't get enough Joachims to auction off. Real money makers.

For a long time Roz's sorrow was intense. "I thought I'd died. I didn't think I'd feel anything ever again, which, according to my shrink, was why I drank – not to feel. I told him to cut out the Reader's Digest crap."

Then she went on some more about Bill Joachim and drinking: "If you like, we could talk about bed-hopping as an antidote to grief. Even though it's known not to work and only deepens depression."

Her thoughts back then were confused. "Life was so fucking

miserable. It was all depression, and then when that lifted, it seemed that life was all trichomonosis, however you pronounce it, vaginitis, cystitis, warts, herpes and pubic lice. Oh and gonorrhea and AIDS, of course, not that we talk about these things."

"And income tax?" I prompted.

"And income tax."

"Have you had all those diseases?"

"Good god, no! They were in some article I read about women. It said these are what we, today's young ladies, get."

She finally stopped seeing another shrink, her most recent one.

"Too weird, he was. He used an electric timer. Can you imagine? – an electric oven timer that announces the end of your session – ping! Made me feel like a pork roast."

She went on, with me making an attempt at writing things down as it came.

"Do you think we should talk about sex and things of that everyday nature? – you know, universal interest? Like when I was younger I got felt up a lot. Enjoyed it too, if I liked the guy."

"We can always edit."

"Little humorous quips?"

"Anything."

"Like: 'Just because you have a quickie with somebody it doesn't mean you want to bear his children.' Although that one's a little stale."

"You don't want to get too many jokes or too much sex into an interview. It starts to get unreal."

"Yeah, life is supposed to be pretty real. Besides, what is there to say about orgasms – that I've been in earthquakes that have lasted longer? Although that's not a bad line."

"It was a great line in 366 B.C."

"That late?"

It was hard to keep her serious but I didn't really try. I was in rebellious mode too and thought the hell with the World-Herald. She said I deserved more than the welfare check the paper was paying me. She was always ready to get back to that theme and how I was frittering my life away.

"It's for salaries like yours that food stamps were invented."

Obviously we were not doing an interview. But I wrote everything down anyway to extract things from later.

"How about putting everything I say into the profile? If there's one thing I hate, it's all those phoney interviews about what some bimbo had for breakfast – publicity department shit. A tell-all, sex life, the whole bit, is what people really want."

"Would you do that?"

"Sure but the publicity department would kill it. To them I'm Miss Blabbermouth."

"You mean, the world's not ready for it yet."

"The world's not ready for it yet. Piss on it."

"You mean the world."

"Yeah, the world."

"What about things like 'Her Hobbies Are'?"

"Like things I do in bed?"

"Aside from that."

"I mostly sleep in bed."

"Apart from that."

"Blow jobs you mean?"

"Apart from that."

I told her I'd be glad to let her read whatever I wrote so that later, when I was done with it, she could weed out anything she didn't want to have published.

"The trouble is the studio regards me as an investment. The

publicity department will kill anything that might put me in a bad light – or cost the studio money, more to the point. Hypocrisy. I'd like to talk about hypocrisy. Fellatio is now in like it's never been in before and liberated women chatter about their vaginas and how nice they taste and how they used to be so hairy before the shaving craze. In the old days they used to hate men for even mentioning such things. Now it's dinner talk."

•

I wanted to write about her way of speaking, as in: she has to wear a fucking babushka just to buy a fucking sandwich. She wonders out loud where in fucking Manhattan she could get good acrylic nails and find a good hair shop (beauty salon) that she could schlep into wearing only sweats or jeans.

"Out West here they all try to be so chic and fucking formal. Very insecure people in Hollywood."

But as she goes on, it becomes more and more obvious that most of this will never appear in print – like her spoofing title of the fictitious memoir she plans to write some day: "Lost Erections, or The Clitoris and I". Her interviews on taped late-night shows never reached the public intact: all that the public saw was what was left after the studio's publicity department, by formal contract, censored them before allowing them to be aired.

She tells of the first time she became aware of being stared at was when a kid tried to look up her dress and she thought: "Wow! I'm turning him on." Few things impressed her as much. "Pussy power! I could just look at a guy and get him hot."

There were some details about entering beauty contests and she was once Little Miss Sunshine somewhere in New England. After being educated at Spence, which I gathered was New York's most expensive school for girls, and Bennington, she did summer stock before landing a small part in a Spielberg TV miniseries that moved her into the big time.

"At the beginning I would have kissed ass to get to where I am."

"You kissed Spielberg's ass?"

"Oh no! Absolutely not. He's a really nice man. He assured me I had talent and there was a role he could use me for and surprise surprise he fucking did. Unlike the others, there was not the slightest bullshit about him. He's Jewish and married, and Jewish men are always faithful to their wives because they have this deep racial feeling about Jewish mothers, or something, but some of these other directors – they hire you just to have you sashay your ass around the set while they're shooting so they can look at you and feel they're big shots – you know, as though they own you. They want you to parade up and down in a skimpy bikini to satisfy their mental lusting. Just to feel the power they have and have others see that they have it. But Spielberg gave me a real part, and not just a walk-on either. I spoke eighteen words and appeared on the screen large as fucking life."

She likes Martin Scorsese and Steven Spielberg and Max – Max most of all. He creates a gemütlich atmosphere on the set.

"He's not a shitbag, which is one of Max's favorite terms and a useful one in Hollywood for you to learn. He also likes to call the bigwigs mo-ghouls. Anyway, Max is as good as Spielberg and may even be a tad smarter than him but that could be argued."

"In what way, smarter?"

"In general. I like his wisdom. He says, 'We love life because that's all there is.' That's pretty profound when you think about it. But not if you think about it too long. And: 'You have to undream your dreams.' Although you never do undream them, of course – you're too busy dreaming."

It was as I was gathering material for her profile that I learned how extraordinarily unruffled Roz can be and I had to find a way to convey that to readers without upsetting sensibilities. As we're having drinks Roz talks as she makes trips to the john rather than interrupt the flow of talk and confers on me the ultimate female compliment of unzipping her shorts while still just leaving the room and settling her movie-star derriere comfortably (as I imagine it) on the velour-covered john seat out of direct line of sight but with the door not quite closed. We continue chatting over the background sound of a woman's hazy whiz and I see her, in my mind, enthroned in the peach-colored marble room with the sunken tub and glass walls looking out to a private rug-size sunbathing garden and high protective hedge: Roz at home – laid bare, as it were. Her behavior comes with the endorsement of her best friend (Inge) and is completely trustworthy, making her inhibition threshold somewhere near zero. Good friends piss together. What's so unusual about that? So I happen to be a male. Big deal.

Commenting from the john: "Americans spend two billion a year on toilet tissues and manufacturers pay thirty million a year to advertize it. Did you know that? Just to wipe ourselves, can you imagine?" She sounded astonished. "That's why the economy of the poorer countries is in trouble."

"Why is that?"

"No toilet tissues."

"But think of the forests not being leveled."

"There's a tradeoff. Think of all those unwiped bottoms."

She returns looking prim and proper and we get back to the interview. I ask her about the last film she made and her leading man.

"Lee Robinson was snorting coke again. On the set. I'll admit it relaxes him, especially in the love scenes – you know, slowing his pace. But you don't want to kiss anybody on amphetamine."

"Is it true that drugs are common on movie sets nowadays?"

"It's written into contracts." It's a well-known fact the way she says it.

"You can write coke into a contract?"

"It goes under transportation."

"You're kidding."

"Transportation hides all sorts of miscellaneous things."

"Like?"

"Like location hunting. An assistant producer wants to take a trip to Paris. He records it as 'location hunting'. He already knows the film is set in Mexico and will be shot entirely in Mexico with a lot of Mexican people in it. But he wants to take his wife and family to Paris on a spring jaunt, so he works in a trip to Paris as location hunting."

"Doesn't anybody call him on it?"

"If they do he explains there's a sequence where the hero's thinking of taking a quick trip to Paris and needs to hide away in a hotel so posh they'd never think of looking for him there."

"You're kidding. He checks into the Crillon?"

"Naa, someplace really posh."

"You're kidding."

"On the Île St. Louis. Fifteen grand a night. Another scam example: if you just bump into somebody on the street and have a brief chat, you could describe it as a conference and claim it as a production expense."

"A scam like that? Are they that naïve?"

"No, they all do it."

Reminding her of our plot to get Max involved in a film about women who disappear I ask: "After that last meeting, what do you think our chances are?"

"Nada, I'm beginning to think." She looked a little embarrassed saying that.

"What?"

"Because ultimately nobody gives a damn about a woman who goes missing. The family maybe but not other people. They don't have the time – or really they don't know what they could do, if anything. When you hear about somebody's disappearance it seems sad, but it doesn't exactly hit you hard, does it?"

"How about the police?"

"An adult has the right to take off and never be seen again. People drop out of sight all the time. To get away from a wife. Hide from a lover. Or they sometimes just want to change identity You have the right to walk out of your life."

"The police can't do anything about it. No crime has been committed," I corroborate. No body, no evidence, no suspects. No signs of foul play.

"Right. No crime has been committed. People disappear. What crime?"

•

On Sophie's day off (I imagine her haggling at a downtown panty swap), around lunch time, I'm in Roz's kitchen when Roz rolls in saying, "I've been fucking with my hair all morning but no use – it's going to be frizzies all day."

No hair is out of place that I can see. But then women see things that men can't.

Thinking of Inge had made me feel homesick and now, inspired by Roz's unexpected arrival, I fixed us some hors d'oeuvres the way I sometimes did with Inge.

"Like the thing you made the other day," Roz encourages.

Which was to assemble a few black olives, some cucumber spears and cherry tomatoes – no big deal. She bribes me telling me she admires men who can cook and I tell her this isn't really cooking. But I don't need much encouraging to go all out on the main course: slice a sourdough baguette lengthwise and paint the insides with olive oil and rough-rub the surfaces with a fat clove of garlic. That was the way I had seen Inge do it. Then, placing tomato slices on the two lengths of sourdough and drizzling mozzarella bits over the tomatoes, I put the baguettes into the microwave and watched the cheese melt into an orange goo as the kitchen filled with the rich smell of eau de garlic and Roz moaned mmmm Jesus and saying how good it smelled. I removed it from the microwave, cut it into slices and served. She took a chewy bite and said, mouth full:

"This garlic bread is the tastiest fucking thing I've had in weeks. You've got to tell Sophie how you make it."

She asked whether Inge and I were really as happy with each other as we gave the impression of being.

"She's my life partner, as far as I'm concerned."

"How really in love with her are you?"

"I'm crazy about her."

"Why don't you two get married, then? Or am I being charmingly old-fashioned?"

"Inge says men have this thing about marriage, where I've always thought it was women who had this thing about marriage."

"She's still turning you down? I don't believe it."

"Provisionally."

"I've gotta talk to that girl."

"She'll change her mind when she changes her mind."

"Yeah, men think that women are still sitting around waiting for somebody to come along and marry them, even though that idea goes back to the horse and buggy."

"How about back to Ancient Egypt?"

"How about the Garden of Eden? I know a lot of women who wouldn't get married if you paid them. Of course a lot of men wouldn't marry them either, not when you have pussy emporiums around."

"There are a lot of brothels out here?"

"Not like the old days, with Billie Bennett. There's nothing like that now."

"Who's Billie Bennett?"

"She was a very attractive madam who specialized in leading-lady lookalikes. I'm surprised you've never heard of her. If you wanted to fuck Ingrid Bergman she set you up with an Ingrid Bergman double."

"You're kidding."

"Even Bergman's husband, when his wife was off with Rossellini, would occasionally go over and by proxy exercise his conjugal rights. There's a story that an MGM exec once brought someone from the New York office who wanted to fuck Jean

Harlow, so the exec fixed it up with Billie, who told him: 'But you better tell your friend that if he gets inspired to go down on her he's going to end up with a mouthful of peroxide.' She was said to be quite generous with money loans to people who were desperate."

"Do you think she's in a brothel?"

"Billy Bennett? She's dead, honey."

"Karen."

"Oh, Karen. Do you think so?"

"She's never been found, and if she's alive she could be anywhere."

We have another discussion about how Inge has gone crazy looking for her friend.

"She realizes that people around her are going a little crazy too hearing her talking about not finding her."

"She doesn't do that with me. Not lately. She mostly talks about our movie and how it's going."

We bat that around a while, putting ourselves in Karen's shoes.

"Wherever she is she must live all day with a yearning that never ends."

Roz shivered.

I told her of a story I once read.

"It was about a woman, a sole shipwreck survivor, on a little speck of an island in the Pacific who one day hears a plane far away. It's just a tiny dot on the horizon and so far away she can barely hear it. The dot crawls along the horizon and crawls along and gets smaller and smaller and then disappears, and for hours the woman keeps looking at the place where she saw the dot. I don't think there could be any greater loneliness than that."

Roz: "Now you're making me crazy."

•

The librarian, Ms. Highsmith, was by now a fan, a conspirator. Whenever she sees me arriving she greets me with a smile that says we're in this thing together.

She has been doing research of her own: sex slavery in Asia. She shows me a Sunday supplement.

"In case you missed it," she says, simultaneously pointing to a chair. "You have to read this thing."

A friend sold a young girl to a trafficker in Mumbai for $800, and to win back her freedom, the girl had to work for five years to repay the trafficker's "costs". The article explained that prostitution in India is legal if it's voluntary, but I wondered how an eight-year-old girl could volunteer to become a prostitute. Or why if she saw a dozen men a day it would take her five years to pay off a debt of $800. Well, of course, it turned out she had not volunteered but been kidnapped. But if she had been kidnapped, how did she incur a debt of $800?

The article was the usual gathering of facts and figures. In India an unscrupulous man deceived a girl into marrying him and as his wife she became his property and legally he could now put her up for sale. It was so easily done that some men made their living kidnapping girls and selling them. They would visit a brothel, choose a nice-looking girl working there, promise to marry her and liberate her from the terrible trap she's in. He would be her savior and they would be happy together once he put up the money to buy her freedom. And that is what he does. Her joy is great – freed from slavery! And then he sells her to another brothel for a nice profit.

I glimpsed Ms. Highsmith looking at me as I continued to read. I read that a large percentage of sex slaves were children, six, seven years old. The parents of these children lived in the mountain villages up north. They were illiterate and naively believed the glamorous tales they heard of city life. They imagined the luxuries they could buy if they sold their daughter, sold her to someone in the city who knows the ropes. The nice gentleman or the nice lady would place her where she would soon be posting money back home to them once she was settled in. The fortunate parents would then start enjoying the good life they had always dreamed of having – and get a nice TV antenna.

Everybody would be happy.

There was another side to it. Sometimes selling one of their daughters was an economic necessity. The family would then have one less mouth to feed and the other children would benefit. Often the little girl that was sold was never heard from again. The mother and the father felt sure they would eventually get word, and that was when their good fortune would start. They understood that these things required patience.

Information was skimpy. Statistics were rare in places where births were not recorded and a girl's disappearance often went unnoticed. That explained why it was not possible to guess how many girls were sold. But that was not important. What mattered was that the parents were satisfied they had placed their daughter in good hands. They had made every attempt to verify the person's credentials and were certain this was someone they could trust, not just anyone. And now that they had sold their girl, money would start coming in, but only if they were patient. They had heard that city life was different from country life and things there could take a little longer than they usually did at home. Getting the good things in life required much patience.

16

When the hospital discharged Max, doctors warned that more monitoring and testing would be needed. His headaches were not migraines but they could not yet determine their cause. A precise diagnosis required further analysis. That's what Max said they'd said.

Back at work, Max seemed glad to be with friends and reassured everyone he never felt better. I understood that to mean it was best to give the studio only good news.

But he really did seem to feel better, and in this happier mood suggested I go with him to the business meeting he had once mentioned. It was just coming up and was to be a discussion of a film in trouble. It would be instructive and might also provide material for the profile: an insider's view of the life of a director.

"Two birds with one stone. This is not a meeting of second-string producers and so-called creative executives, " he would have me know. "Or, put it another way, it's not a gathering of hustlers. It's a meeting about the single most important thing in Hollywood – the budget."

The invitation renewed my hope for our project when he said I could see for myself the kind of thing he would be up against with our movie idea. So our film was still viable? Even if it was not, I would have material for the Max profile.

He instructed me to show up at his office and we'd go from there. Max warned not to expect much. The meeting might be nothing at all or it might offer a glimpse into the hard-nosedness of the studio. He had mixed praise:

"In Hollywood's early days, producers were little Napoleons and would literally strut around the studio. The strutting's all financial now. They look harmless now, and are probably just well-intentioned schmucks, but they know money."

"This film, will they cancel it?"

"Oh no. There's too much riding on it."

•

I took these notes of the meeting by hand:

East-West Love Fest

Oak-paneled room: a long table holding Perrier, Vichy water and a pitcher of lemonade and a tray of upside down glasses. A slim young woman that Inge would cattily describe as Bimboesque soundlessly trolleys in a giant carafe of iced coffee and a dozen cups. She dresses and acts boffable. And appears happy to look the role. Maybe she'll be discovered and get a small part, and after that . . . Who knows?

The men: what is striking in their appearance is their identical café-au-lait tans. Tennis tans.

The meeting:

They exchange amenities about their recent vacations in Europe and places in Southeast Asia where I didn't think anybody ever went. Max says a few introductory words about me to put them at ease at my presence. I'm with "the great New York World-Herald," and as he builds me up he promotes me several ranks to Sunday senior features editor. (The longer I stay in Hollywood, the higher my rank goes.) I try not to smile at my new status as all but one greet me with a warmth that exudes a very good resemblance to genuineness. The hold-out says: "We'll see a copy of whatever you print before it hits the stands, right?" I make noncommittal sounds as I try to imagine the paper waiting for the approval of somebody in Hollywood..

The discussion begins with an action-hero film that, it is hoped, could go up against the James Bond franchise. The studio thinks it's hubris – that's a word used often out here – but has approved the project, and now with principal photography only half done, the film has seriously overshot its budget and studio execs are discussing how to avert disaster. Cleopatra and At Heaven's Gate have never been forgotten – or allowed to be forgotten.

Someone named Maury – a studio head, Maury Samuels – says: "I've been looking over the costs that the studio as a whole has been incurring and it's the most alarming report I have ever read in my forty years of picture making."

Keynote speech, sounds like.

Max sighing theatrically: "Maury, costs keep rising."

Maury: "Then profits have to keep rising too. The costs of set construction are double what they were ten years ago. And I'm not even going to mention labor costs."

Max: "But – "

Maury: "Hollywood is no longer in its infancy. We don't throw money around anymore."

I'm impressed that Max falls silent. Deferential? Or feeling futile? Or a tactic.

Someone (an associate producer?) mourns the fate of a film released a few months earlier. Looking back on recent history he laments: "Our release positioning wasn't bad, but we hadn't counted on that fucking Sky Dome. How the fuck could we know it would be practically the number-one grossing film of all time. Our film had no legs from the get-go."

"We were too optimistic opening in eleven hundred theaters at once," one suit argues. "Big mistake."

Dull laughter when someone else says there goes the billion-dollar club, followed by some talk of an eve-of-shoot budget. Then, after more discussion of what has gone wrong, there's a brief digression about how the Academy Awards "meat parade" is "becoming a marketing exercise. It's all a first-weekend business now."

"It's a producer's medium now. This is all of our own making – we brought it on ourselves." He doesn't sound unhappy.

"True. But what makes it these days are still all those high-concept films like Batman, for crap sake." This opinion is delivered by a short, fat, sad-looking man. "Or crash-and-burn junk. Using films as money machines. They crap out money."

"C'mon, Dave, when have they ever been anything but money machines?"

"They used to pretend to be something else. Where has art gone?"

"You know, we're not in this just for practice," somebody with a large Adam's apple says.

"Desperate times call for desperate measures," a man who as a teenager had had a bad case of acne declares, and, cliché or not, all concur with feeling. One of the main budgetary problems seem to be the number of days spent filming on location, especially the one in China.

Max's attention revives when one of the execs proposes that its principal photography be shortened from six to five weeks.

To this Max objects with feeling. "I know Wilkinson's work. He's working as tight as he can."

"We have to keep expenses down, no matter what the cost."

The exec suggests in that case eliminating the Hong Kong sequence.

"That would mean a radical change in the story."

"The yacht is the whole heart of the story – the luxury yacht scene, where she flaunts her ass."

"That golden ass," someone murmurs. "What I wouldn't give if my wife had an ass like that."

"She could always flaunt her ass on a smaller yacht, couldn't she? She could flaunt it right here in L.A., for that matter."

"If the Hong Kong sequence is not retained, then the number of extras will have to be cut and that nice crowd scene on the mountainside will have to be dropped."

"If you take out the scene on the mountainside, there'll be nothing left. What you'll have left is The Sound of Music.

Without the music."

"I wish we fucking had the Sound of Music."

There was talk of economizing on set construction, especially redesigning the whole New York street going into the Bergdorf scene, but that of course would "bring the unions down on our necks."

"Well, we gotta resolve it soon."

"How about a small yacht off Hong Kong? Couldn't it be a moderate-sized yacht?"

"Can't we fake Hong Kong? There must be a place we can use – some place cheap – that can be made to look like Hong Kong."

"Yeah. Long Beach."

"This is like pushing boulders up a hill and watching 'em go down again, like what's-his-face."

As the meeting drags on some of them seem as bored as me

"Hollywood," one of them says. "Nobody in Hollywood is honest in what they say. They all have agendas."

Someone in reply: "It takes an incredible number of skills coming together to produce – what? The same old product again."

"The same old film."

"The same old product," he insists. "We have to learn we're in a new Hollywood. And as for what's happening to Hollywood social life nowadays," he adds irrelevantly, "forget it. You go to a party to meet new people and what do you see? The same people you saw at the last party."

"What about Sutliff? Let's get back to Sutliff," someone says.

"Oh fuck Sutliff."

I wonder who Sutliff is when one of them groans: "Bastard has us over a barrel, with the clock ticking at $200,000 a day."

"What's he want to call it again?"

A disgusted silence. It's too ridiculous to bother answering – it's too horrible. In the heavy silence someone jokes quietly:

"Eating Pussy."

Apparently it was a familiar joke. It's given a polite titter.

"Eat shit, you mean."

"How do you know Greenberg's doing the film?"

"He's developing a script on it."

At this Max breaks in with a laugh. "Greenberg develops seven or eight scripts for every one he shoots."

Dave: "Yeah, but Kellman optioned a generous fifty thousand on this last one, and a lot more on signing."

"What's a lot more?" Max asks. The question sounds genuine.

"Seven hundred."

"The story's that good?"

"Enchanted his pants off, he said."

"There's miles to go before we sleep on this one," one of them murmurs.

They eventually drop budgeting and move on to their favorite topic, which surprisingly is not pussy, though references to it multiply. It's films as something people want to go see.

"Which is different from films that make money, right?" one of them says playfully.

"We should make films as though they qualified for a Nobel Prize."

"For films? It'll never happen"

"Ah but you're wrong. Someday there'll be a Nobel Prize for great directors and great writers. Why should some crappy poet from Baluchistan get a Nobel Prize for poems nobody's ever going to read and then turn around and not give an Oscar to – to Jean Renoir?"

"Renoir? Renoir wasn't a writer."

"He wrote and directed. A jack of all trades the likes of which we don't see anymore." His dark lined face looks simultaneously defiant and dejected.

A quiet quip: "What exactly is the latest market-share report from Baluchistan?"

In the silence someone murmurs: "South or North Baluchistan?" No one laughs.

"Baluchistan makes me sick. All you need is a sound bite on CNN of some armpit-smelling flag-burner with a missile up his ass and the Dow drops three hundred points."

"The only smart move the studios have made in recent years is to give writers some of the status accorded to directors and actors – above-the-line people. Even then, they were forced into it."

"But the poor bastards are low on the food chain. They can sometimes give you a finely crafted screenplay but then the producer and his Aunt Martha change it around."

"A great degeneration set in after Battleship Potemkin."

"Don't you think we're straying from the subject?"

"If we could combine Potemkin with Ernst Lubitsch –"

"– Christ, you'd have a winner-and-a-half!"

"The Sound of Music is what we need."

By the sound of it, the meeting is limping to an end. A book is mentioned – for possible adaptation.

"The main difference is in literature you've got to be a little boring for your book to be considered a masterpiece. In movies you can never be boring. But you notice that comedies never win Academy Awards."

"What we ought to do is write a comedy about Academy Awards."

"People think comedy is lightweight."

"It is lightweight. You're not moved by it."

"The Academy Awards is a comedy."

This goes on for a while longer. But the substantive part of the meeting is over.

•

Leaving, Max suggested lunch at Spago's.

"You may think they don't sound very intelligent, and I grant you they don't. They're playing the game. Ninety percent of what they say can be safely ignored, but the trick is to recognize the other ten percent. They know what they want: a more disciplined approach that involves the budget department, the distribution arm, publicity, and the input of them all together that will guide the strategy of making a film. Does that sound like film making to you? Strategy – distribution – input? Is that how a story gets written? Is that how you photograph a film? But you have to treat them with respect. They have business savvy and with their connections they could destroy you in three minutes if they felt like it."

He made a small laugh. "OK, now you've had an insight. Given these factors, go make a movie."

17

To keep Umpleby, last of the Great American Journalists, satisfied, or at least off my back, I sent him the notes on the meeting along with sketches of what I'd been doing so far. From his perspective I was never doing much. He was always slow with his response so I didn't expect to hear from him for a few days.

Meanwhile Inge was vacillating, simultaneously telling me to just enjoy myself while I was in California but also nagging me to get on with the Karen story.

"How's it going with Max?"

"He seems undecided."

"What does it take to decide him?"

Catching her in a happy mood (relatively) I related a conversation I had overheard at a crowded downtown L.A. barbershop with three barbers. It was exactly the sort of thing I knew she liked – urban anthropology. Two guys talking, waiting their turn, and one of them says::

"She was once a nun but gave the best blow jobs in Orange County."

"She was once a man, you mean," the other says.

"No, nun. Oh wait. Could have been a man. Wow."

And in another conversation, a man laughingly related the story of his life as his hair was being cut, the barber laughing with him like old-time friends.

"I was nuts in those days. I think I still am."

"What do you mean you were nuts in those days?"

"Well, I'll tell you, I was seeing two psychiatrists at the same time."

"You were seeing two psychiatrists at the same time?" It sounded like a vaudeville routine. "That cracks me up."

"Yeah, I was seeing two psychiatrists at the same time. I was so paranoid I would try to find out from the second psychiatrist what the first one was getting at. You know, compare notes."

The barber cheerfully supported him: "Yeah, you sound nuts all right."

"You'd think there'd be some agreement between them. I mean, I'm the guy with the problem, right? How could they have two different opinions about what's wrong with me?"

•

Roz recently started a blog showing portraits of Karen and Karen's fashion shots, plus the lovely eye-catching picture that had made her famous, that gorgeous nude of her. Roz soon realized her mistake when the nude picture generated an ocean of spam. One was about enlarging Roz's penis ("A bigger dick in 4 weeks! why wait?"). Someone in Nigeria offered to send her two and a half million dollars if she deposited $5,000 in a certain bank account to show she could be trusted. One persistent email promised her a cleaner colon and the most abdominal relief she had ever experienced. Nothing in the one-week tide of spam pertained to Karen Bryggman.

Roz thought I should write articles not about Karen but about our Karen story and how it wasn't working. "It might open doors."

I couldn't see it. "Without a recent hook, there's nothing newsworthy in a story about someone who disappeared two years ago. Who'd print it?"

"Relate it to someone who's recently gone missing, then."

With her overblown opinion of my abilities Roz wasn't convinced. She took the view that as a journalist I was secretly a frustrated novelist. Books were what I should be writing.

"Hemingway was once a newspaper reporter too, but he got out of journalism as fast as he could. Ergo you should too."

I reminded her I didn't have Hemingway's talent, ergo I couldn't.

•

On our evening phone call Inge brought up her Doomsday Book again, a project I always encouraged. I thought of it as her safety valve. I suggested she also do an "anger anthology" and hoped she'd let me read it someday. She said she'd already started one. Topics were organized alphabetically – S for sociology, P for pissed off – ready classifications for convenience.

"It's my controlled emotional outlet."

Under D (disgust) she planned to include "the idiotic chatter of the world in all its petty interests." She had been reading poetry and had a Byron quote: "The more I see of mankind, the less I like them."

I tried to reply supportively, injecting a heartiness in it that I hoped wasn't too false, "Old Byron, eh?"

"When you rang I was just writing F for fucking monsters."

"F could be for fucking anything, couldn't it?"

Ignoring me: "This kid, this girl – can you imagine such a thing?! – taken from her home in the middle of the night."

"What girl?"

"This evening's news. Don't they give you the evening news out in California?"

"What happened?"

"Some guy stole into this child's room as she was sleeping, wrapped her in a blanket and was seen driving off in a van."

"What guy?"

"I dunno" – irritated. "Some guy. Or maybe a gang. This was all some time ago and they just found the girl today. She had been there all along, right there in Utah for the entire eight years. The people who had her – it was a husband and wife who took her – they trained her to walk alongside cattle, but that was only later, when she was a little older. Her job was to make sure the cattle didn't stray. She had been taken so young she no longer remembered what her life had been like before or where she lived. She didn't know who her parents were. She had been three years old and all she knew was that her name was Beth."

I said: "This is depressing. Aren't there other things in the news you could be watching on TV?"

Silence. Then quietly: "Yeah sure. Bomb throwers, wars. There was a suicide down in the Village today."

•

At the library a bald-headed man was sitting at the librarian's desk. Ms. Highsmith was attending a funeral.

Browsing the stacks, I found a book on writing and it fell open to "The New Journalism". I read a few paragraphs hoping I'd learn something more about writing for newspapers but the author barely touched on the subject. He referred the reader to recent changes in writing and to look on the internet for his forthcoming book on Modern Expression. It would be out soon.

A passage on fiction caught my eyes. It said a writer had to know what the hero wanted, and that, whatever it was, he had to want it more than anything in the world and be willing to fight to the death for it. I thought: if I were a hero what would I want more than anything in the world? Inge. Which didn't sound very heroic.

The author went on to ask: how does the hero go about attaining his goal? "In a love story, the hero's unrelenting persistence pays off. Persistence: through thick and thin, he remains undaunted by obstacles. He persists. The plot gradually emerges from his never letting up. Persistence is the key."

I'd have to tell Max persistence was the key. If we persisted in our search for Karen the ending to our story would emerge.

About that bridge in Brooklyn . . .

•

Reading the papers over espresso at the Café Français on the Strip this morning and still thinking about that kidnapped girl Beth, I came across the obituary of one of the oldest survivors of the Nazi death camps. As background the author of the obit recalled the French government minister Laval saying "Les enfants aussi". This Laval had become famous for keeping parents and children together when he sent them to Auschwitz. It would have been too heart-breaking to separate mothers from the babies in their arms. The only humane thing to do was to kill them both.

In Disneyland police discovered three video cameras that voyeurs had been using for "upskirting" and "downblousing". The acts were considered misdemeanors, but past punishment had not kept the offenders from pursuing their hobby, as the voyeurs called it. The addiction had become so widespread, there were now global fan clubs for upskirters and downblousers. Authorities, deciding something had to be done, raised the jail term from 30 days to six months. But it didn't seem to stop it from happening. A small local paper even carried an ad: "Buy your girl some platform shoes – look up an old friend tonight."

Next I read of a young widow in North Hollywood who had the ashes of her husband sewn into her breast implants and offered reporters the touching explanation: "To have him forever close to my heart."

•

Back at Roz's place Sophie and I put together a lunch. She hated being in the house all day by herself. It was a luxury prison cell. Her life was spent in comfortable, cheerful rooms but with nobody to talk to. She was starved for conversation. I couldn't look at Sophie without flashing on Roz's panties downtown. Or via eBay, in Tokyo by now.

Sophie was obviously an eavesdropper. She sounded confiding: "The police are never gonna find that girl again" – meaning Karen.

"Why not?"

"They never do. Those cases go cold."

"The cases may go cold and some may take a long time but they sometimes get solved."

"Few of them get solved. Especially when you have umpteen millions of them around the world. The police would be all tied up just chasing after missing women."

Phoning Inge was becoming an obsession but it was my way of being with her and being in New York. I was beginning to fight a horniness whose intensity was commensurate with separation length. With the sudden hots for Inge, visions of her lovely pussy floated through my mind. In moments Sophie, with her black black hair, was beginning to look good and she sensed it too, plump and aproned and secretly happy, laying on the compliments as sly encouragement. She told me how Easterners seemed so gentlemanly compared with the cowboys out West. She said that excited her, that gentlemanly quality.

"Westerners are not too bright," she said. In case I wasn't getting the message: "I like a guy who is intelligent."

In her opinion, the bumper stickers of Westerners revealed not just their personal philosophies but the smallness of their minds.

I told her I thought bumper stickers were highway amusements breaking up the dullness of travel. "For example, 'Cement Workers Stay Hard Forever.' "

She laughed. "Ha! Such egoists, men are."

" 'Court Stenographers Do It With Their Fingers.' "

Delicately pink-faced: "Yes, well, we're more realistic."

I kept mentioning Inge for two intertwined reasons. One was the ever-ripening of hormones in the human organism, in this case someone I'm extremely close to and who bears my name, namely me. And the other was the accuracy of the bit about absence making the heart grow fonder, although I could not have been fonder of her than I already was. Also I didn't want to give Sophie the impression that I could eventually be available, that it was only a matter of time. I didn't think it would be honest to be encouraging or even just give the appearance of being encouraging.

So, to keep things clear, I told Sophie I'd check with her later and went over to the bungalow and gave Inge a ring. I just wanted to hear Inge's voice – have at least that. She was sympathetic and understanding of us poor males for always being sexed up as a part of our evolutionary function of keeping the human race perking along, reproduction-wise. Well, in that sense, I told her, I was feeling extremely moral these days and wished to place myself at the service of the evolution of the species, if there were any takers. Even my banter was getting crappy, a sure sign of horniness.

In the absence of the usual anger from her I told her about a dream I woke up from, repeating the phrase as I opened my eyes: "Fun memories bind us pleasurably." The words were attached to the thought that families were what make life beautiful and gave it emotional richness. The whole thing was strange. She agreed. She thought it sounded like I was going round the bend, but she had thought I was slightly odd many times before.

She was on a rush commercial assignment – still that Vogue thing – and had to hang up. Bad timing.

So I stretched out on the bed, thinking about important things, like going round bends, going off my rocker, the thoughts getting mixed up with memories that drifted back to the orphanage, or the little I remember of those earliest years, my earliest feelings really, and wondering as I sometimes did what kind of a life I would have had if I had been raised the way other kids were raised, and what my real mother and father were like, where they lived – if they were still living . . .

A very pleasant Trish Hooligan phone call interrupted these thoughts: Max was inviting me over for another session but not till late afternoon and hoped I could make it on such short notice. It would be just the two of us this time.

I made myself coffee and, looking for something to do, was

preparing to get down to work on some column stuff when Trish called again. It was to apologize that Max couldn't make it today.

How was I? Was I okay?

•

So back to TV and there was a news story on the crime syndicates of Eastern Europe making millions smuggling women to Britain with forged papers and forcing them into prostitution. Member states agreed that things were going too far. Action needed to be taken They would meet once again and report on their findings and see what conclusions could be reached.

There was another item. Three Lithuanian gangsters known as "the Little Doctors" had recently been arrested for controlling four prostitutes brought to England from their homeland. It was a story about teenagers abducted from Yugoslavia, Albania, Lithuania, Poland, Hungary, the Ukraine – really all of Europe. Some of the money brought in by these women was split between the gangsters and their Eastern European counterparts and the remainder was deposited in numbered accounts on offshore islands or in Swiss banks. This too would be looked into. Member states agreed it was something that needed to be stopped.

It sounded like the world had gone mad. Police learned from an escaped Polish teenager named Katia that none of the girls smuggled into Britain ever saw a penny. It read like the usual story, and out of habit I took out my notebook and noted that women were promised they could earn huge amounts of money in London and then once they were in England they were told that to see the money they had first to repay their kidnappers for their air fare ("Do the little bitches think flying in a plane costs nothing?"). And until they paid up, their passports would be kept from them. They also had to pay for their three meals a day and for daily living expenses in things like condoms, toothpaste, toiletries, soap and, for sanitary reasons, a personal hairbrush – a seemingly never-ending bill that was always larger than the money they were earning. And always too there was the threat that an attempt to escape would mean their families back home would be hurt or killed. One girl kept thinking of her three-month-old baby, left behind, and she passed her days servicing clients but longing to be with her baby. The girls worked a 16-hour day and serviced 50 men a day. Quickly figuring at an unrealistically low $20 a throw, each girl brought in $1000 a day, which was held for them "for safekeeping".

I tried not to think this story was getting old. Some reports stated that the numbers of girls and women involved was increasing, and I noted again that the member states agreed things had gone too far and something needed to be done and they would meet again for further discussions. This was not a subject by any means closed.

With the day warming up I got drowsy enough to take a nap and woke up later thinking "Umpleby, Bumblebee" and, with some incoherent connection that I couldn't put my finger on, felt that all the research I'd been doing in the library could actually make a good series in the World-Herald as a shock report on the slavery of women. Even if we didn't make the film I could at least do that. The facts begged to be given wide circulation.

So despite not hearing from Umpleby the last time around, I picked up the phone and called him and outlined what I was thinking. He wanted to know what was so new or different about sex slavery that would justify running an article. I rattled off a few of the statistics I had gathered: 27 million slaves, children and teenagers kidnapped from malls, 100,000 U.S. girls missing each year, sex slavery now $32 billion a year, captivity maintained by threats that family will be harmed if escape is attempted. When we hung up he said he would think about it, providing I didn't abandon the profiles of Max and Roz. They came first. Of course, I said. Max and Roz came first.

I quickly knocked off an outline, or really the sketch of an episode, and emailed it in. I didn't want to give Umpleby too much time to think and maybe come up with objections to running a story. He was a skillful objector. But he was also a good newspaperman and I was sure he would see it, if not up-to-the-minute newsworthy, then as a feature.

Consulting library notes, I whipped out this draft on a new

batch of material:

RESEARCH NOTES

• In Sudan the British Christian Charity Worldwide (CSW) buys enslaved women and gives them their freedom and returns them to their families. A slave woman costs $90. The charitable act of buying them and liberating them creates an ironic cycle. Roaming militia kidnap girls and women just to collect the reward of liberating them. It has become a cottage industry of crime. Charity workers face a moral dilemma. If they don't pay the reward, the women are kept hostage. Paying the reward promotes a cycle of slavery.

• In Mumbai, 200,000 young Nepalese girls work in brothels, according to one estimate. Each year five to seven thousand girls are smuggled across the border from Nepal to India. Half of them are believed to be under age. It is hard to locate the underage ones. They are kept hidden, and having no passport or visa or any form of identification, they don't officially exist.

• The whole thing is sometimes disguised. For example, palaces recruit girls from Kathmandu to serve as maids but they are really there for the sexual service of the palace staff. To the young girls it is made to seem an exalted tradition and an honor to be chosen for the role with the Ranas. The Ranas were feudal despots ruling Nepal and liked girls of fair-skinned beauty. It's true that the lovelier maids were occasionally promoted to concubines or even queens, which was alluring and tempting, except that a Rana prime minister could have thousands of maids, hundreds of concubines and a dozen queens. Families who gave over their daughters to the Ranas overlooked all of that and saw only the money they were given. Money meant a lot not just economically but in social status. There was no other way they could ever make that kind of money.

•　　New girls were needed each year to keep up with the palace's needs and also to fill vacancies in the various brothels around the countryside. In mountain villages apparently it was easy to tell which families had sold their daughter. Their houses had a nice shiny new tin roof.

•　　It came as a surprise to learn that sometimes, after years of working and despite the pain of their own suffering, the girls themselves became madams and, life no longer meaning much to them, cynically went back to their own villages to recruit fresh victims.

•　　If a new girl in a Mumbai brothel refused sex, a hot chili pepper was inserted into her vagina and after that objections stopped. Often they beat her, sometimes so hard she lost her "pay" until the more obvious bruises had healed. If her minders accidentally broke an arm or a leg, they sold her off to a low-price brothel or, if no one wanted her, dumped her body in the poor part of town among the homeless. A girl with her arm broken or a leg that wouldn't heal was of no use to anyone.

•　　The police raided the brothels every three months in visits that were announced in advance and well prepared for by the brothel. Their reports were always the same – no working girls were found on the premises and there were no violations of the law. Then, before leaving, the inspectors were serviced by the girls of their choice.

•　　In her first months of life in a brothel a girl might still yearn for her village, where she had sometimes gone hungry but at least had not been raped ten or twenty times a day or beaten for an infraction of rules she barely understood. But gradually the happy memories of her former existence faded as she grew into a woman and accustomed herself to the squalor of her new life. She began to accept that she had crossed over a line and become a woman so bad that no respectable man could ever want her, not even as a concubine. And too there was the question of disease. She couldn't know for sure if she had caught anything but in any case she lost any wish to return home. To go back to her village would mean a shame too great to bear.

•

I felt sure Umpleby would see the article possibilities and have no trouble getting authorization from the bigwigs on the fourteenth floor. I awaited his reply.

18

One morning I happened to catch an old "Columbo" rerun on TV. I saw Peter Falk, the actor who plays Columbo, having a bowl of chili while chatting with a murder suspect. Watching him enjoying eating gave me a yen for some chili too. So I got in the car and drove down to a hole-in-the-wall restaurant I remembered seeing on the Strip called Chili Happy Chili.

It was the lunch hour and the place was jammed. There was one unoccupied seat at the counter and I sat down. I looked at the guy next to me and it gave me a start. His resemblance to Detective Columbo was uncanny and to top that he turned out to be a private eye.

He laughed. "I get that all the time. They even ask if I'm Peter Falk. Peter Falk would have to be about a hundred and nineteen years old by now. I think he's dead – isn't he dead?"

He said the specialty of the house was a syrupy short stack of waffles. The server behind the counter, a woman with very wavy-blonde hair, smiled at me and I smiled back. She was assembling an order on a square blue platter. It had some chili separated by a divider from two strips of dark-brown bacon. It looked good and I ordered the same.

Columbo told her, "I'll have a steak rare with French fries." He turned to me. "Where you from?".

"I'm from New York."

"Can you beat this weather out here?" he asked.

"No," I said, supplying the needed endorsement.

"It can't be beat."

His name was Al Kiernan but everybody called him Columbo, so he didn't mind if I called him that too. Chili Happy Chili was where he hung out and during quiet afternoons, when the place was empty, he did some of his work over at a corner table. Management apparently liked him and didn't mind his sitting there and doing his paperwork. People who worked there liked him too and told him he was good for business. People would keep asking if he was Peter Falk.

"I+s that true?" he asked when I told him the story of the disappearance of Karen Bryggman. He was intrigued by the idea of making a film to whip up public awareness of the crime of women being abducted.

"The girl's never been found but you feel there's still hope after all this time?"

I told him yes, in theory. Inge had gone a little crazy looking for her friend Karen and now wouldn't talk about it whenever she sensed she was becoming a bore about it. But she would never give up the search.

Columbo seemed interested. He advised me to look up people who knew her and interview them. Somebody had to know something, have some clue. He knew one person he himself occasionally used as a help in tracking people – a middle-aged character named Pignatelli.

"First name Henry but everybody calls him Pig Knuckles. He's a good gumshoe and knows a few Hollywood people and even knows somebody who is connected with Mossad – somebody on the inside, can you believe that? All hush-hush of course. You know how secretive Mossad is. For all I know, you're Mossad."

I told him I didn't want to just come right out and admit it and he laughed.

He described a recent case that bore a similarity to the Karen story.

"They came to me after the girl was presumed dead. Never found. This goes back a good, oh, six, seven years – a cold case. Very sad, about a young girl. It's always a young girl or a young woman. Men don't go missing much. I mean, they do, but you don't hear about them unless it's a teenager or something."

He finished eating and after mopping up the bacon grease pushed his plate back.

"Any woman, or a young girl of legal age, has the right to

just take off and go away -- disappear. You know? -- it's a free country. Here's the rule: if she's of legal age, has no criminal record and is not taking medications and is no threat to anyone, the law says she's not legally accountable to anybody. She has the Constitutional right to just take off for Tasmania if that's where she wants to be." Bringing it back to Karen Bryggman: "As far as the law is concerned she has only disappeared, so there's nothing they can do. Where's the crime?"

Columbo was obviously familiar with the point and said the toughest cases he'd ever heard of were where there had been traumatic bonding.

"I don't know if you know what that is. That's when a girl – it's always a young girl – has been held hostage for so long she begins feeling emotionally close to the kidnapper, sort of like emotionally tied to him in a way, and is afraid to do anything that would make him unhappy."

I said I'd heard that that happens and remembered the famous Patti Hearst case and how she even joined her abductors in bank robbery.

"It's like she's gone over to the other side. They're buddies, you might say. There're cold cases like that, and my theory is that the traumatic bonding is self-protectiveness. I don't know how else to figure it. When the girl is eventually liberated, it takes quite a while to, what they call, deprogram her before she feels safe not having her captor around. Strange, isn't it?"

I told him of the FBI's report on runaways and how discouraging it was, and of the powers the UN has. Or doesn't have, judging by results. And the Interpol shakes its head almost in embarrassment over its own poor track record in tracing people, even people known to have been taken into slavery. The practice is so established in Africa that there are slave routes that are openly called slave routes. Those methods of kidnapping and selling women, and men, have come down to us from antiquity. Obviously things haven't changed much.

He knew all that. Columbo looked impressed when I mentioned Petrov and Roz and told him about our project. He didn't know who Roz was.

"Lorna Beach!" He knew that name, all right. "And Max

Petrov the director, right?"

I explained the connection and told him about Karen, a fashion model friend of Inge's. I explained that Inge, who is a little older than Karen, feels responsible for her disappearance. Even now, two years later, she sometimes wakes up from a bad dream.

This Columbo, it developed, was divorced and had a daughter the same age that Karen would have now – assuming she was alive – nineteen, and if something like that ever happened to his daughter and if he were rendered powerless to rescue her, he would go bananas. I knew how he felt and told him Inge seemed in fact to have gone bananas, or was well on her way.

He was very likable and a detective and I thought there was much I could learn from him. Before I left I asked him if he ate there often.

"Practically every day."

●

On the phone, Inge was sounding more pissed off than usual, saying the progress Roz and I were making was "dismal" and we were letting her down. Then, becoming aware how unreasonable that sounded, she took the curse off: "Don't you think it's dismal?"

Her anger at our getting nowhere was always there now. But, I explained, we'd been doing all we could – certainly Roz hadn't been loafing. And my library research could only help the cause (if we could get Max to listen). Still Inge kvetched.

Her unreasonableness could be excused – she was depressed. To lighten things up I told her a tidbit of local Hollywood news about Marilyn Monroe. Actually not news but I had only just heard about it – Monroe's stay at the Roosevelt Hotel back around the beginning of her career. After her death, to honor her memory (management claimed), the lobby had been permanently installed with her wardrobe mirror. It was there now for the world to gaze at in wonder, imagining la Monroe putting on her makeup. One visitor declared that if you viewed the mirror from a certain angle you could see Marilyn's face in it. Interestingly not Jesus' face – no sign of Jesus, although an oatmeal cookie had recently shown up in a Santa Barbara bakery of a Descent from the Cross and was bought by a museum in Las Vegas. I sent it in as a clipping in an upcoming "Out of This World" column but Umpleby deleted it. He also deleted a Jesus Christ spotted on a dog's butthole. Inge liked the stories, though, and her mood changed a little.

Speaking of which, sightings seemed these days to be going in waves. Perhaps in compensation, quite a few Michael Jacksons had been showing up recently, twice in Nashville, three times in Vegas, and once way the hell up in Alaska where the pipeline begins. Some of the Michael Jacksons have been ebony, some sepia and some white, possibly reflecting America's increasing maturity in accepting multiethnicity. Or maybe Jackson's surgical evolution from black to white. All the Jacksons clutched parasols, and in the sighting in Alaska he was outfitted with a snowman's battered top hat.

Encouraged, I reported these events to Inge and listened for her amused reaction but there was only silence. Then in a quiet voice:

"Let me know if anything develops with Max and Roz."

Leaving me now a little pissed off at her.

What the hell did she want from us? We were doing all we could. And after I went through some eloquent interior ranting, like the crazies in Manhattan who stride down the street in a violent argument with someone not visible to others, I decided I needed a break – a feeling that lasted about two minutes, because at just that moment an email arrived from Umpleby including another attached file of clippings as column fodder.

So now my anger shifted onto Umpleby, and that was probably where it belonged in the first place – well, some of it. So I sent him a letter to deliberately provoke him, saying I liked doing a column but not crappy three-dot journalism. My aim was to get him mad enough to fire me so I'd be forced to look for another job. My message was unambiguous and concluded:

"Fuck columns, fuck everything, goodbye and good luck – rhymes with fuck. Oh and fuck the World-Herald."

A rare display of eloquence. Naturally as soon as I sent it in I thought: "Great, what are you going to do now?"

Before I could seriously start worrying about looking for a new job, there was a reply from Umpleby saying obviously I was having a nervous breakdown and needed time off.

He wrote, "Calm down and cut out all that resignation shit – and by the way, how's the article coming along?"

So. He was still hoping for something like 5000 words on Lorna Beach, making it obvious that my principal and possibly only value to Umpleby was my closeness to Roz. I hadn't realized how desperate he was to get an interview of her. Net conclusion: I was still working for the paper.

At least I tried.

And still not a word about the draft I sent him about prostitution in Asia.

19

It was nice to have a hold on Umpleby, though. After cooling off a bit I decided to let him think he was right about my just needing time off. I went down to Roz's garage and began to feel a lifting of the spirits just revving up the Mercedes and backing out, hearing that classy sound that cars make on gravel driveways. At the front door I left the motor running and went in and found Sophie to tell her I would be taking a trip up north and didn't know when I'd be back and to please tell Roz. Sophie said to wait just a sec and reappeared after a few minutes with a picnic basket of Belgian duck pate and two quart thermoses of menudo.

"Menudo? So fast?"

"I always keep some frozen for emergencies."

I didn't know what freeway I got on but I headed north and then on an impulse turned into twisting back roads with occasional highway signs obviously put to good use by locals for target practice. Octagonal STOP signs were clear favorites, the word "stop" showing the most bullet holes.

By the time I got to Wheeler Springs I was tired of driving and I stopped at a place called The Roadside Inne. The orange neon sign outside read: "Happy Ho r 2-9 PM – Famous Cold Beer," and I wondered if the missing letter was meant to be a cryptic message.

Coming in from a brilliant California sunniness to the gloom of a low-ceilinged dance floor I made out only one person in the dark, a woman of around twenty-five who in a brighter light could easily have passed for thirty-seven. Genus Bimbo Bimbo, principal habitat Southern California (definitely not an endangered species). Possibly she was the happy hor. She wore a black tank top, or possibly the latest in women's lace underwear. Slightly overflowing it was a pneumatic cleavage. She looked away, a knowing smile forming at the edges of her mouth.   I imagined her thinking, "A mysterious smile is seductively playing about my lips, intriguing him."

"Sure, siddown," she replied when I crossed the thirty-five feet of dance floor between us.   She indicated a chair and I joined her. I had the fantasy it would be fun to talk with her and forget about Inge. There was a hard look behind her baby eyes.

"My name's Sharon and you sound like you're from the East.   I been to Denver once.   Nice friendly people in the East.   Y'ever been there?"

"No."

She asked: "Wanna buy a girl a drink?"

She ordered what she'd been having, a martini on the rocks.   It came with six or seven large ice cubes in a half-pint jar.   I ordered a Virgin Mary.

"Karl always makes doubles. I think he has a thing about doubles.'"

Comparing plans we found that by one of those extraordinary coincidences we both had the whole evening free.

"Is there much in the way of excitement in Wheeler Springs?"

"Sheesh, you have to be kidding," she said.   "Wheeler Springs is not as dead as it looks. You can do anything you want in Wheeler Springs, that's the kind of place Wheeler Springs is."

It developed that a gentleman like me would have no trouble finding fun ways of occupying his time in Wheeler Springs.

"Maybe we should order another one of these.   Nobody makes martinis the way Karl makes 'em. He's also good with a Naked Lady. Would you like a Naked Lady?"

Not being much of a drinker, I wondered if Naked Lady was the name of some new drink or code for a fun way of passing an evening in Wheeler Springs. I told her I'd stick with the Virgin Mary.

Her middle name was Cassandra. I asked if she foretold the future and she said she doesn't do tarot.

In the scintillating company of Sharon I was just beginning to have second and third thoughts about the World-Herald when my phone rang. I got the phone out of my shirt pocket and held it to my ear. Inge. I was obviously not going to get away from her and I only hoped this wasn't another scolding.

It was not a scolding. She was calling to give me a shocker. Her dear friend Mr. Maki had just died. He was an old retired Finn she had been helping write his memoir. More death. They had been working as usual, rounding out the story of his life with a fresh memory of the Eskimo woman, Asiak, when he paused searching for some exactly right word to express what he was feeling, and as she waited, looking at the stringiness of the backs of his hands, he interrupted himself with: "Curious, in old age you begin to view life as a very pleasant place to be – a place, not a thing. It's a place you're familiar with and you'll be leaving it, and you finally get used to the idea that others will live 'in' it after you've gone, and there will be people who will never know you were once a part of it – that you even existed."

Words to that effect. Inge said she had paused in her typing, her eyes down at the keyboard, waiting for him to continue and wondering whether what he had just said was part of the book or a comment he was making to her, and when she looked up she saw him staring at her strangely, gazing into her eyes in a very odd manner – and then with a shock became aware that that was no longer Mr. Maki sitting across from her but a corpse.

"He was dead – he was . . . dead. It's hard to describe the coming of death if it happens like that, while you're sitting there and you actually see it. He was seated in his chair talking to me and he just sort of . . . went dead. I don't know how else to describe it."

Listening to her, I wanted to reach through the phone and put my arms around her, to kiss her and comfort her.

I said what I could and put the phone back in my pocket and got up to leave. The girl, Sharon, had made a tactful trip to the john while I was on the phone and she was just returning when I told her I had to get back – unusual circumstance – must run – apologies – and left the barman a fifty-dollar tip on the table that I knew Sharon would pocket the moment I was out the door. I hurried back south toward L.A., not seeing but feeling the vast blackness of Pacific Ocean somewhere way off to my right, and kept driving until the luminous sky of the horizon ahead of me slowly congealed into clusters of light blazing the western edge of North America: L.A.

In Roz's kitchen Sophie, peeling a potful of potatoes, gasped as I came in.

"Don't tell me you ate all the menudo!"

•

I phoned Inge as Sophie prepared something to eat. Inge's voice, businesslike, said to leave a message and she'd call back.

The next day, Sophie's day off, I made lunch for Roz and me – Roz hating cooking. I was becoming quite a chef out here in Hollywood, and I thought Inge would be proud of me.

I did a repeat of my one showoff specialty: the platter of pitted black olives, small cucumber spears and sliced vine-ripened cherry tomatoes – that number. It wasn't exactly what you would call cooking, but still. As I had done before, I arranged them symmetrically in a colored pattern and decorated the platter with fresh leaves of sweet basil. The eye appeal in appetite arousal got praise from Roz, and I explained again I was just copying what I had seen Inge do. The main course was another repeat performance: my sourdough shtick of baguette topped with mozzarella, tomato and garlic, shoved under the broiler.

"Jesus," Roz exclaimed. She bit off a piece of baguette. "This garlic bread is pure heaven. Nothing like garlic." I asked if I should have added anchovies and she exploded: "Jesus, no! How anyone can stand anchovies is beyond me."

Taking coffee on the patio on the other side of her house, we settled comfortably in matched deck chairs. The property was high enough up for stout Cortez to have a peak at Malibu. We could see the Pacific, soundless and misty way off in the distance.

After lunch Roz took me round to a gallery having a show of

Bill Joachim's early works – fragments, small sketches. His work bored me so I worked my way through the few visitors dutifully walking from glass display to wall display and studying printed notes affixed to the walls. Slipping through a half-open door into a smaller gallery space, I was surprised to find an Edward Hopper not on display and next to it an undersized powerhouse John Marin watercolor. The Hopper was a big brown box car sitting on a siding, and I felt the same amazement I always felt by Hopper's ability to imply the blazing heat of the sun just through light and shadow and one small telling detail. Really amazing.

●

The rest of that day nothing much happened. Roz had some appointment to keep and I hung around the bungalow. The pool's smooth surface looked inviting. I took a dip, showered, and enjoying the eucalyptus-scented air got out the bungalow's laptop and did some work for the paper on the latest squibs that Umpleby had sent. I remembered Max once asking me how someone became a writer, meaning a print writer, not screenwriter, and I told him that from what I had ever seen or learned you spent your time doing jobs you hated and felt your spirit destroyed day by day as your coworkers gave you funny looks as though you were someone who needed help finding the bathroom. That's how. Max looked at me strangely, not knowing whether it was meant to be facetious, funny or what. He asked how my job was at the newspaper and I told him about my running arguments with Umpleby.

"Who's he? Is that his real name?"

"Managing Editor, unofficial gadfly and in the long run a very likable pain in the ass."

"Bright man? Do you get along?"

"Not particularly bright, but the Italian cliché applies."

"The boss may not always be right but he's always the boss."

To give Max a sample of Umpleby, I told him that in one

column I mentioned a Frenchman named Vauvenargues because I liked something I had found of his in an old anthology and thought it would liven up the column and maybe even raise its tone a notch. Vauvenargues wrote: "If all errors were clearly stated, they would perish by themselves." Umpleby read that and asked, "Who the fuck's Vauvenargues?" I told him he was an intelligent Frenchman and that was all that mattered. The reader didn't have to know who the fuck Vauvenargues was. He gave me a funny look so I went on to explain that if you give a quote by Archimedes no reader ever asks you who the fuck Archimedes was. Then, shortly after the Vauvenargues "contretemps" (Umpleby's word), I happened to use one of my favorite quips of Oscar Wilde's: "Meredith's a prose Browning, and so is Browning." I thought it was funny. Umpleby wanted to know "who the fuck's this bimbo Meredith?" He got embarrassed when I explained that Meredith was a he, not a she, and after that, Vauvenargues became code between us for something a little embarrassing but amusing. At least I could kid him and get away with it.

Max laughed at my story and said it must be quite an experience being a writer and working for somebody like that. Oh, I said, it was priceless. Except that I wasn't a writer, I was a journalist.

•

Anyway, the newspaper clipping sent by Umpleby that I began to focus on was: "A new publication for people who yearn for life without the curse of television was launched outside Westminster Abbey yesterday. The White Dot is a newsletter which claims that it reflects increasing concern about the damaging effect of too much television. It argues that the population should be 'meeting people and falling in love' during their leisure time rather than staring at an electronic box."

I liked the falling-in-love part but I could think only of commenting, "Hear! hear!" or witty words to that effect.

Stubbing a footful of toes I went to the kitchen to make a late-afternoon snack for eating outside in the cool dry California sun. A bird with a pair of lungs like an opera singer blasted out "McFEE-View" and I wondered what kind of a bird it was that made so lusty a cry, "McFEE-View . . . McFEE-View". He sounded overjoyed to be himself. I ate listening to the bird recital, enjoying an Inge-style snack of sardines on pumpernickel and reminding myself that things could be far far worse.

Watching the sun sink low in the sky, almost to the horizon, I phoned Inge. Not home. I left the message that I had called and stretched out on the bed to read. California was becoming a place where I ate and read. And felt lonely.

●

Sophie had obviously overheard our discussions about women disappearing, or kidnapped, so as I lazed in bed and thought about life and the usual crap that most newspapers print, she arrived with a token knock at the door and breezed in with a tray of toast and marmalade and a glass of milk.

And a happy-face grin of a smile: "I thought you might like a snack."

Seeing me in bed apparently made her feel apprehensive for me. "You might become too California laid-back. I have to watch out for you. The danger with you Eastern guys coming to California is that you go native and end up with brain rot. Don't laugh, I've seen it happen."

I told Sophie I've been known to get work done even in bed, a habit learned from Inge, who leaves bed only at gun point. As I was saying this, Sophie slid in beside me. I couldn't believe this was happening as she cozied up against me, finding as much skin contact as possible.

"What're you doing?" I was genuinely shocked. A little thrilled too at the smoothness of her skin. I had a sudden yearning to caress her body.

"You look lonely," she declared. "I'm lonely too. I know you have a lover but she's far away and, you know, the mice will play? Am I too forward? I've been told I can be too forward." Her face indicated her fear that this time she might have gone too far even for her. "I can't help it. You're beyond hot. I'm the type of person who can be very forward sometimes."

I was still formulating a tactful way to turn down what was being offered on a platter when she said reminiscently:

"At one point I thought of throwing my bathrobe belt over the beams and ending it all. No more washing, no more ironing, cleaning, dusting, mopping. Sometimes I think I just hate myself for the kind of life I lead, but then I think of all the poor people around the world and it doesn't seem so bad."

I tried to think how to get her out of bed. She spoke in a lulled voice as she continued:

"I didn't get along with my father back then. I wasn't married and got very pregnant and then lost the poor thing. My dad's friends were over one day and taking bets whether I could squirt my breast milk into an ice bucket in the middle of the table. My father absolutely died. He got up disgusted and left. Which was of course the reason I did it."

She looked at me. "Your girlfriend's so lucky." Then beginning to understand I wasn't anywhere near tempted and fearing she had made a tactical miscalculation, a sudden sadness came over her.

"I talk too much. They tell me that I'm too forward sometimes."

I told her that sometimes people had other reasons for not hopping in and out of bed with each other.

"Like what?"

Wondering if she was joking and feeling we were slipping into some kind of role reversal, with me making the objections women normally raised: "Like love, for example."

She thought that was "wonderful – and noble too," but it was pretty obvious the substance of the message was not registering, as she now helpfully continued her campaign:

"We could be working in bed. You know, talking about

these women who go missing and all that human trafficking. A lot of them, you know, come up here from Mexico, and I could maybe teach you something about how to find that girl you're looking for. There's this radio actor in Mexico City, he's somebody I know very well, and he could get word out down there. He's always on the radio and he's got pull."

Slipping out from the sheets, I playfully suggested she hop into bed with him and she shrieked: "Oh! He's my cousin!"

20

The next morning, after a breakfast of crepe suzettes prepared by a sadly smiling Sophie, it was off to downtown L.A. to put some distance between me and surprise drop-ins. After driving around a while, thinking of going to Chili Happy Chili I sneaked back to the bungalow and my laptop and tried to knock out an interview of Roz, thinking to propose it as a draft to the World-Herald, not for publication. It was crap stuff but I was reaching a point of not caring. I knocked it off in the format of a first-person rambling meditation and would let Roz read the draft to weed out anything that might prove embarrassing and also to get her to talk some more. Plus she's a friend. I wouldn't want to publish something unintentionally hurtful or that she might dislike.

Also I'd tried to anticipate any reservations the publicity mill at East-West Studios might have. Or any possible stink its watchdog lawyers could raise over trivialities, as I knew they could and would. Lawyers sometimes went out of their way to object to dozens of unimportant details and things they thought might be construed as insinuations or hint at scandal. It would give their clients great peace of mind knowing they had retained the best legal watchdogs money could buy. And by the time they were done the article would be lawsuit-proof pabulum.

Anyway, this was what I gave Roz to read, to see how she felt about the direction an interview might take before we went back over it together and filled it out to read more smoothly:

(NOTES: ROZ INTERVIEW)

A DAY IN THE LIFE OF LORNA BEACH

(World-Herald Exclusive etc.)

She's wearing vintage Gucci boots, tan Capri pants and on

this cool California day a royal-blue Lycra top under a cream cable-knit cashmere sweater. Never makeup offscreen. As she nervously fidgets with chic sunglasses – typically perched on her forehead and pushed occasionally to the top of her head – she sounds and looks relaxed.

OK. what would you like to know? – what is my life like? Well, for a long time I didn't think I'd ever get over Bill's suicide. I was on self-destruct from all the falling-down juice I used to put away in those days, which all changed after Bill died. Back then I thought I was drinking to keep myself alive but it was just the opposite. I was killing myself. My heart still aches and that is probably why I got involved with Laszlo, who, though not exactly a Princeton graduate, was fun while I weaned myself from memories of Bill. Nowadays everybody talks about Bill Joachim and how much greater a painter he was than Jackson Pollock, but I never cared much for the work of either of them. Just being honest.

And Laszlo? He came into my life right after Bill died and I was feeling adrift and I dunno, I just wanted a man in my life. I had grown used to it and missed it. Laszlo happened along and I felt a visceral response. He liked that, he told me, and then asked what does visceral mean. His cock is on steroids, which is what his brain should be on. But I liked him. I liked his ignorance, which sort of grew on me, even though his personality needed a transplant. I once told him about something that required a little suspension of disbelief and he laughed and said, "Yeah," and then a second or two later said, "A little what?"

He was a pushover but then most men are, and pushovers can be fun. I don't know if we can talk about this in a family newspaper but it used to amuse me to give him a hand job in the limo en route to some big-star dinner where I knew there'd be nothing but drop-dead women and it was a way of castrating the poor bastard into happy contentment. It was amusing, actually. It kept him trailing me all night. At one of those events, just as we got there and were being let in by the maid I whispered in his ear, "Oh fuck! I forgot my underwear." It was a magic potion.

It seemed to mesmerize him and kept him from eye-fucking every woman in the room, eleven tenths of whom were practically openly signaling availability. Men are so easily tempted but then they're also so easily controlled.

I saw so many people fall in love when they were young and they got married. Then they became famous and people began treating them differently. Stardom changes everything. It's difficult to explain. You have this endless attention and a kind of respectful worship.

Sex is funny, isn't it? The women who start out in life puritanically avoiding a roll in the hay end up decades later not getting enough and just lying there presenting themselves for a good old-fashioned hump. In contrast, men who start out strong and urgent and can't get enough, end up decades later too tired to think twice about sex because it involves all that humping. Talk about asymmetric fucking! The sexes seem almost designed to be divergent – and would be if it were not for love. Love comes to the rescue and makes all the difference – if you're lucky enough to have it. Here I am, talking about love.

This sounds incoherent and of course it's only one woman's view, and not a very original view but something, in my case, that came originally from my mother when I was growing up. She was a beautiful woman – I'll have to show you a picture some time. She had her midlife crisis at 29 and got it over with. When I was a kid I could look at her for hours, just gaze, you know. Couldn't get enough. But her beauty was all wasted in that lost town where we ended up living in the end, all pizzas and parking. Grandma too – they were both lost, this was in the hills of Pennsylvania. Grandma was French and quite a knockout in her day, with tits to die for. By her eighties she had stray chin hairs and always wore long white gloves and a low hemline on her dresses, with everything just comme il faut. She ended up in a hospice, raising her nightie to every grinning male attendant who passed her room, giving her great pleasure in knowing that so simple a gesture as allowing them to look under her dress cheered them all up so much. I'm a descendant of a long line of sluts. Not that it matters. We all end up in the ashes department.

What else? My father was in the diplomatic service, so actually I grew up in Italy, Peru and Paris and was sent to college in the States. Which accounted, people said, for the inflection or whatever it is they claim to hear in my voice. They said I spoke with American consonants and British vowels. They pointed out that I always spoke highly of the French and French culture. I do.

My view of life? Extremely positive. The glass is always full to brimming even if it's a quarter of an inch from the bottom. What do I do to relax? Nothing, actually, just sit on the deck and gaze at the Pacific and breathe the air and think. Let the mind drift. Sometimes I go to a hospice nearby and read to an old blind man. If you do little things like that you could never feel down. He's a nice old man. He asks if I'm beautiful and I tell him I'm a knockout. He looks happy.

●

Admittedly thin stuff, some good but some of it too hot for the World-Herald, but at least a start, to see how things might sound.

We liked what we had of the interview – at least Roz said she liked it, and I know I did (as a first draft) precisely because it rambled on exactly as she did. Hard-to-believe stuff and almost pure raunch. Her only comment was: "It's nice, quite nice."

The praise sounded so little like her it screamed disappointment and only my insistence got her to admit that there was, well, just one small thing, come to think of it, a little detail that did trouble her.

"Am I really that dull a person?" Her surprise sounded sincere. "It makes me sound awfully fucking sad, doesn't it? Do I really sound that sad to you?"

She protested that it gave no sense of her as a person. "I sound like an unhappy freak. Blah, as in blasé. Also an unhappy sex freak. Surely you wouldn't want to print that."

Later, when I went back and reread what I had thought was a light, almost a fun piece, I agreed with her.

"And there's nothing in it about Hollywood," she added. "How can you write about Hollywood without mentioning

Hollywood?"

"Did you want to say something about Hollywood?"

"Anecdotes help – make it more real that we're living in Cloud Cuckooland. You know, the usual crap that people eat up."

I remind her that it was part of her expressed goal in life to always say what she thought, and to hell with those who were offended by the rawness of her honesty. I got nowhere with that argument. My curiosity piqued, I asked what crap did she have in mind.

"Made-up crap. Like what happened that time with Billy Wilder."

"Really? Billy Wilder? You never told me about that. What happened with Billy Wilder"

"Nothing happened with Billy Wilder. You fake it. Wilder's not going to object to a little fun."

"Especially since he's dead."

"Or Scorsese. Scorsese's alive."

"What about Scorsese?"

"He's a genius in the kitchen, the way he makes meatballs, did you know that?"

"Does he know that?"

"And he makes a marinara that'll bring tears to your eyes. Don't look at me like that. Who cares if it's not true? Do you think all those Hollywood stories are true? People love anecdotes about Hollywood. Do you know what Moss Hart said about Hollywood? 'Hollywood is the most beautiful slave quarters in the world.' Throw that in and you have our sex-slave connection. And speaking of slaves, Ben Hecht said about starlets, 'A starlet is any woman under thirty not actively employed in a brothel.' The whole thing could be an amusing piece. Especially if we can get in stuff about women in brothels."

"Fuck the truth."

177

"Exactly! Fuck the truth! You stretch things a little. Wouldn't that be more fun to read? Real-life anecdotes?"

"Real made-up anecdotes."

"Well, you know . . ."

Hearing her get into her normal flip mode, I switched on the recorder, whose batteries I had remembered to change, as she started now about a passionate affair she had once had in Turkey with a married Turkish villager. He seemed to be a deputy mayor of the small Turkish village overlooking the Aegean Sea. She thought he might have been one of sixteen deputy mayors of the tiny mountainside village. Was this true? Oh yes it was true. He tried to throw her off a cliff when she told him she was going home, leave him – you know, my little holiday is over, time to say bye-bye, honey – and his attitude was "If I can't have you, nobody's going to have you."

"Was that really true? Throw you off a cliff? With crocs below?"

"From a cliff, no crocs below, just rocks. He explained it all very reasonably. The Koran teaches one to respect women as a matter of great honor. It assured you a place in Paradise. He would not be caught dead treating me, a much honored and gracious lady, with disrespect and explained something about family honor. The more he talked the more I realized it was I who was wrecking his family honor. I would be breaching it by walking out on him after the wonderful time we'd had together. If I left him, he would be laughed at. No virtuous and well-placed family man could tolerate such disrespect. What was interesting was that he had some kind of defect in his cremaster muscle – quite an unusual case, in fact. It had even been written up but I forget where. It was interpreted as an omen of some kind but just looked like real low-hangers to me. "With his pants off he looked like a stud ram in season after a good morning's workout with a flock of ewes."

"What the fuck's a cremaster muscle?"

"It's the muscle that controls the rise and fall of the testicles. It's funny what men don't know about their balls."

"What's funnier is that women do."

"Not all women. It's just that I once read a friend's graduate thesis on testicles. She had already done mucho field research in the frat houses, so it was like combining business and pleasure, you might say."

I had trouble believing that one, thought she was pulling my leg, and didn't believe it would go in the interview anyway. But she went right on, hopping from one subject to another in what to me sounded like a better interview: "I once had an old cat who brought things home with her. Once it was a pair of men's shorts, another time it was an artist's paint brush clenched between her teeth that she deposited on her milk bowl, and one day she even brought home a fried egg. A real old dried-out one. How the egg held together I don't know but she dragged it in like a trophy. Or brought it in like a kitten between her teeth. And then sat on it."

Then, slipping into reminiscent mode:

"Hollywood makes sense when you understand it's just a money machine – a beautifully tooled, well-oiled money machine. Occasionally, almost incidentally, somebody makes a film that's not only worth seeing but worth seeing twice . . ." (Shrug. End of topic. She looks to see if I'm taking notes. I'm not.)

"How come you're not taking notes?"

I point to the recorder.

"Oh."

Collecting her thoughts: "Okay, how about my ambitions as a child? At twelve I wanted to be a firefighter so I could rescue cats."

"A nice detail."

"Or we could go into my hobbies."

"You have hobbies?"

"My big secret is that I take weekly violin lessons from the great Jascha Mariansky when I'm not on location."

"Jascha who?"

"Boris Mayakovsky. Does it matter? Jacob Malinowski."

"You play the violin?"

"Absolutely not. I mean, Jesus, what the fuck would I do with a violin?" She looked horrified.

"We could always say you went through a crisis in your young life. You felt torn between Carnegie Hall and Hollywood."

"Right. I agonized over it for months. But without growing bitter. You have to put that in. I never once got bitter about life."

"What stopped you from becoming bitter?"

"I think it was the fear of becoming bitter."

•

What I had left out of the interview was Laszlo and all the stuff Roz had told me about him, and I wanted him in as part of some larger picture. Although I had never met him, I thought he was funny and could be good for some lines for the column. The problem was to figure out a way to make him seem relevant without making Roz look dumb – or the whole so-called interview sound fake. Laszlo called himself a teamster which to me sounded like gangster. If you jokingly asked him what the difference was between a teamster and a gangster he'd say boy there was some difference, all right. So right from the start you knew you weren't dealing with a particle physicist. He's a Hungarian-Australian, and he came into the picture when Roz feeling adrift after Bill's death had the crazy notion that she wanted a man in her life and chose him because he would not be hard to get rid of when she got tired of him.

"I had the fun of feeling in love for a bit. He reminded me of the way things were in my crazy household growing up, fast, loose, zany, not very bright. Laszlo had those qualities and I gave up much just out of the puppy love I felt for him for a while. Lust, really. Some of my friends are still shocked to see how I fell for him for a short time but I actually did love him in the sense that it gave me pleasure to please him. But they were right, I should have listened to my instincts." And: "Here's a funny thing that happened. Laszlo had heard of Max's interest in War and Peace and was thinking of reading it and I told him it didn't come in a pop-up edition. He said, 'You're kidding, right?' I said, 'I have to admit that was a joke.' He wanted us to get married but I couldn't see a lot of little Laszlos running around America, the country being politically hopeless as it already is. On the other hand, I did hope to find somebody. I couldn't indefinitely put the family thing on hold if I was ever going to have one. I had about six eggs left by then, and anyway things seemed to change and, I don't know, I just no longer wanted to see him, which broke him up, the poor guy. I think he had seen me as his ticket to some mythical Hollywood inside track that outsiders think that all us charming glamour girls must have. He saw himself as Arnold Schwarzenegger redeviv – redev – whatever – reborn. He began stalking me, I mean in a friendly way, and I finally had to tell him to stop being so adolescent and accept the reality that we were no longer an item. He threatened to expose some nude images he had made of me, claiming he had even been approached about them by one of those shitty little tabloids that airheads buy. I told him to go home and give his three brain cells a rest. I knew he wouldn't do anything as mean as that, and he knew me well enough to know that when all is said and done I would actually have been delighted if he had published the photos – I mean, talk about free publicity. Afterwards he apologized, saying, 'I was thinkin with my little head.' I said, 'You mean your other little head.' "

" Oh wow, you're really funny sometimes. Ha ha."

"I told him we could see each other from time to time, that he could always find me at upyourass dot com, and he thought that was extremely witty."

"I'm going to borrow that one," he said. "How's it go again?"

"His IQ matched his humor. He thought he was complimenting me the first day we met when he said every time he heard people talking about the Big Bang he thought they were talking about me. Big grin on his face. Then to avoid any possibility that I might think he was being rude he added: 'You know I'm only joking, right?' "

Laszlo stories: wanting to know if a certain starlet dyed her hair blond, he peeked while she was showering and confirmed that "her carpet matched her drapes." (His term for cunnilingus: "munching the carpet.")

Roz was fascinated by what she called his "navigating the English language, which he frequently got right. I told him he makes being emotionally dysfunctional into an art and he took it as a compliment." She said that when he tried to read his lips got tired. "I'm just glad never to have to see his Malibu place again. Imagine a beach house with empty pizza boxes all around."

She ended it when he wanted her to wear biker-slut black-leather outfits. "In bed."

To bring the Laszlo episode to an end, she changed her phone number and email address and the locks on all the doors and gave him a parting gift of $100,000 credit at his favorite men's shop on Rodeo Drive.

"Boy!" he said.

•

"Maybe I'm talking too much," Roz says. "The hard part about interviews is sounding fresh every time the same old questions are put to you. You have to make it sound as though nobody has ever asked you the same deep philosophical questions about what you had for breakfast. That's especially on publicity tours for the studio, when you get a question in Appleseed, Wisconsin that you just got done answering that morning in Crotch Haven, Arkansas. In the hundreds of interviews I've given, only one question has ever interested me over the years because it was so different. A Parisian journalist, some name like Maya Charpentier or Chapoutier, asked, 'Who are you?' and it made me stop and think. Who am I? It really threw me. I finally said, 'Fuck if I know,' and, good old France, they broadcast it without bleeping it.

Over there I could horse around in an interview and crack a joke like, 'Well, vaginally speaking, . . .' and nobody sent for the riot police. The atmosphere in France is so much freer than here

– but don't get me started on comparative mores. Over there they seem interested in more than the usual idiotic stuff they ask over here – you know, the color of my underwear, whether I go to bed in the buff, what I think of women shaving, who my favorite Hollywood star is, and all the rest of the crap that passes for journalism. The funny thing is they never ask about the really juicy stuff, like my college days and our little Phi Delta group called the "Cucumber and I Society". But I don't think your nice newspaper is looking for world dildo reports – although I doubt that there's even one female reader left, including or maybe especially milfs, who isn't a happy owner of at least one new pair of Christmas-gift vibrators."

●

I sent Umpleby these stubs of Roz interviews, just as sketchily and wild as written here, with the Laszlo notes appended, knowing that Umpleby would cut much of it, maybe all of it – after enjoying reading it. And then fire me.

No response from New York, a habit I was getting used to. I began to feel like a Kafka character who suffers from the delusion that he works for a New York newspaper called the World-Herald.

We were in Roz's kitchen, now our regular meeting place, with Sophie doing Sophie things in the background and Roz saying she was not surprised. She said the interview fell short of ideal.

"Don't most things?" I heard Sophie say at the sink. She was washing out a baking dish, trying to do it quietly so she could hear our conversation..

"Lao-zay," Roz said.

I maintained it was my lack of skill as a journalist, but Roz insisted it was just that she talked nonsense.

"It makes people laugh when it's all dished out orally and I'm spouting the garbage. But when you put it in writing it doesn't come out funny. It comes out stupid or nutty. More demented."

"It's up to Umpleby. And they have some pretty good rewrite guys. I'll ask that you see it before it gets published. Demand it as a courtesy or you'll never speak to them again."

"Send in an article on Max at the same time – absorb some of the shock. Or schlock."

Roz was just off to see Dave Two Commas, the "great new love of my life." Then she was going shopping.

Dave Two Commas was her agent – two commas and eight figures, as in $20,000,000. That was what he got her for her last film, and with that established a new floor. Max was another two-comma client, but with a paltry $7,000,000 per film. But – big but – he also got twelve percent of the gross. Roz got two percent, usually described as a "whopping two percent", the amount adding up to another few million. I asked her how many million more.

"I don't know."

"Don't you care to know?"

"I pay people to know."

"I didn't iron your yellow dress," Sophie threw in at this point. She looked tentative, sounded reluctant. "If you can wait a minute I'll do it right now."

Roz picked up her cue. "'Ts OK. I'll wear the green one today. Green dress, yellow dress. These are questions I wrestle with."

Roz changed and left. Sophie, observing me sideways: "What you need is comic relief."

I agreed with her, that in fact I did.

Fussing with a teapot at the sink, she scooped out the tea leaves at the bottom, adding: "Some kind of relief." Then in case I was still not getting it: "Something emotional – you know, bring it all out."

That getting nowhere, she went on.

"Like it would be better for your health."

Progress meter on her face: zero.

Back to cleaning the teapot, looking over at me reproachfully, with emotional-blackmail eyes.

"You'd go to bed with her, though."

"I have a rule about not going to bed with virgins."

At least I got her to laugh.

•

Talking with Trish Hooligan at East-West Studios. She was dabbing things on a face that grimaced back at her from the mirror.

"With y' 'n a minute." The words were pinched out through lips being applied with gloss.

I was behind her and took in her long sleek legs and imagined their hidden upward continuation and could almost feel the always surprising heat where the thighs met at the nest. The room reeked of a wild cologne. In the mirror her seductively pursed upper and lower lips were forming an oo as she twisted her head for sideward-approving glimpses.

"I have a question about Max."

"You bet."

"Who's his press agent."

"Max doesn't have a press agent. He has a public relations counselor."

"Could I speak to him?"

"You could speak to her for sure. It's her job. Downtown" – handing me a business card with a Wilshire address and chattily asking if everything was going okay.

Trish lived in Burbank with a Johnny Pagano, a part-time jazz trombonist who began life as an animator at Disney but got tired, he said, of Sir Michael. She knew Laszlo, or rather knew of him, and thought him amusing.

"And a little ridiculous. Know him through Roz only. You know how they say men think about sex every ninety seconds? Laszlo stops thinking about sex every ninety seconds – well, that's according to Roz. She said she finally had to put something in his drinks. Apparently he's just a pair of balls on legs. Oops, sorry. Her description, not mine."

Trish wanted to marry the trombonist to change her name. "After a lifetime of being a Hooligan, Trish Pagano sounds like music."

"Means pagan, doesn't it?"

"Love it."

"When's the wedding?"

"First he has to get a divorce."

"When will that be?"

"Well, first he has to discuss it with his wife."

"Doesn't she know yet he wants to leave her?"

"He doesn't want to give it to her in one big shock."

"It must be difficult for you."

"Well, I'm not planning on having a self-pity party."

I told her that sounded pretty level-headed and she smiled. "Did Max call a meeting?" she asked.

"That's the message I got."

"Well, I'm afraid he's gone again. He'll be back."

"Is this his usual way of doing things? – calling a meeting and then canceling?"

"No. Right now a lot's happening."

"Not all bad I hope."

"From the little I know, it's not all good."

21

This habit of Max getting called away at the last minute was annoying, but I didn't say anything. We waited together and I think she felt glad not to have to pretend to be busy. She brought up the Karen Bryggman film project and hoped it was materializing:

"If it's for the cause of women, I'm all for it."

She asked about me and my life in New York and I told her my standard line about being born posthumously.

"Go on!"

"My critically-ill mother departed from the world while pushing me out into it."

"Go on!"

"A childless middle-aged couple adopted me from the New Jersey New Hope Orphanage and Foundling Home."

Trish staring at me, taking in the words – and to see if I was kidding.

"Do you get along with them?"

"Why would I not? They're good people."

"And they're the only parents you have."

"Exactly."

"There won't be any in-law problem when you get married."

"Just step-parent-in-law problems."

"Oh go on!"

We were still exchanging autobiographies when Max arrived. He was in a rare philosophical mood, almost high. I recorded most of it on my iPhone as Max launched in with a family background of his own.

"My grandmother once told me that everybody should leave

something behind before leaving life to bear witness that they were once here. You know, we're here and then we're gone but we leave the world a slightly better place. And that, she used to say, is terrific because 'slightly better is a lot.' But you know what we really want? A caress, some words of love, a little warmth, a little security. But the strange thing is the moment you put those feelings into words it all sounds corny. Yet it's all we really want."

"Not power?"

"Without love, power is empty. St. Paul. He was right."

I was mulling over this sudden shift in subject when, again without transition, Max began talking about his plans for a film of The Death of Ivan Ilych. Although interested, I only half-listened, waiting to break in with a request that we continue with, or better yet conclude, the profile of him for the paper so that we could at least have that to leave behind.

I think I managed to hide my impatience, both with him and increasingly with California. My thoughts were mostly in New York, and I was snug in bed with Inge when I heard Max say "Oh" with an ugly sound and saw his hand move to his head as if someone had just bashed in his skull. The look of pain on his face was so genuine I suggested calling off our interview session. But no no, it was all right. He was learning to live with this migraine horror, or whatever it was.

The phone rang. His cheeks looked pale as he spoke to the caller.

"No, not Clint," he said. Speaking in a low voice: "It's Sid. Get Sid." Then with extravagant annoyance: "Not that Sid. Sid uh – you know the one I mean. Names!" he muttered angrily at the unreliability of memory.

Turning toward me, with a shadowy sadness in his eyes, and silently mouthing unintelligible words, he indicated the sofa.

I made a show of not overhearing the phone conversation, studiously examining the paintings on his walls: an old visually complex Vasarely and the junk art of a forgotten craze. So Max had good stuff and bad stuff both. From Matisse and Pissarro to this. The junk brought to mind the headlines of the newest sensation at the Tate: a refrigerator stocked with human organs. It showed, a London critic admiringly commented, "a rare poetic sensibility for reality."

I had to tell that one to Inge, for her collection. I remembered a similar comment a few years earlier about bronze castings of elephant dung decoratively arranged in a row of three heaps on the gallery floor . . . so sophisticated. And it was in such contrast to what Trish once privately showed me, one of Max's most personally valued possessions, a Courbet hidden behind a panel that only special visitors were permitted to view, "The Origin of the World" – or rather an oil copy of the original in the Musée d'Orsay. A luscious dark-haired vulva.

Max suddenly yelled into the phone, "Well, do you know where he is?" An impatient pause and then his voice going acid with sarcasm. "Would you please please have him call me back?"

And hanging up loudly he yell-muttered, "Motherfucker" and made a face "He's a first-class prick but a good writer. You can have all the superstars in the world coming out of your ass but if you don't have a script that's well structured and tight, you've got nothing." A growl from his throat. "No more borderline personalities for me."

"What's that, a borderline personality?"

Max tried for a laugh. "It's anybody you don't like."

•

On the basis of several conversations I tried to piece things together. He wanted this Sid person for a film currently in development hell. Development hell – Roz was my informant in these things – was a project kicking around for years and so hopelessly bogged down in conferences and revisions that it risked being abandoned. The implication was, in development hell a story idea was pretty much doomed. In this case it was a film about the unhappy story of Shalimar's death. The idea was to make the center of the story the Taj Mahal itself, not Shalimar. Shalimar dies, but the Taj Mahal that commemorates her life – that lives on. It sounded like it merited its own special development hell.

"I should have done things sooner, things I wanted to do," Max said. "It's painful to look back and know you've blown the whole thing." And then the afterthought: "My life in a way has been so unlucky."

I reminded him of the good films he'd made. "People have lined up three deep in queues circling round the block." I felt strange giving moral support to the Magnificent Max.

"All shit," he said, dismissing a lifetime of work. "Good for making money. The critics are right -- except that they can't see that I still have the ability to make a film that'll be talked about twenty years from now."

"Which pictures would you say you've made that ca – "

"Actually I never made even one. In that sense I've betrayed myself. Maybe the Tolstoy, if I had ever got around to making it. I shouldn't have listened to anybody. The only way to make a film is to dream, just let your mind wander wherever it wants and not worry. In the end you'll find a way to pull it together. The Long Way Round, for example. Halfway through The Long Way Round, there were some shots of sunlight over a sea of tall yellow grass going out to the horizon. Nebraska. People may or may not remember that bit, but you know, it was the only reason I wanted to make that film, to get that lonely but beautiful prairie feeling, that spaciousness and light. The rest was all there to advance the plot and satisfy the audience's need for a story. It wasn't worth a pygmy's fart. But that field of golden yellow – that was for me."

Then his dreamy thoughts apparently still with Shalimar: "There's something deathless about an unhappy love story. Unhappy love stories survive the ages. Troy and Helen."

And back to Karen again. He asked if the story about her was true and I assured him it had been in all the New York papers. When – boringly – he again pointed out it had no ending, that every story needs a third act et cetera, I again – boringly – had to tell him that that was the whole horrible point of the story. Not knowing the ending. That was what made the story so frightening, and real, because that was what happened in life and why a film of its kind would be worth making. There was no third act. Couldn't anyone see that? Did people think life comes with an Act Three? A woman disappears – or a man, or a child – a human being disappears. And apparently there isn't much anyone can do about it beyond contacting the police and the missing persons bureau and checking with civil or law-enforcement authorities. And none of them are of any help. I tried to explain that what made the Karen Bryggman story real for me, with or without a third act, what gave it the pain of reality, was what Inge was going through after two years, long after people had forgotten there had ever been a Karen Bryggman or that a "tragic incident" had once happened. For Inge, Karen was still alive somewhere, still suffering, still dying every morning and dying every night with never any hope of being free again. That was real life, and I never could understand why Hollywood never dealt in real life. Why did it crank out shit? Did money always have to trump morality? And life as we know it, does it just brim over with happy endings? Where's the happy ending in Hamlet? Othello? King Lear?

And while I was saying all this (and feeling way out of line – and not very intelligent) I suddenly had the reverse thought, Oh fuck! none of this ever gets through, what's the use? Max is right and I'm the one who's wrong. Nobody in his right mind would ever sit through a library of statistics and facts. Even I got bored as the über-efficient Ms. Highsmith handed me more masses of UN reports on rape, abductions, killings, and genocide. The sheer amount of the reports leached any horror out of the reality. Feelings, human fate were reduced to cold administrative matters. The murders and rapes were something "to be looked into.". They were "to be studied" – "to be moved to the top of the committee's agenda." They were "to be investigated further". In the end that was what we had left: a thing to be investigated further.

Which was both life and not life. In life what held our attention was story and only story. We want to know what happened. And then what happened? And, of course, how did it all end? Max was right about that. Life itself, the whole messy thing, was only a story – or it was nothing. Which was where we were: we had nothing. We never got beyond the fairy tales that a haremful of Scheherazades were sitting around telling each other while quietly nodding off to sleep before reaching the end.

And flashing in and out of these thoughts was the growing conviction that this project of Inge's and Roz's was not going to work. If all our problems could magically be resolved and we could finally start making a movie, we would still not be given a green light unless we got two superstars to commit to the film, or actually now only one superstar since we already had Roz. Because without the essential elements contractually locked into place, the people in New York would not bankroll it. So as sorry as I felt for Karen, as miserable as I felt for Karen, I thought the hell with our whole idea. Not the idea. The idea was good but it was pissing up a rope full time. And I wanted out. As Max had stressed, no third act, no film, so OK, no film. The. End. And fuck Shalimar – and if she had a cousin, fuck him too.

But I have to say she had to have been one helluva wondrous piece of ass to have that Taj Mahal built to honor her.

•

An anger that was building in me began to edge over into disgust. Somebody goes missing and all we say is, "Oh how terrible! – what an AW-ful thing!" – and then forget about it. I appreciated even more Inge's analogy of her Aunt Leena's goldfish. Inge would tap her fingertips against the glass of the little aquarium and the tiny fish would panic in flight. "Flight" meant darting an inch away and slowly drifting back, as though anchored to the earlier spot. When she tapped again they startled away again, always that same inch, and floated back exactly the same as before. No matter how often she tapped on the glass the behavior of the fish didn't change. Their memory of past events seemed to last all of one second – Inge commenting that apparently the feelings of goldfish have a built-in statute of limitations, and me adding, "If only human feelings could have that same statute of limitations."

22

I don't know. I felt my life out here was in some kind of limbo, on hold, you might say, with meetings going nowhere. Or else we were kept waiting for the next meeting to be called and then have it postponed.

In desperation I spent time on the diary I had started, thinking of it as maybe being an entertaining read some day. I thought back in New York I could mine it for any frothy stuff that might be usable in the column. Meanwhile doing it had a calming effect.

•

22 September

Hopeless feeling continuing. Our great film idea is ending before it ever got started. Too many things oppose it. The consensus was that it was a great but unworkable idea. Aristotle: beginning, middle, and that other thing he kept yapping about.

I'm being careful not to let our Hollywood adventure bring me down or give me the feeling it was pointless coming to California. A case of self-dislike and self-defeat becoming twinned. In the earliest days of my analysis, when I was seeing Yeblon four times a week, I started suffering attacks of self-dislike just popping up. And as corny as that sounded, or maybe not corny but crazy, my feeling then was that I didn't think anybody wanted to know me. Who am I? Scorn and self-disparagement would wake me up at three in the morning. But Yeblon gave it a positive spin. He said it was a hopeful sign. It was the analysis doing it – raising buried questions about myself. My psyche was being stirred. And sure enough, surprising stuff started coming out. Before then I had been living with the feeling that my life was vanishing day by day and all that would ever happen was that I would waste whatever time

I had. I felt I had not yet begun living but was preparing myself to live – someday – when the time came.

That is, until I met Inge. I think she saved my life. I met Inge through Vicky, an NYU math major and nonpracticing Catholic. Vicky came originally from somewhere in the south of England and lived in the East Village – sandals, beautiful buck teeth (I had, briefly, a thing about buck teeth, god knows why), the long waviness of her golden hair the most attractive part of her and – only because I preferred it and for no other reason – she would shave her legs ("but not the pussy hair – that stays"). She took two or three showers a day, ending up with the fragrance of a Yardley's English lavender factory – not much of a turn-on. She offered friendship with benefits, the first time I had ever heard the phrase used by the woman offering, accompanying it with the warning: "If you think you can handle it, because I sometimes get very horny, I mean it's Krafft-Ebing time." It was all gropings and penetrations for a while and then one day I said something that pissed her off royally and brought things to a halt. We were free to do what we wanted. But it had no effect on her horniness so we became "enemies with benefits". She liked the phrase so much she kept it, extending it eventually to men, women and the whole human race – enemies with benefits. I was young enough to be amused by her extreme views, that, for example, Dante was a good Catholic but a pedophile to go for Beatrice, a nine-year-old kid. Nuttily she believed this. She didn't believe that customs were different in his day or that Dante admired Beatrice from afar and wasn't looking for a preteen boff.

She belonged to a Mood Disorders Support Group – I checked: the name was real – and she was the one who suggested that before I threw the rest of my life away to go see a shrink. It would help me get over the shyness I suffered from that was interfering with my new job as cub reporter on the World-Herald. She herself was in her seventh year with someone named Yeblon and swore by him – and swore also by yoga and by Pilates. Finally, almost to get her to stop bugging me and by now somewhat curious too, I called Yeblon for an appointment, and it was there, in his waiting room, that I first glimpsed Inge as she came out of Yeblon's office. There was a quiet conservative beauty about her.

Later we bumped into each other at Rory's Bird in Hand and on parting Inge boldly put it out there: "Do you think we could see each other again?" Wow, I thought. My heart flipped – a new feeling for me. It wasn't just the heart but a jolt in the groin, and incredibly, from our very first chat, I had the sense that my life now was set on a different course as I felt feelings I never knew existed. And that wonderful Finnish face! – so difficult to turn my eyes away from her. I thought how amazing Finland must be to produce such creatures. I imagined I smelled her fresh northernness, the lakes and pine forests of Suomi, and I thought when I was with her I had passed into some happy psychotic state – and didn't care that I had. If this was psychosis I loved it and couldn't get enough of it. I would get even shyer with her than usual and when she told a joke I would laugh more than I needed to. I wanted her to see I was interested in her. I was completely nuts over her and acting silly and knew it and couldn't help it. And when we started living together it didn't take much for me to love even the small things about her, like her saying "hopingly" instead of "hopefully", or "a bull in a Chinese shop," or once, while I was lying in bed anticipating snuggling together, hearing her breathlessly whistling "Finlandia" as she showered and toweled down in the steamy-mirrored bathroom. And our zany conversations, which were so much what I needed in those days to get me out of whatever I had sunk into, made me want this new life of screwball comedy and Finnish sex. And in fact as it developed, things turned out to be so right for both of us that I just moved in with her and our crazy-manic days took off from there, and no one in the whole world was ever more happy than me.

•

23 September. Roz still hot and heavy on the project has persuaded Will Jamison to commit to our film. A coup. Much jubilation. Jamison is big box office too and I was surprised Roz got him so easily. I suspected it took a torrid Palm Springs weekend in the sack with Roz to boff him into it. (Jamison lives in Palm Springs.)

So now with Roz on board and Will Jamison in the wings,

Max has his two-star minimum for tentative New York approval. If the okay is given for the next step, the film as a project stands a chance of becoming a reality and not just an idea for some day. All that would remain to do would be to find the right person to play Karen, and as always the great fear was that the front office would insist on some bimbo – plus of course a body double for the inevitable public-pleasing nude scenes – there would have to be some stupid nude scenes. Still, for the moment, at least, what matters is that the film looked to become viable. Barring Murphy's Law.

My take on this was not optimistic: I think Max was telling us yes, yes, the deal is on but possibly it's just to get us off his back. It was hard to tell. I didn't know where he stood and that may have been the way he liked things to be. I've been warned that his style is to call for more and more meetings and keep raising new obstacles, and after a certain time throw up his hands and say, well, he tried. I've been told this is one of the better-known ways projects are abandoned here.

For me, the wisest thing to do of course would be to just leave. I would have to deal with Inge's reaction and too there would be the wrath of Umpleby to contend with, compared with which, the wrath of Achilles was a childish tantrum. All Achilles wanted was to win the war against Troy. What Umpleby wanted was to scoop the Times Sunday edition.

I found Max now more interesting than his films, especially since learning of his passion for Tolstoy. I was surprised when I learned also that Max had been orphaned as an infant – he too. That made three of us. Tolstoy had been orphaned later than Max or me. For Tolstoy it was at the age of two. I remembered reading he had only a single pleasant memory of his mother and then her sudden disappearance and at seventy-eight he still yearned to put his head in the lap of some consoling woman who would comfort him. I wondered if Max had similar feelings about his life, and if that connected with his making love with a succession of dark-haired Shalimar-scented "assistants" – each a morning's pleasant memory after a sudden disappearance.

•

24 September.   This morning, still undecided whether to continue to play a part in our enterprise or cut bait and head for New York, I bumped into Mrs. Petrov.

I had arrived to meet with Max at the agreed hour but was met in the foyer by Mrs. Petrov informing me Max would be along shortly.   She appeared to be in her beginning fifties without attempting to hide it except to add charm to it. I could, if I wished, sit and wait, showing me, as she said this, a waiting room of decorator's chintz, mirrors tinted pink, cheerful orange wall hangings multiplying the glowing sunshine – a California and what-the-hell-am-I-doing-here feeling the room gave me. Or better yet, she said – (a social chirp thrilling her voice) "yes, because this is for the article, isn't it?" – I might find enjoyment in being shown round the house and seeing where Max likes to relax in the comfort of his home. She again said he'd be home shortly and if we just looked around . . .

"Are you expecting him?"

"At home and unbuttoned."

She said this with a stilted laugh to win over the journalist from New York, although she really had no need to be afraid. I had taken an instant liking to her after hearing the story of the parrot she and Max had briefly owned in the hand-to-mouth early years of their marriage.   Max had acquired the parrot, Rheingold, from an aging widow of an old sea captain retired to Sausalito who claimed she was parting with Rheiny only because she needed the money. Max discovered – too late for a refund – that as visitors walked in the door the parrot's joyful salutation was "How the fuck are you, mate?" Regina's women friends thought the parrot was priceless as a door greeter but Regina had other plans for it. She had a huge dislike of religious people ("the abracadabra people") and she took her revenge by gifting the parrot to the next Jehovah's Witnesses who arrived, a mother and a girl of eight, who knocked at their door the following Sunday.

"I felt sorry for the little girl, but they'd been around once too often. Too much religion is creepy. Oh dear, I hope you're not religious."

"Me? No."

"Good. Lew, you know, is very devout, the poor dear. He says the Bible is the word of God and when I asked him how he knew that he said well, it says so in the Bible." She gave me a look.

Bypassing the spacious living room and the by-now familiar pool outside, I was led by Mrs. Petrov to another room. following her in a wash of Shalimar. What I saw was not the usual movie screen quietly descending from the ceiling as louvers self-adjusted to darken the windows but a 42-inch plasma screen majestically levitating from the floor in spooky silence.

"So this is where he watches films?"

"No, he mostly just sits here and meditates."

•

I was to see only the smallest part of the splendor of the Great Cotswold's twenty-seven ritzy rooms.

"I don't know that the World-Herald's readers would be interested in bedrooms," she said – a sentiment I didn't agree with but was grateful that it meant skipping a half dozen or so rooms. "Things like Louis Cans chairs."

But nothing of the rest of the house seemed it could serve in any sense as a place of relaxation for Max. We passed an ornate bronze candelabra held arm's-length high by a white-turbaned slave of mixed ethnicity guarding a room with a table seating twenty-four ("bought from the set of Citizen Kane"), a small humidity-controlled room consisting of shelves of intricate cabinetry nestling individual Steuben cut glasses and goblets and purple-velvet-lined boxes of gleaming silverware, a separate room of china for every conceivable formal and informal service, the tour none too soon ending in, if I heard correctly, "our little gift-wrapping room".

I was absorbing slabs of information (gift-wrapping room?) when Mrs. Petrov led me into a glassed-in thirty-foot-tall solarium she called the South Porch that looked out on a lake of a lawn that swept past a helipad to a manicured garden in the distance.

"To conceal Max's 16-car garage and private showroom."

"Private showroom?"

"He keeps his Bentley and a prize Lamborghini there. He's never driven them, not even once!"

I said there was something wonderfully extravagant about that – or words to that effect, trying to sound sympathetic. I found out later that she omitted telling me he had once given her a $285,000 Ferrari for her fiftieth birthday.

Apart from the garage, a 10-car motor court lay somewhere near a wooded area of rare Madagascar trees and . . . and I no longer remember the other loopy details of this incongruous Shangri-La until we came finally to a rose garden and a toy waterfall lazily cascading into a koi pond. Two swans (high Regina laugh: "Genuine English swans – kidnapped in Oxfordshire!") glided in our direction for a possible handout. Disappointed, they swiveled their heads back in swanny dismissal and sailed snootily away

Gracefully Mrs. P. indicated more grounds and "a little bosky wood" and further out I could see a bowling green and six tennis courts – and I kept thinking: "People actually live this way" and almost said aloud, "Just six courts?"

"And there you have it. Just beyond are the staff's quarters, where we're forbidden to go!" A staccato shrill of noblesse oblige. "Out of respect for their privacy."

I tried for something so obviously fake she would understand it was a joke, like "My!" After so grand a tour, something was needed to get us past the embarrassment at having nothing to say to each other.

"Some layout!" I said and she laughed an accommodating laugh. I think she was noblesse-obliging me, but whatever she was doing, there was something sweet about her, and although she was old enough to be my mother, I tried imagining her in bed. I see all women as wild between the sheets since meeting Inge, who sometimes has to retrieve duvet and pillows from the floor and remake the bed after some of our sessions.

With a formulaic dishonesty that shows how well brought up we both were, I thanked Mrs. Petrov and hoped we'd see each other again blah blah. I'd soon be far from genuine Oxfordshire swans and little gift-wrapping rooms, and if it was here that Max liked to relax in the comfort of his home, there must have been an unbuttoned-comfort room that we missed.

•

25 September. Unusually hot morning. It's becoming pretty clear that the film project will probably go nowhere. But I'm more interested now in Max and film making and so I continue gathering and learning whatever I can about both. My hope is there's an article in it, something that Umpleby, in announcing it in the paper, would probably hyperbolize as "an in-depth profile" and stretch into a week-long "chronicle of a life." At the World-Herald anything longer than a thousand words passes as literary endeavor, and with little daily cliff-hanger breaks, a story that barely makes it as a short human-interest item is sometimes spread out into three days of the thinnest shit in the belief that that's what people like. And people probably do.

I'm ready to accept Roz's judgment that I could do better than write junky three-dot journalism but I don't think I would ever want to be a screenwriter. "Why not?" she asks. "It's an easy life. A screenwriter sleeps late, has a leisurely breakfast with a little Colombian coke sprinkled on his grapefruit, spends a tranquil hour reading the trades before going down to the Strip to meet an old buddy for lunch and more coke to get through the afternoon. The last thing screenwriters do is write." But she's only kidding. "Naa, don't get into that life."

Max is interested in "our" article. He enjoys hearing me complaining about newspaper writing and its "unmatched insignificance" (a phrase he got from me) in the cultural life of humans. He seemed to take that as a challenge and said we would try to make our article different. He's surprised that I enjoy reading memoirs and wants to know what I find in diaries. The occasional raunchy detail, I tell him, the small daily fact that is usually omitted in other forms of writing. The nitty-gritty, especially intimate things. The socially unspoken. Opinions, judgments.

He was surprised I was reading the autobiography of an English butler, of all people, but I assured him it was "very un-butlery in spots" – as when the butler says that his idea of pleasure was to enjoy breakfast tea and toast as he lazed in bed reading the Sunday papers with cunty fingers. Max laughs, relieved, apparently, that I am after all normal (but probably at the same time wondering in fact if I am). As I sometimes wonder too.

•

26 September. This morning's spam: "Find a local slut near you and fuck her tonight! She's dying to put out!" But no offers to correct my erectile dysfunction for several days now and I wonder what's up.

Speaking of intimate details, a squib emailed from Umpleby:

"Bill Thurston paints with his penis. A saucy self-portrait for a Swiss art show won him first prize. He works under the name Pricasso." Hard to believe that one was true but it was true.

Another email, part of a batch: "A Czech railway bridge was reported stolen. 'It's the first time we have dealt with this type of theft,' a police spokesman for the Czech Republic said." I wondered if he expected a serial bridge thief.

"Bishops Search for Condoms in Girl Scouts' Cookie Boxes" – headline. Boston.

And this from China: "Eggs hardboiled in children's urine are a traditional treat in Zheijiang province, China, and now officials want to export them worldwide. 'The urine is gathered from local schools, and the very best comes from boys under ten,' said a local chef. 'They pee in buckets and we collect it fresh every day.' The eggs are said to fight disease and boost brain power. 'We are having a big export push because we want people outside China to fully appreciate the delicacy of our cuisine,' he added."

Life is not all shark fins, then. Piss on that story. Everything in China, edible and inedible, is either good for the general health or fights off disease. Estimating here: with 100 million boys ten or under peeing into, say, 10 million buckets, with a dozen eggs per bucket selling for $5 per egg, how long would it take a rocket to get to Mars if it slowed down ten feet every 100 meters?

Umpleby, who is of an older generation, sends email instructions modeled on telegrams as though each internet word cost money: "More to come. Column still once weekly." Also suggests that I occasionally throw in quotes from historical figures "to give it zip but no Tibetan shit about the meaning of life."

I put the squibs in a drawer. The penis painter had possibilities, but a Czech railway bridge? The motto of the World-Herald: "To those with a sincere interest in the events of the world and our time." It of course could be argued that that included everything in the universe, including railway bridges and the piss of young Chinese boys.

Later more squibs popped up on my laptop screen:

"In Zimbabwe a bus driver was taking twenty mentally ill patients to a hospital. He stopped for a drink in a bar and returning to the bus found that the patients had escaped. He went to a bus stop and offered a free ride to twenty people waiting there. He drove them to the hospital and told the staff that these were the patients and to handle them with care because they were all terrible liars."

That story, at a conservative count, has been made into at least three films and first appeared in Joe Miller's Joke Book.

Then this: "The policeman took the woman by the arm and assisted her into the police car. She was accused of killing her lover. As they left she said, 'We had a date to meet his mother. So I guess that's off now.' " That one had possibilities.

Another: "When six-year-old Ursula Tompkins, hearing strange sounds, barged into her parents' bedroom, she asked in amazement why Daddy's penis had suddenly grown so huge. 'Because Daddy likes me,' Mrs. Tompkins said."

And I instantly like Mrs. Tompkins.

Pressure now from Umpleby the Indefatigable adding to Inge's pressure, he complaining I'm falling behind in returning squibs with punch lines added. The World-Herald likes to have a bank of five or six weeks of squibs and I'm down to two weeks. Umpleby says that the suits, the philosophes on the fourteenth floor, suggest I get my ass in gear.

Fact, from Los Angeles Times: In Mauritania it is illegal to discuss or mention slavery or even talk to foreign journalists.

Later: That's when a man is drawn to a woman because of her mind. I think the reason I didn't fall into a deep depression at this point was my regular nightly phone call to Inge. I missed New York pretty bad. And I missed horsing-around with Inge – just the usual verbal fun, like going out the door and she calling after me: "Where you off to?" and me saying, "To observe the world and attempt to impose an order on the perceived chaos we call reality" and without missing a beat she says: "You get that feeling too?"

•

27 September. Waking up after a nap with the insight that history is a monstrous soap opera with no ending, I relegate the thought to a note I'll never look at again. I want out of our film project though still sympathetic to it.

At the local supermarket, a blonde woman to her female friend: "Where do you stand on toilet tissues?" "Toilet tissues?" "Yeah, shit paper." "Where do I stand? I don't. I sit." They laugh.

On Facebook: "The fucking thing I fuckin like most in the fucking English language is that you can fucking put the fucking word 'fucking' every fucking place you fucking want." (Source: "Intelligent, Classy, Well-educated Women Who Say F*ck a Lot." The humor in "F*ck".)

Posted on line: the "greatest suicide note ever written: 'All this buttoning and unbuttoning.' "

Also on line: "While the food of Vietnam has been influenced to a certain extent by the cooking of the Chinese, it would not be mistaken for Chinese food, for true Vietnamese food has a character and flavor all its own. Instead of using soy sauce, there is the universal use of fish sauce, nuoc mam or nuoc cham, which is added during cooking. Nuoc Man is more pungent than other Southeast Asian fish sauces. If it is not available, add a little dried shrimp paste to Chinese fish sauce for a good substitute. But nuoc mam sauce which is served as an accompaniment with practically everything, is based on nuoc mam with the addition of fresh chilies, garlic, sugar, lime or lemon and vinegar. The flavor is sharper and more pungent than anything the Chinese cuisine has to offer."

I'll never look at a Vietnamese dish the same way again.

Tired of the newspaper notes. What good are pissy little bits and statistics about railway bridges? They have slowly become a list of horrors. They are all jokes and faintly amusing and I dump them into my diary of meditations, which also I will never look at again in a scrapbook habit picked up from Inge. She comes from a family of journal keepers. Her father is a professor of history at the University of Helsinki and she probably got it from him. And the latest scrapbook Inge has started, her Doomsday Book, regards the term "doomsday" not as something heavy but farcical. She hopes I'll send her more cult stories. By email I send her the World-Herald's squibs to use in any way she likes in her Doomsday farcical scrapbook:

" 'Germany has declared war on Russia – Swimming in the afternoon.' – Franz Kafka."

That one appeals to me. Kafka's diary writing is the diary writing I like. Put down spontaneous non sequitur-ish little shockers like: "Bought gun to blow neighbor's head off, but then thinking of the price to pay if caught, took Inge to a new off-Broadway comedy and then fucked all night." That might hold interest with a capper: "A day well spent."

Sent one to Inge, recently received, about the Supreme Court in Spain overturning an assault conviction that had been handed to Henry Osagiede, a Nigerian national. Osagiede, who was facing ten years in prison, had been picked out from an identity parade in which he was the only black man.

And this one: A woman claimed to police that not only had she been physically abused by each of her three former partners but all three were still stalking her. Then one night as she was happily fondling her latest playmate, soon to be her fourth former partner, she squeezed his testicles a bit too hard and he was put on pain-killers for two months. Impatient at the man's slow recovery, she dropped him and went back to one of the earlier partners, the one, as it happens, who had abused her the most. When asked why she had returned to somebody who had broken her nose and sent her to the hospital with a split-open lip and a forehead requiring six stitches she said: "I got a card from him on my birthday. He remembered."

23

I had felt it coming on and this was it. Basta.

Fed up with the project and fed up with waiting, I wanted to quit but do so without letting Roz and Inge down. How?

The great plan had sounded good. And it was good – on paper. But the money people had their needs and their needs didn't coincide with ours so why go on pushing against a stone wall?

Phoning Inge before bed, I again brought up marriage – partly to avoid the subject at hand. But Finns have a special gene for intransigence.

"What difference would marriage make? You'd still be out there and I'd be here. Are you still madly in love with California?"

"I'm definitely, positively and terminally not in love with California but I do have to admit my skin is improving out here. Possibly it's the climate. Or is it just that I show more skin out here and have more time to examine it?"

"There's nothing wrong with your skin. And I miss its smell."

Then more chitchat, concluding with my telling her I love her and missing her and that Roz sends her love too.

"What about my buns? You haven't mentioned my buns in a while. You used to sound like you were writing sonnets to my ass. Sonnets with ruffled underwear."

"How beautiful are thy buns," I say. "You have the most beautiful buns on the Upper East Side of Manhattan."

" 'In all Europe, madame, in all Europe.' You used to say my breasts were a twin row of boobs, or something along those lines. Why do men get biblical about tits? I remember you once also asked if there was anything more loved on earth than what's between a woman's thighs."

"It all depends on whose thighs."

"There's nothing like pussy to make men go all poetic."

At this point I sneaked in the thought that I sometimes wondered if I should go back to New York and just give the whole project up. But her response was violent. No! Absolutely not! That was definitely and unchangeably not an option.

So back to Roz and Max and unfindable film endings. I've begun hating Aristotle and his idea that every story had to have an ending. Does life have an ending?

Well . . . yes. But let's not go there.

•

Meanwhile, to avoid any help from the dread Ms. Highsmith and for a change of atmosphere, I went to Chili Happy Chili hoping I'd find Columbo there. His home away from home.

I parked on Sunset and heading toward the chili parlor I passed an elderly bearded hippie who looked, I would guess, about sixty-five and asked if I wanted to buy some trainers for a dollar ("worn only once"). They looked a perfect fit for a nine-foot-tall basketball player. When I hesitated he said: "These're legit. They're not stolen." I gave him a twenty and told him to keep the trainers, they were not high on my list. He yelled as I left him, "I have a smaller pair. Size five."

At Chili Happy Chili the server behind the counter shouted over the heads of four diners as I walked in, "Hey! New York!" A gleam of white bra peekabooed between the buttons of her blue uniform. She volunteered that Columbo had not been in yet.

An abandoned newspaper on the counter was folded open to a story about the periodical cicada. Waiting for ham and eggs I read that a periodical cicada has a plump body and four three-inch-long transparent wings and is the longest-living insect "known to man". I wondered who else might such things be known to.

Skimming the article, I tried to work up interest in periodical cicadas, hoping there'd be something about their love life. My eye was caught by a detail: every seventeen years the periodical cicada emerges from the ground, does its schtick and disappears again, and I thought: why? I further thought: who hangs around for seventeen years to clock its appearance and disappearance?

And then of course it hit me – the number seventeen. I tried not to make the connection with Karen emerging into the fashion world at seventeen to do her schtick and disappearing.

And while I was thinking crazy thoughts like that and that I should get out of Hollywood before it was too late, I saw Columbo approaching, hand extended for a shake. He couldn't wait to tell me about a divorce case he was working on in which the wife had recently transgendered, and boy! were there ever legal complications. He was full of stories. A man died in an internet café and his death was not discovered until nine hours later.

"Kinda world we live in."

He too had been doing some research for me and had statistics he had run across. World-wide, 36,000 women were trafficked each day, which came to 13,000,000 a year – numbers that to me felt more and more unreal. I was surprised at how much Columbo was picking up on the subject.

"These things happen right around here in our midst too but you seldom come in contact with them." He said about the missing Karen: "She could be in L. A., not Morocco. You'd be surprised at what you find in L.A. Sex slaves, pimps, the dregs of society. You got a daughter?"

"Me? No."

"You wouldn't want her to get involved in the kind of stuff that happens around Hollywood. I've had only one sex-slave case, you want to call it that, gruesome. Well, not really a sex-slave case. Some nice Filipino woman held against her will. Can you believe that?"

At this point, I assured him, I could believe anything.

"The cops sprung her in a raid when someone ratted on the

creep, who turned out to be a pedophile with a string of divorces behind him and who had mail-ordered her over from the Philippines with a lot of false information about himself."

The story was the local authorities arrested the man and temporarily moved her to safety.

"They moved her to a building a little on the cruddy side, and so this poor woman, who was wondering what the hell she was doing in the good old U.S. of A., sends for her mother just to have her there by her side. So now the mother comes over from Manila to be with her daughter and is napping in bed one afternoon, and an intruder – some hood, some neighborhood piece-a-shit addict – not expecting to find anybody home, comes in to do a little afternoon shopping, you might say, and, holy shit! there's this white-haired little old lady staring at him looking like she was some kind of wild woman, cursing at him in Spanish. The shock scares the creep half to death and he goes berserk, grabs a kitchen knife and stabs her about nineteen times like some crazy person that can't stop, and then the topper – with that same knife he carves out every gold tooth she has in her mouth."

He paused to let me absorb that interesting bit of information.

"It was days before anybody could calm the daughter down."

Fortunately he got busy eating. Reverting to our conversations about the missing girl Karen, he said: "You can't help feeling a little guilty, can you?"

Was he questioning or accusing?

"A little. Inge definitely does."

"It doesn't do any good, though, does it?"

"No, but feelings are feelings."

"Yeah," he agreed with that. "You can't just turn feelings off."

"No."

"You gotta be careful, though. You can't stop feelings but you can control them and not let them wreck your life. If you take on somebody else's pain you can get into a lot of trouble."

But how could we not feel another's pain? If I knew of a way I'd tell Inge about it. Here was Karen, a beautiful young woman appearing in the world one day making people feel happy just knowing her and feeling almost a gratitude toward life for knowing someone so innocent and young and lovely, and then they go and kill her.

It was not possible to feel another's pain, I thought, but how long did we mourn a missing person? Did we mourn a day, a month? A year?

He asked what do I remember of Karen?

"I think of her as a nice person, a very nice person, but you know, I have to be honest. How can I seriously mourn not seeing her again if I never really actually knew her? I never met her. She was never a part of my life."

●

I was certainly glad I had gone to Chili Happy Chili. Columbo's message always seemed to be that death was always there, affecting us at all times. Listening, I couldn't stop staring at him. His resemblance to Peter Falk was so uncanny I found myself trying to determine which eye was his glass eye.

"You want to stop the abduction of women?"

The question was abrupt. He watched me, letting it sink in.

"How do you stop the abduction of women?" I asked. Maybe he had an answer.

"You make everybody rich. Praying aint gonna do it."

"Make everybody rich. Right."

He continued more meditatively.

"Life can be a terrible experience. But, no matter how bad it is, you go on living. Aside from death there just aint no alternative to life so there's nothing to compare life with. Which means there's never any choice involved. We don't choose to be here. We're just here and that's all there is to it." Then: "Do you know why we're here?"

"No. Why?"

"We're here because we're here because we're here."

The old marching song.

"That's all I remember from being in the army," he said.

I smiled to see him looking happy. Karen was fading away. I asked how it felt to be a divorced family man, suddenly wifeless, and he grinned.

"Listen, with a secretary like mine you don't need a wife." Then suddenly serious: "We don't call them secretaries any more. She's my personal assistant – my P. A." The smile reappeared. "Although I don't know what the fuck the difference is."

We left Chili Happy Chili together and were walking down the avenue when a woman with a handbag the size of a valise stopped us and asked Columbo if he was Peter Falk.

"No." He made a small polite laugh.

"Yeah, I was pretty sure you weren't," the woman said. "You're not wearing a raincoat."

Columbo took off down a side street. He was supposed to meet someone working with him on a case. I turned the other way and stepping from the curb crashed into a woman hugging a potted hyacinth plant. She did an Irish jig to get around me and incorrectly sidestepping her twice I wisecracked, "Shall we dance?" and she smiled and murmured, "Oh, yes!" and as we passed I got a whiff a brandy and saw tears swimming in her eyes.

At home there was voice mail from Inge: "Please light a goddamned fire under Max – and if I'm saying please it's only as a concession."

•

I thought it would be best if I let the library cool off for a bit and just go on with my diary to pass time between meetings with Max. I had begun to feel spooked by the library. It was a place of horrors. Horrors and Ms. Highsmith. I pictured her waiting in the doorway with an armload of articles to hand me ("We live in a world of violence").

So I kept busy writing down random thoughts as possible ideas to develop for the column. Umpleby liked an occasional philosophical summarizing statement, saying it gave the column ballast (his word), but nothing too "snooty or self-important". An example of snooty or self-important was what "Harold Pinter said about Sam Spiegel: 'He's a modern-day Robin Hood. He steals from the rich and steals from the poor.' " Umpleby felt that was communist propaganda cryptically expressed and he was not one to be fooled.

I also spent time reading, especially diaries, in particular the diaries of authors I admired. There was always, or rather there often was, an absence of bullshit in diaries. A diary was like talking to yourself. There was a Frenchman named Stendhal who said he started a diary to provide himself with something entertaining to read in later years. I made a note to look up to see who Stendhal was. I knew exactly what he meant.

●

The for Max just to hear him say No! again was getting me down. And watching TV, it wasn't all that compelling to learn that the shepherds of the Andes have sixty words for the color brown in the coats of sheep and I wondered what they did about black sheep. I switched to another program that explained how people over eighty wake up in the morning feeling a strong impulse to just stay in bed and not get dressed but laze half awake enjoying doing nothing and I got to wondering how that was different from certain unnamed people from Finland who lazed half awake in bed doing nothing and were only twenty-eight. Except that she was incapable of doing nothing, my Inge.

I turned off the TV and turned back in my notebook to browse earlier notes and found the phrase "racing toward a sad conclusion" and wondered why I had written it down. I remembered liking the sound of it as a general phrase but couldn't remember what I had thought it meant. Or why I had thought it worth writing down.

Another note squirreled away was about prostitutes and Frank Sinatra. I must have thought I could use it someday. Sinatra's bodyguards were said to have pimped him a new woman every day at $300 a lay, a generous sum when the going rate then was $50 for first-class call girls. A snooping tabloid reporter researching a biography of Sinatra asked one of the women a direct question about his boudoir performances. "He doesn't exactly sing down there," she said. That would be the unauthorized biography.

I took out the old banged-up copy of a biography of Sue Mengers I had found in a secondhand bookshop in Westwood. As one of the more powerful movie stars' agents in her day she made more money than some studio heads. That plus her tactics made her – I should have known it was coming – "legendary". Skimming the book for anecdotes for possible use in fleshing out the Max Petrov profile and also to get a little background for the period, I discovered a witty line she had once come out with, commenting that a certain misguided actress had "fucked her way to the middle."

•

I woke up the next day with what was becoming a constant thought, namely what the hell was I doing out here? I felt very alone and began thinking of my adoptive mother – to me, Mother. Maybe it was the warm sunniness of the day that reminded me of my visit to her grave in Westwood, New Jersey. In the cared-for ground, patches of snow and a recent powdery fall had been absorbed into the pale spring-green grass sprouting from the brown soil on the surface of her grave. Just underneath that, only a bit further down: that was where she was lying, hands folded on her chest, looking restful. I wasn't religious nor was she and I just stood there looking at her grave and thinking about her, knowing she would have understood how much love I felt for her, and too how much gratitude for the life she had given me with her warmth and closeness. I thought of the monster I could so easily have become without her love. I really missed her.

●

Email from the Great Umpleby urging me to get a move on. More clippings attached, one an upbeat one about a woman in Mozambique who had given birth in a treetop during a great flood in 2000. As the woman hung on to a branch one person held her baby and another the placenta with the baby tied to it. A helicopter hovered above the violently trembling, shivering branches to lower a medic, who cut the cord before airlifting mother and baby to safety. I liked that one just as it was and didn't know what Umpleby wanted me to do with it. I decided we should just run it as is.

Another clipping was strangely connected to our film idea – U.S. Federal agents breaking open what was being called the largest and most complexly organized international child pornography ring ever. On a social networking password-protected website for pedophiles more than 1000 men traded over a million sexual images of children forced into performing sex acts. Thus far 26 members had been arrested and 16 children identified. Members excited others by discussing how they had personally abused children. It was a well-organized ring.

Another clip described honor killings but this time the killing was in reverse: a woman stabbed her brother to death. She repeatedly plunged a kitchen knife into his chest while he screamed, "Why? Why are you doing this?" She had just killed their mother. "So I had to do it," she explained. "He had seen me do it and was a witness."

And this one from Newark, New Jersey, about a girl, Jane Doe, found dead. She had been wrapped in a blanket and dumped naked behind a church. A church member who knew her had identified her to police. Her name was Stephanie. She had been staying at a shelter for homeless youth, where some local hood had got her onto drugs and then began pimping for her so she could continue to afford the drugs he kept supplying her with.

●

Trish phoned from Max's office to say he's slipped away to Nevada for a few days but before he left he suggested Roz and I meet him on his return. She hoped it was okay and I said it was. I asked Trish about her trombone player and his divorce.

"It's going slowly."

The trombonist's wife was becoming all clingy at this late stage and that was creating a problem. Trish was positive, though, it didn't undermine his resolve. She said their love for each other was very deep and I wondered if she was just saying that to reassure herself. But she sounded genuine. Somehow we all think "But this is different" when we're involved.

There not being much for her to do while Max was away I proposed lunch and she suggested Morton's.

"It's a very business-focused show-biz restaurant. See how the other half lives. Oh wait – that's a dinner place."

I said how about Musso and Frank's. I had heard about them and it had been mentioned in Sue Mengers biography.

"That's a good place. You get two martinis in one without asking. But the spaghetti costs about two dollars a string."

We settled on Ma Maison, a small garden restaurant with umbrellaed tables close together.

I assured Trish about the Max profile, that I would try to make it a good one, favorable, positive. She was interested and I could see she was quite protective of him.

"It'll probably work out," I said. "I keep wanting to write about Hollywood but it's so complex."

"That's what everybody says."

Loads of authors had written about Hollywood: Scott

Fitzgerald, Nathaniel West, Lillian Ross, John Gregory Dunne, even Mario Puzo – a small library.

"Part of the problem is that there isn't just one Hollywood."

Each was a mutation of an older Hollywood. There was the old filmland of the silent nineteen-twenties. In the thirties it became the Hollywood of social content. After the war there was, for a while, the decline of the studios – that would be during the fifties. Then the coming of the indies –

"You should say something about the video assist," Trish suggested. "Max pioneered it."

"What's a video assist?"

"That's that little monitor that the director sits in front of and sees what he's filming as he's filming it. You know, sees the finished film on a little screen in front of him so he can reshoot it till he gets it the way he wants it. They've been using video assists for a long time now."

"If you're unhappy with what's happening, you just redo it."

"Exactly. You just keep doing it until you get the result you want."

She thought she should get back after lunch and I went up to Roz's place, to my bungalow. I was thinking more seriously now that I should jump ship. I might just as well be in New York for all Roz and Max and I were getting done.

•

I took the plunge. I told Roz and Inge how fed up I was with our missing-persons movie assignment, not the assignment but the way it was going or not going. It seemed too hopeless. So I submitted an ultimatum. I said I'd hang around for one more meeting with Max, my secret purpose being to see if I could get just enough more material for his profile to round it out and then – New York! And if I didn't get a promotion out of it, journalism was going to lose one of its stars.

Meanwhile I tackled the vignettes and clippings from

Umpleby partly as relief and partly to keep from going bat-shit crazy in California. I tackled the "reindeer stop" one. How many readers knew that a sleigh of reindeer must stop every 60 kilometers for the reindeer to do a wee? Reindeer cannot peepee while moving because of something in the genitourinary tract. And stopping every 60 kilometers of course must be sheer hell on Santa's itinerary. I was about to put that aside till Christmas, when it occurred to me that Inge could find a place for it in her Doomsday Book: Life in Lapland. Or possibly Reindeer Travel Habits. Or: On Reindeer and Lappish Urination. If I knew Inge, it would probably be filed under P for Piss. I wondered if the Chinese could get a cure for Alzheimer's out of young reindeer peepee.

24

It came on a news bulletin that Trish happened to catch on TV. She felt a shock looking up from her work and seeing him on the screen.

Max had not shown up at his usual time that morning. By noon she had begun worrying and then the worry turned into panic when she saw his face and a bulletin intoning that the famous film director Max Petrov, most recently of Millie in Love, had suffered what might be a heart attack, real cause not yet known. Regaining consciousness in hospital he complained of dizziness and confusion. A hospital spokesman stressed to reporters he was not suffering a heart attack, but nothing could be ruled out, and it was important that he remain in care. The present attack was similar to a recent incident except that this one gave indication of being more serious in a way yet to be determined. Details would be forthcoming as soon as they were known.

Trish, flustered, phoned to fill me in, in case I hadn't heard. A quick exam had led doctors to believe he had suffered many TIAs, which were transient ischemic attacks, but they were not uncommon. They were not uncommon but doctors understood them to be a warning signal and, when they came in series, thought it best to remain alert to the possibility of a stroke. More tests would be needed before releasing him. Specialists made arrangements for a brain scan and until those results were in, there was nothing anyone could do.

Trish promised to call me back in a few hours and she did, to say it appeared that Max was going to be okay. She had tried calling him and had finally been put through.

"He sounded in a strangely jokey mood. He said, 'It's mysterious but not serious.' "

Then he said: "I'm entering the third act of my life and all that's left now is to work out an ending." And then apparently laughed at the private joke.

Trish added: "He said to be sure to tell you that last bit, that you would appreciate it."

I asked her what she was going to do while he remained in hospital.

"There are always things to do. He has a private payroll I was just preparing."

The detail of checks being made to a private payroll surprised me – surprised me that there was a side of Max that only Trish and, apparently, his wife Regina knew. I don't know what astonished me more, learning that Max had on the side a fictitious business called "Silver Fox Enterprises". Or that its ghost staff were relatives whose "job" was to receive a monthly subsistence from a fictitious fund, the Max Petrov Foundation.

"Silver Fox is a private charity," Trish said, "a family charity, you might say. And you wanna know something funny? One of the relatives is somebody he's never even so much as heard of. Max calls him his schnorrer."

Which was my first inkling that Max was Jewish, not Russian.

"It's become our joke. Max suspects that the schnorrer is just one of the other relatives he's paying and this guy is cashing in under two names. He says that that guy alone justifies anti-Semitism."

"Why doesn't he lop him off?"

"He says he admires his chutzpah. Anyway, he says the guy's a 'landsmann'."

●

The next thing I heard the doctors were saying that the original, tentative diagnosis had been wrong. The truth was disturbingly worse. Now it came out: Max had a brain tumor. What was puzzling and what had earlier thrown doctors off was the absence of the symptoms usually accompanying brain tumor, such as headaches, vomiting, dizziness. He had complained of headaches but nothing else. Fortunately they had discovered the real problem: a scan showed a walnut-sized malignancy in the left inferior frontal lobe.

And that had the doctors seriously worried. The lump was just far enough back to threaten Broca's area. That was the region associated with the muscle movements necessary for speech. There was now the risk of aphasia, and in an operation that was deemed imperative the surgeon would have to exercise extraordinary care not to accidentally damage neurons that could impair speech.

•

As soon as Max was allowed visitors I went to see him and was surprised that he appeared in excellent health. And he swore he felt fine.

"In every respect. Except that lying here with nothing to do makes you have a lot of crazy thoughts."

"Like what?"

"Like feeling guilty about unimportant things – you know, little everyday choices involving events of thirty years ago. My thoughts keep going back and wondering why I sometimes did what I did. We harm people without intending to."

No doubt through personal associations, he switched without transition to East-West.

"They say the studio's a bear pit."

I wondered what he meant. "Who's the bear?"

"Me." He made a silent laugh, his head moving up and down. "You know what the studio heads call me when I'm not there? The Dark Prince."

"You don't seem to mind?"

"Oh I mind, all right. It's too close to the Prince of Darkness. But I have to admit it's amusing to think I have that much effect on people. Especially the higher-ups."

He spoke of other directors and of the friendly rivalry between them tempered by appreciation for each other's work. Enjoying reminiscing he spoke of Billy Wilder.

"One of the greats, you know, but with all due respect, that shot of Marilyn Monroe with her skirts shooting up is obscene. Not morally obscene – who cares if you were to see her snatch? The obscenity is in its appeal to sex-starved males, the pitiful nebbishes of the hinterlands. Can you imagine how regressed a population must be to think that Bimbo Number One coyly, puritanically, holding down her up-blowing skirts, is an erotic image – I mean, to the point of practically making her into a national treasure?"

"You don't care for Marilyn?"

"I'm probably one of three people in the Western Hemisphere who never thought she was even beautiful. Or sexy. If you ask me was she was photogenic – yes, very photogenic, which is what matters. For that she was terrific. Stand her in front of a lens and the camera falls in love with her. But away from the set – nothing. Intelligent and talented? Maybe – who knows? Maybe if she had lived long enough . . . but I doubt it. Jean Harlow had more talent. And more personality."

"Did you make any films with her?"

"Monroe? No. That was before my time. I did see her at a party once, at the end of her life."

"Did you talk to her?"

"I was young. To her I was a nobody."

The doctors of the generously-endowed pavilion were Hollywood pros, skilled in avoiding publicity. For Max news of his illness could mean being denied insurance. No studio would entrust a film to him when films nowadays took months and sometimes years to complete. The return on investment of an unfinished film was zero.

"You're looking good." I could see he knew it was a lie.

"I feel pretty good," he said. "I read and watch films on TV."

He had enjoyed seeing an early Hitchcock again: The Lady

Vanishes. He noted that getting away from his usual work left him plenty of time to think about our Karen project. He hadn't given up on it

"Not yet." He seemed to be laughing at himself. "Needs more work."

Back at the bungalow, I tried reading the World-Herald on line, hoping it read better in California than it did in New York. But crap was crap. There was an article about the writing of Japanese memoirs but the two memoirs that were excerpted were about death and I didn't need to learn anything more about death right now.

•

As promised, I sent Umpleby column fodder from small local papers and free community handouts and suggested as part of our column a subcategory called "Life in Hollywood". Surprisingly he seemed to like it. I suppose film-industry gossip represented a radical shift for the World-Herald, a condescension to low popular taste (lower than its accustomed one). Possibly the fourteenth-floor bigwigs hoped a spike in Sunday sales would lead to a boost in weekday circulation and ad revenue. There was a new concern over the internet at social media: those new resources had the paper worried shitless. The world was changing. Thanks to the internet the public was openly sharing the latest news through free blogs and websites or via Facebook and Twitter before newspapers could set it in type and charge people money for what was by then second-hand day-old attempts at sensationalizing dead stuff. As for TV, it had become mostly a vehicle for movies and chat shows, with a new yellow journalism being served up as news entertainment. News entertainment consisted of opinions, distortions, spin and propagandistic overstatement, with an occasional high-speed car chase or a nice new college campus mass murder thrown in for audience relief. And all the rest was a tsunami of commercials.

At first Inge felt betrayed by my abandoning the project even though I explained:

"It has stopped being a story about a missing girl. It's now becoming a story of the difficulties of making a film about a missing girl. The person's gone. We have only production problems."

I don't know whether she got hit by lightning while out photographing one day but she began coming round to understanding my feelings – or so I thought until on one of our phone calls she screamed, "Shit! shit! shit!" and sounded like she was about to slam the phone down. I quickly attempted to calm her with things I knew she liked, the "everyday anthropology" of amusing scraps of civilization, like internet spam on erectile dysfunction, G-spots and their location – sex-sex-sex. I managed to get her distracted enough to laugh as I suggested a book called G-Spots for Dummies.

I emailed her things Umpleby had sent me for the column, about subjects I knew were favorites of hers and that the paper could easily do without. She was going through another one of her phases of crazy laws on the books, like the one in California about the ordinance making it illegal in Pasadena for a secretary to be alone in the office with her boss, and New Mexico law demanding the removal of 400 "explicit" words from Romeo and Juliet before allowing the play to be read by the young. If you can believe that. Then there was the ten-year-old boy in Kansas making a model electric chair for a school project, and a frat in Illinois hazing freshmen by making them insert their penis into a light socket. My personal favorite was the Rhode Island man who, claiming to have found the secret of life, predicted he'd live to be 150 and on his 47th birthday succumbed to a urinary infection. I thought his last words to worried hospital attendants would go well in her book of epitaphs: looking at his nurse, he said, "Hey, I'm perfectly okay. Watch this.". He shut his eyes and never opened them again.

•

My decision to opt out troubled me and I told this to Columbo. I made him into my conscience as I defensively explained, "I'm still working on a profile of Max. And too there's the column."

He was surprised I'd give up on a film project with a big gun like Max Petrov behind it. But he didn't know the problems involved. He asked if I had been following the series on CNN, the Freedom Project. It was a documentary about ending slavery around the world.

"Really horrible stories, and not just women. Kids too."

"What's the program about? What's it supposed to achieve?"

"It raises consciousness, that's what it's about. It raises consciousness so you'll go out and act."

"Does it say how? Like do what?"

"Like write to people. Speak up."

"Write to people and speak up?"

"Yeah. Write to people. You know, speak up."

•

The TV series had pretty obviously raised his consciousness. He handed me the morning paper with an article he said was "in line with" my interest. It was coming in now from all sides.

It was a very long article about Iraqi girls sold into slavery. The Iraqi part sounded like it might be interesting so I promised to give it a look, though privately I felt reluctant. But once I started reading the report I couldn't stop.

It was about two teenagers. Zeina and Fatin. Zeina's father took her on a visit to her grandfather in Jordan. But the girl quickly suspected that the story was just a cover and sure enough, instead of taking her to Jordan her father took her to the United Arab Emirates, where he sold her. The man buying her dealt in sexual slavery – her father must have known that for the kind of money he was paid for her. Horrified at being betrayed by her father and seizing an opportunity to escape she fled to the local police. But because her passport was held by her father she was told she could make it back to her home only by traveling on forged documents. When she attempted that, she was arrested for carrying forged documents and sentenced to two years in jail. The jail term so mortified her parents that to preserve their family honor they felt it legitimate to kill her. But feeling kindly toward her the parents chose instead to give her the lesser punishment of forbidding her to return to school and not ever leaving the house again. To keep greater control over her, her father forced her to marry a bachelor cousin twice her age and someone they trusted. Encouraged by the parents this cousin, who moved in with them, kept telling her how lucky she was that her father had not killed her after all the shame she had brought down on the family.

That was pretty bad. The other one was worse. The other girl in the report was seventeen-year-old Fatin. On learning that her father was attempting to sell her into slavery she begged and beseeched her mother not to let that happen. The mother, who was equally horrified at having her daughter sold into slavery, took her to the safety of a lawyer and a court in Baghdad. As they were awaiting proceedings, the father discovered where his daughter was hiding and raped her. The girl, maddened with rage, impulsively killed her father. The court weighed all the circumstances and decided to be kind to her. Instead of ordering her to be killed, she was sentenced to fifteen years in prison. The prison they sent her to was notorious for guards who routinely raped women prisoners whenever they wished. There, as the years went by, she fell into a deep depression that never lifted and a hopelessness at living never left her. When she was set free after the fifteen years were up, she said: "What right do I have to expect any man to want me after what I did to my father?"

These new stories inside me, I checked with Max about our next appointment and was told by Trish that he would be tied up for the rest of the week – maybe longer. Was it something that could wait?

Frustrated, it was down to the library again, and my intrepid unpaid P.A., Ms. Highsmith, who seeing me walk in jumped up.

"Hi."

I knew when I saw her face it was a mistake to have gone there. She had saved a story for me about a young girl lured by a "16-year-old friend" on the internet to a sleepover but was met at the hotel rendezvous by an older woman and her "kindly old divorced father" and after the girl sipped from a glass of water, she woke up being raped by several men. I was barely inside the door when I was told all this.

Since our last meeting, the fearless Ms. Highsmith had undertaken research on her own.

"So important do I find the subject."

I knew what the appropriate response was: gratitude for work done on my behalf. But to be honest I could have done with less misery and felt more determined than ever to give the whole project up and just get the Max profile and the Roz interview done and head back to New York and lemon growing.

Ms. Highsmith handed me photocopies of documents she felt I should read. Pretending to be engrossed by the shitload of reports I would probably never look at without a gun pointed to my head, I accepted the pile of papers, thanked her and turned and walked out as though I had accomplished my sole purpose for stopping in that morning.

As bad as I was feeling, I didn't need more horror stories and tabulations and charts and statistics. They would all describe the same recruitment techniques and coercive tricks, the methods of deception, and corruption at high and low levels. And the language would all be legal and larded with the jargon of bureaucratic administration and the excitement of paper promises – legislation without teeth or enforceability. Not one of them would state in all these stories the simple truth of what happened: a girl left school one day and never reached home. Her family went mad with grief.

Driving back to the bungalow I thought the hell with the project and the hell with pain and suffering if there was nothing I could do about it. How could I help free a girl in South America or liberate a woman in Asia or Africa or Iraq – assuming that the victim's whereabouts were known and assuming she was not dead? I didn't think such things could be done just by making a movie. If it were that simple then all that authorities needed to do was keep talking it up and showing pictures. But they suffered the same helplessness: "We're doing all we can," authorities said. I was beginning to believe them. "Everything humanly possible is being done." And the pity of it was they were telling the truth. As far as anyone could tell.

After a quick lunch in the kitchen with Sophie I lied that I'd be working in the bungalow for the rest of the day. I had only one wish: drop the project – not think about it.

And having that wish appalled me. I was becoming exactly like the others. A girl goes missing and for all anyone knows suffers indescribable anguish until one day death mercifully comes, and so what do I feel about it? I feel I'd rather not think about it.

To blot out the world and take a break I switched on the TV to a movie channel – and hit an old Columbo rerun and was glad of the distraction and felt somewhat cheered seeing my friend Kiernan, or rather the real fictitious raincoated Columbo in his ancient gray Peugeot, a car in need of immediate burial. He drove up to a posh portico, the program's formulaic conclusion permitting him to rush in without knocking because in the story's final moments that's what detectives do when they've just found the key to the mystery, the unraveling bit of knowledge that the audience is tensed up to hear. They barge in without knocking and swiftly nail the suave son of a bitch upper-class scoundrel in his lair. And in the closing seconds Columbo is no longer the bumbler but reveals that his ineptness till now has only been a cunning subterfuge to disarm the criminal he now charges with murder (the girl is not in Mexico, she's buried among the orchids in the indoor greenhouse, right here where they're standing) and as the criminal surrenders in shock, Columbo's glassy smile freeze-frames on the screen behind the words "The End".

I turned the TV off and, shamed a little by my real-life chili-parlor Columbo's reaction, I read Ms. Highsmith's documents and sketched a piece for the World-Herald's Sunday supplement. I wrote without pausing to rethink or do any correcting, afraid I might get sick of the subject and abandon it.

•

I condensed into an article what someone else might pretty

comfortably have spun into a short book about customs in rural Ghana, particularly a tradition called trokosi. Most of it was about a nine-year-old girl named Mora, and when I got done organizing the main points, it felt way too long. But I decided to hell with it. I would let Umpleby worry about length.

I typed it up and finished it as fast as I could and put the laptop in the car to go somewhere and read what I had written. It would need revising if Umpleby approved and I wanted to be ready. My life in Hollywood was revolving around The Two Columbos, the one on TV and the chili-parlor one, and the car just naturally headed there. Maybe Columbo, the real-life one, would be there and he was. At his usual place at the end of the counter. When I told him what I had just written and asked if he would be kind enough to read it, he said he'd be glad to. He got curious when I told him it was about a family custom in Ghana of selling a daughter to a priest for him to marry her to the gods.

"You've gotta be kidding."

"The priest acts as a holy go-between for the gods."

"Just when you think you've heard everything."

I explained that the nuptial rite had to be consummated here on earth. "That was the only way the marriage would be legally-binding in heaven."

He laughed. "They really come up with some good ones."

"But the priest is not obligated to provide for the girl."

"What's it, up to the gods?"

"When you marry the gods, the gods take on obligations."

I explained she was considered lucky. The priest was a kind man. He gave her permission to go out each morning and poke around a nearby wood to gather twigs to sell for money to buy food for the children she began having.

"Just an all-round decent guy."

"The children came because the gods liked multiple consummations of the legal bond."

"Jumping her once or twice just wouldn't do it."

"It gave proof of the constancy of her love and the priest wanted her to arrive in heaven with a good reputation."

"Altruism."

Columbo was staring at me waiting to see if I would break out laughing, that it was all just a joke.

Gauging to see how he, a reader, would take it, I ended up telling him the whole article pretty much as I had written it. How one day Mora ran to some visitors to the village that she had never seen before. They seemed like good people, so she explained her situation to them, how her parents had said what a good daughter she was and how when they prepared to take a trip to another village, they said that as a special treat she could go with them.

"I was so happy," the girl told them.

Her mother had given her a bath and dressed her up so that she would look pretty, and then when they got to the other village they introduced her to this nice priest. They told her the priest liked her, and wasn't that exciting! and would be happy to accept her as a wife to the gods!

So her parents had left her there, and when she saw them leave she felt so shaky her legs trembled and she began to cry. The priest started undressing her and touching her and she said that was when she knew her parents wanted her to die or they wouldn't have done this to her.

Mora had four children by this priest, and one day, seeing an opportunity, she escaped back to her home, where she hoped her family would take her back in. But then her mother started putting poison in her food and Mora understood. No one can leave the gods, ever, and go back home. That would mean she would just bring the family bad luck. Then one day Mora saw some other workers, white women and men, going through her village and asking questions, and, taking a wild chance, she told them her story and this time she was lucky. They were rescuers from a faraway country and they had a long talk with her mother and father and afterwards came and told Mora they had good news: she was free to live her own life again. Nobody would ever force her to go back to the priest. The rescuers would take her to a safe place where she would be free of the past and, to protect her, not even her family would know where she was.

"So it worked out in the end."

"Not really. At first Mora was overjoyed, but she missed her children, especially her new three-month-old baby boy. And when she was told she could never see him again, it was like hitting her. It was part of the bargain the rescuers had made that the priest's children belonged to the gods, not to her. When they told her she could never see her children again, it made Mora more miserable than she had ever felt before and she no longer cared if she lived or died."

"Jesus H. Fucking Christ," Columbo said.

•

I kept waiting for a response from Umpleby about the notes I sent and meanwhile kept thinking how royally fucked-up the world was, especially given the randomness of victims and the cruelty. Feeling really in a bad mood, every time I thought of the trokosi girl my thoughts went back to Karen's disappearance, a life destroyed so somebody could make money. In moments I wondered whether if it would not have been more merciful if Karen, that lovely seventeen-year-old Finnish model, had just been dumped into a trash bin in an alley like that other girl rather than imprisoned in a harem for the rest of her life. Or maybe she was locked in a brothel. Or had already been sold on to someone as a slave. She was beautiful and young and could have been displayed in a cage, as they did in India. Death would be better than being shown in the marketplace, caged like a human female animal, a girl-woman to buy like property. A woman was put on sale and men haggled over a fair price for her as they poked and examined the strength in her arms and the sturdiness of her legs ("And a nice pair of tits on that one") before putting up the money for her and taking her home. Did the buyer of a woman expect her to go live in his house and love him? She was his property – he owned her. How could a human being own another human being? How did he think she would feel as she lived under the same roof with him? Did he expect her to love him?

After some deliberation I had included some of these additional thoughts to Umpleby, Sage of the Fourth Estate, and even suggested doing a series of articles on the buying and selling of women in marketplaces. He shot back a reply later that afternoon.

"Retain the human interest but drop the documentary slant. And no erotic titillation stuff."

He commented that the writing should be more lively, more now – a story of today. He reminded me that the World-Herald was a newspaper, not a professional journal, and that it dealt in news, not anthropology. He said my notes had the makings of a nice essay but should be more journalistic in feeling and that I needed to be careful not ever to let my writing get turgid if I ever wanted to get anywhere in the newspaper field. He also asked if I was sure the events described were current history and not something I was dredging up from the past to dish out to Sunday readers.

"And cut out the lurid flights of fancy about slave markets and pinching tits and stick to facts. Remember, the World-Herald's a family newspaper."

He also said his patience fell a trifle short of Job's and asked how much longer he was going to have to wait, for crissakes, for the goddamned Max Petrov profile that I had promised. And he said he wanted good family-readership stuff – like where Petrov had gone to school, what his grades were like, who his favorite authors were, what he enjoys doing when he's not working . . . Wholesome stuff . . .

And no doubt the color of his underwear, I thought . . .

•

I was tired of tragedy. I'd had enough of hearing about terrible things happening to people. The next time I saw Columbo again, he came on like a scold:

"Don't torture yourself." When he wasn't scolding. It was all friendly instruction.

"If I could have one wish it would be to feel less caring," I told him/

He scoffed. "But you care. Everyone cares. Do you know how many people go missing everyday – just in America? Twenty-three hundred in America alone. Their families care. How could anybody not care? Even I care."

I asked what people could do.

"You're expecting a happy ending. That's your problem. There are no happy endings. So many women and children are suffering that if you're not careful your life will begin to feel like a giant loony bin. You think nature gives a happy shit about justice? Let me tell you something. It does – not – care. It doesn't give a damn about justice – if in fact there is such a thing as justice, so if you're looking for justice, quit now because you're not going to find it. And if you don't quit now you're just going to destroy yourself. And if you destroy yourself, who is that going to help? And, by the way, tell your girlfriend it may be unbearable but you go on living anyway. She should know that by now. After two years, for god sake. Tell her she has every right to be unhappy but she should also put it behind her."

I had heard all that stuff about nature before. It didn't matter to me that nature was not caring. I don't even know what that meant. I was caring. How was I supposed to stop caring? Or Inge.

"What would that girl tell you if she were here now? She would say you'd be a fool not to get the most out of living. The only thing you can do with that missing girl is remember her. Forget how unjust it is that she's missing. You'll go crazy thinking that way. Remember her."

"The thing is I can't forget her."

"Remember her as you used to know her."

"I never knew her."

"As your friend Inge knew her."

"Inge is slowly going crazy."

He shook his head. "Look, Inge has to choose. She can

either keep worrying about her missing friend and get nowhere. Or she can forget her friend and put it out of her head and get on with her life. Or she can go crazy. Those are her three options and whichever one she chooses, the suffering will be the same."

•

Later I kept thinking, twenty-seven million human beings, twenty-seven million lost causes, my thoughts going back to Karen, trying to imagine her suffering – where? In Marrakech, where she had gone "missing"? In the desert's furnace glare and the freezing nights of the Atlas Mountains? Was she part of a harem, a sheik's concubine? I thought of the desert's loneliness at night: the stars, the cold dark, and somewhere under the sandy emptiness there was a seventeen-now-nineteen-year-old Finnish girl living with memories of "back there", the place where she had come from and never stopped obsessing about. Living for her had stopped. For her, there were no longer days or weeks or months, only this moment now, an awful now that she lived in that would be the same as the now that will go on until her death.

And there was Inge's sorrow – the sorrows of Inge. It came to me then that the only ending there was or ever could be was dying and death. Disappearance had no ending. It just continued: without a parting, without leave taking, or smiles, or hugs, or goodbyes – no ending. Unlike death. Death was different. Death was an ending and endings were a movie formula: The End. But movies were not life. In life, Karen had been there and then she was gone and that was The End. It was a book with the words "To be continued" written halfway down the first page followed by blank white paper.

•

In the midst of all this Umpleby emailed more fodder. It was an Umpleby mystery where he kept finding these things:

. . . A Mr. Polanski handed the police a sizeable fortune in packets of small bills he had found in a plain paper bag on a crosstown bus, and after the police commended him for his unusual honesty he went home to tell his wife about the happy events. She said to wait, she wanted to go tell all the neighbors, and went out and bought a gun and shot him . . .

And this one:

. . . The parents of a 7-year-old Bangladeshi boy chloroformed him, gashed his face and cut his penis off to make him an object of pity so he could beg for coins. In good weather his family took in $8 a day . . .

I scrunched the printout and flung it into the trash, stretched out on the bed, and thinking about Inge and life and Karen I must have fallen asleep and next became aware of woozily rising up, up, through layers of a dream of burnished pomegranates bursting open in spurts of ruby seeds – so real I could taste their juice. And I was in bed with Inge, breathing the fragrance of her hair and feeling the softness of her twenty-eight-year-old still-girlish ass against me as her backward-probing fingers found and handshook the friendly dong with a quiet mmmm as she sank back down into rhythmic-breathing sleep.

•

I would have to leave here, return to New York. Thinking these thoughts I dialed Inge and even before the first ring of her phone her voice spoke a soft inquisitive "Hello?" – she having picked up her phone to call me at the precise moment I had dialed her number.

Drama Critic Inge, off and running: "Act Three happens

only in the theater and you know that life isn't theater. Life doesn't know much about art."

Sparing her and to make talk and to hold off telling her I was quitting, I asked her what she thought of Scott Fitzgerald's comment about second acts in life.

"Who's Scott Fitzgerald?"

"He said there are no second acts in life. Or maybe, I forget, maybe just not in American life."

"He was wrong. Life is all second act. And then curtain. There are no third acts in life."

I told her I was deficient in sisu. Sisu was a Finnish word meaning fortitude. I had learned it from her. It meant the ability to walk slowly through a block of red granite. I told her I could easily do that but only after four vodka collins served by Mama, the seventy-year-old barmaid at Great Scandinavia with eyes that had bags under their bags. I asked Inge if she still dropped in to Great Scandinavia.

"Not since Mr. Maki's death."

"Do you still have nightmares about kidnappings?"

"No."

"Good."

"Yes."

Silence.

"Are you keeping it in your pants?" Her voice smiling.

"Yes."

I asked if the Vogue thing was going well.

"Yes. I'm getting help from Hal. He took me out to the Russian Tea Room and told me the latest on all his models. We had a really classy red wine – Côte de Something. Quite tasty."

"How is Hal?"

"He's going to Paris on a shoot. Again. He can be quite boring. People who go to Paris feel they're special, as if it's their place. They come back and tell you about a little Left Bank boulangerie they found that makes the best croissants in Paris. Or usually not a boulangerie – a restaurant. And it's always a little restaurant. And it's always just around the corner."

•

The way I was feeling, I decided I'd wait till Max was out of the hospital and then go right up to him and say, "Look, Maxie, is this fucking film going to be made or do we just continue saying it needs more work?" But I knew I wouldn't do that. It would be heartless. The poor guy was in doctors' care, and besides, what right did I have for recriminations? He never promised anything.

In the morning, slipping out of bed, I stepped out for a dip in the pool under a flawless blue sky. The fucking California sun was too early-morning-intense to be normal. In midtown Manhattan you saw the sky when you stared up between buildings and caught a sliver of it and felt lucky if it was blue-ish. Besides, in New York, even on a cloudy day, even if it suddenly pissed rain nonstop for two hours, you didn't give a damn because at least you were in New York. So cut to the chase: it was time to go back – after tying up a few loose ends.

I was having these profound thoughts when the phone rang – Roz. She had just talked to a very excited Max about Carpenter and Rubinstein.

"Carpenter and who?"

"Rubinstein. The scriptwriting team. They have an ending to the story."

"No kidding! What's the ending?"

"Two endings. One is that Karen, suffering from amnesia, shows up in New York wondering where she is – doesn't even know she's a top fashion model or that she's Finnish or that her name is Karen. Or if that doesn't do it, a possible second ending is she escapes from her captors and shows up at the Finnish Embassy in Cairo or Nairobi or maybe Southeast Abu Dhabi, I don't know, somewhere, and she's joined there by her family in a big airport reunion, with Karen babbling happily but incoherently -- end of story. Whaddya think?"

I was too stunned to think. I couldn't believe that that was the best that the famous duo Carpenter and Rubinstein could come up with. That was an ending? Hell, why not have aliens from outer space kidnap Karen so she can procreate human babies for their clandestined invasion of planet earth? I mean, why stop at family reunions at airports? Or at least have a Karen closeup at the terminal clutching a stuffed doll in a freeze-frame ending, one tear halfway rolled down her cheek.

Roz patiently waited for an answer, to get my reaction, then said: "Yeah, me too."

"So now what?"

"It's very discouraging. Without Max . . . I don't know."

"What was Max's reaction to the endings?"

"He said the amnesia sounds good. He likes the amnesia. But it needs more work."

"With Max everything needs more work. That's his middle name."

"Yeah," Roz conceded, "Max himself could use a little more work. But at least, he said, we had an ending. We get the girl back. True, she's brain dead, but only temporarily. The doctors can fix that."

"Was he serious? The doctors could fix her up? And that's the end?"

"He was very serious."

"I think he should stick to Ivan Ilych. Ivan Ilych needs more work too. And it'd be hard for him to screw that one up."

" Oh yeah? You don't know Hollywood. If Romeo and Juliet were not written by somebody named William H. Shakespeare they'd bring Juliet back for the sequel Juliet and the Curse of the Capulets."

●

So: Romeo and Juliet again. I sat on the bed with the laptop and looked up the play for a quick glance-through. I googled it up to see if I could find the four hundred words that needed to be deleted before New Mexican school kids could feel safe reading Shakespeare. Flipping through I came across this soliloquy by Juliet:

Spread thy close curtain, love-performing night,

That runaway's eyes may wink and Romeo

Leap to these arms, untalk'd of and unseen.

Sneaky stuff, especially that "love-performing night" bit. And – ah: "Runaway's eyes winking." That was an easy one to spot. "Leap to these arms" – "untalk'd of and unseen". Clues piling up here – and in just the first three lines I looked at.

Then: "amorous rites" – we were getting somewhere. Rites, phew. Maybe we should open some windows, getting steamy in here. Because face it, we're talking two teenage Italian kids, juvenile delinquents with the hots for each other.

Lovers can see to do their amorous rites

By their own beauties; or, if love be blind,

It best agrees with night.

You see what Juliet's getting at? These wild teenagers like doing it in the dark. It's all about sneaky back-seat-of-the-car stuff where nobody can see what they're up to. OK, parents sneak in all kinds of things at night too but only after the kids are asleep. And let's note too that the parents have first done the decent thing of getting married. How old is Juliet? What? How old? Are you fucking kidding? She's thirteen? Ho-o-ly shit! Fucking thirteen? No wonder New Mexico is on high alert. Wait! – wait! There's the word maidenhood. Is that the same as maidenhead? Close enough. Whichever it is or both, this is a play about a pair of "stainless maidenhoods" or "-heads", and not only that, these maidenheads or –hoods are about to get stained. (Boy, it's getting really warm in here.) We're still talking pre-boff. These kids haven't boffed yet, they're still in the feel-her-tits-and-ass stage, and unless you were born yesterday you know where it's headed and how it's all going to end. I only hope Romeo doesn't go in unprotected. Verona pharmacies don't have morning-after pills yet, and you don't want Juliet ruining her nice Capulet dreams by becoming the first unwed thirteen-year-old mother in Verona . . . hot-blooded Italian teenage girls being what they are – sluts.

Come, night [no comment]; come, Romeo [NO-O comment];

come, thou day in night;

For thou wilt lie upon the wings of night

Whiter than new snow on a raven's back.

Come, gentle night, come, loving, black-brow'd night,

Give me my Romeo . . .

Aarrgh! . . . I slapped the damned laptop shut and flipped the thing over to the bed. Fuck New Mexico. Fuck Romeo too. Just give us our Juliet. All our Juliets.

25

Apparently there was nothing more that could have been done, we were later told. Max suffered a painful headache and as it lifted, another more violent symptom appeared: dizziness with vomiting and his thinking became confused. But the doctor said Max was so lucky. If the back of the brain had been the affected part it would have been fatal. He had seen cases like this before. Yes, Mr. Petrov was very fortunate.

Events caught everyone off guard and when I was there visiting him it suddenly, quietly went bad. The doctor was present, being aggressively cheerful at Max, saying what good genes he had and then added as he turned toward me that this might perhaps not be a good time for visitors.

". . . too tired . . . best to leave . . ."

"Tired shmired," Max said softly.

Taking that to mean he was in a good enough mood to talk I said, "What're you doing? Pulling an Ivan Ilych?"

With an acknowledging smile he said: "Don't we all eventually? But there's no curtain yet. I have a contract coming up."

I told him The Reporter was running an admiring series looking back on his cinema.

"I don't do cinema. I make movies. Cinema I leave to the critics."

Before visiting him, I had decided to tell him I was quitting our project, that my job in New York was at stake and, putting it as gently as I could, all plans were on hold. But seeing him lying there, a neat fold of sheet on his upper chest, I couldn't.

I saw him looking at a monitor to his right, a small black screen with green numbers. Below the numbers a graph of smoothly jagged lines sliding to the right. The nurse standing beside his bed looked at me and smiled.

"Know what you're not getting?" Max asked, speaking with trouble. "Don't take this badly – it's just friendly criticism." I awaited his wisdom. "Your fault is it's not apathy you're fighting. Apathy you can overcome – not a problem. But money you can't fight."

I was expecting something of greater profundity but he stopped.

A second nurse stepped into the room and stood just inside the door. It was a hint: time to leave. It didn't matter. Conversation seemed futile. Everything seemed futile. I had the feeling we would only go back over ancient history. I had the nutty idea of not wanting to put Max to the discomfort of saying a definitive no.

"Let's hope for a speedy recovery," I said.

"Actually I never feel better," he said in a quiet voice. Hearing how peculiar that sounded he corrected: "Having never felt better – feeling better."

A noise came from his throat while simultaneously he frowned, shutting his eyes. The nurse at the door came over. I turned and left.

Going out the door I heard him say to her. "Why does my head not clear?"

I walked to the end of the long corridor and out to the sunny street.

The drive back home seemed long and I remembered the last words he had directed to me: "Feeling better." I liked its irony and saw it fitting into the column.

The phone was ringing as I walked into the bungalow. It was the hospital. I had left Trish's number with the ward nurse, and mine too, in case of need. Mrs. Petrov had an unlisted number. I heard a woman's voice saying sorry . . . happened peacefully . . . arrangements . . . .Moments later Roz, at East-West Studios, called to see if I had heard – she had just been told. Speaking calmly she said she'd be there as quickly as she could.

Sophie was preparing tea when Roz arrived and the three of us sat at the kitchen table. Roz agreed it would make sense if I returned to New York, and when she asked my plans – Sophie's eyes making a quick glance at me – I said none, just leave.

"Go back," Roz said. "We'll think of something else. I don't intend to quit. What are you going to tell Inge?"

"Nothing to tell. Max died. End of project."

"It won't make her happy. Maybe she'll have some ideas."

"I doubt it," I said.

"I doubt it too."

"I have to go downtown, " I told them. "I don't feel I owe Ms. Highsmith anything – except that she's been so helpful."

"Who's Ms. Highsmith?"

I explained.

"Sounds like we could use her on the project. You going back to your column?"

"I never left it."

"You have no idea how much that thought depresses me."

•

I recalled, looking back, the day when Roz said that nothing was ever futile – so long ago. I had only one goal now, to get away. In an accumulating gloom I went over any loose ends so that I could leave without guilt, or not more guilt than usual.

The Roz interview had yet to be done, that is, a real Roz interview, not the jokey silliness we had taped, and my impulse was to abandon that along with the rest – just drop everything. And if that got me fired from the paper, then it got me fired from the paper. The way I was feeling, things like that didn't matter anymore. No interview of Roz would have shown her as she is, a flip champion of freedom and nonconformity, more alive and fascinating in life than any interview or portrait on paper could ever show her. Something, you might say, commensurate with her talents.

But it was more than that. Our project was no longer on hold. It was dead on arrival. Which was what I tried explaining to Colombo, that Max's watchword "no ending no story" had transmuted into no director no movie. Without money, there was no story. The only ending there now or ever was that there was no ending.

I told him this on one last visit to Chili Happy Chili. I wanted to express my gratitude for his commiseration and understanding and how much I appreciated his support in believing our film idea was a good one and for his continuing to believe it could still work.

"It's an important story to tell," he assured me.

All I could think to say was that I agreed. I stopped short of adding: "But it needs more work."

Roz took it hard and I had to remind her that I had to work for a living and had already been away from the paper and the "crap job" for longer than agreed. In a final attempt to keep our collaboration alive and me in Hollywood, she suggested placating the fourteenth floor with a zany series of anecdotes about the life of a movie star that we could have fun fabricating.

"Raunchy horseshit we'd make up. That paper is founded on crap and we'll feed them all the crap they can handle. We'll out-Sunday-supplement them. We have to keep the project going. We can't quit."

I was about to ask how but didn't. We were pushing against a stone wall. But then I changed my mind.

"How?"

"By talking about it – keep talking it up. You're a journalist. Write about it."

"Talking it up to who?"

"To whom."

"Talking it up to whom?"

"Yeah, well, that's ..." Her voice trailed off.

•

Inge took it the hardest. She understood finally but that only made her feel worse. I tried consoling her, telling her that when you got right down to it, I had long felt something I had resisted saying out loud, things being hopeless enough as it was – that ultimately justice was only a yearning.

The obit on Max was that he was born in Secaucus, New Jersey back when that piece of meadowland was still a big stench of pig farm that motorists hurried through, and the only Odessa Max could claim knowledge of whatever he got from Tolstoy. I no longer remember who went to his funeral. It was of course a legendary affair but to be perfectly honest I didn't give a damn.

•••

About the Author

Hiag Akmakjian is the author of several fiction and non-fiction works, including the novels *Name Dropping: The Cedar Bar in the 1950s, Cleo* and *30,000 Mornings*.

Readers who would like to learn more about the narrator of this book will find *30,000 Mornings* of interest as it forms a sort of prequel to *Snow on a Raven's Back* as the narrator and Inge appear prominently.